"I asked for the truth."

"What truth?" Stormy felt contentious.

"Is something happening between us?" Tyler asked.

The question, totally unexpected, seemed to hover in the air.

Her gaze met his and held. His face was so carefully devoid of expression, she had no hint of where he meant to take this or what her answer should be. "Are you asking out of curiosity or for verification?"

He put a fingertip to her lips, traced the shape of her mouth.... It took several heartbeats for her to come to her senses. "Stop that, please," she said, moving away.

He followed her with his eyes. "You know I want you."

Stormy exhaled. "Do you believe I had anything to do with the bank robbery?"

Tyler went silent....

ABOUT THE AUTHOR

Jackie Weger loves to travel to research the
fascinating places and professions that inspire the
stories she shares with her readers. She was born
in Mobile, Alabama, and has lived in half a dozen
states so far. Jackie and her husband, H.A., are
currently renovating a big, beautiful Victorian
house in St. Augustine, Florida.

Books by Jackie Weger

HARLEQUIN AMERICAN ROMANCE

289—FULL HOUSE
344—BEST BEHAVIOR
363—FIRST IMPRESSIONS

HARLEQUIN TEMPTATION

181—EYE OF THE BEHOLDER
207—ON A WING AND A PRAYER

HARLEQUIN SUPERROMANCE

227—BEYOND FATE

Don't miss any of our special offers. Write to us at the
following address for information on our newest releases.

Harlequin Reader Service
P.O. Box 1397, Buffalo, NY 14240
Canadian address: P.O. Box 603,
Fort Erie, Ont. L2A 5X3

JACKIE WEGER

MAN OF THE MOMENT

Harlequin Books

TORONTO • NEW YORK • LONDON
AMSTERDAM • PARIS • SYDNEY • HAMBURG
STOCKHOLM • ATHENS • TOKYO • MILAN
MADRID • WARSAW • BUDAPEST • AUCKLAND

**Many thanks to Norman Batson
for all his help, guidance and fleamarketing**

Published April 1992

ISBN 0-373-16435-1

MAN OF THE MOMENT

Chapter One

"Your mug shots don't do you justice."

At the words, a nervous tremor shook Stormy Elliott's hand as she entered the living room. The man who'd uttered them was tall, his shoulders broad, his stance relaxed and still, as if he'd spent the moment waiting on her gazing out the window to the beach. It was a view, Stormy knew, that seldom failed to garner an appreciative comment. Yet the man's stillness did not invite the usual impression: that he was mesmerized by the panorama of foamy waves rushing ashore beneath a cloudy March sky. Rather, his stillness suggested that of a predator, a silent stalker avoiding motion to catch its prey unaware.

A lowering gray cloud scuttled across the heavens and the room suddenly darkened. Stormy switched on a lamp.

The man moved away from the window, taking a step toward her. She saw a gleam in his very green eyes, a slight lift of an eyebrow, and watched as an ironic smile tilted his full lips.

The tension inside her expanded, gripping her limbs, but misfortune had taught her how to present an unruffled facade, so she glared at the man, taking him in, assessing him even as he assessed her. His light brown hair feathered back from his face, his eyes sharply defined. Parallel ridges under his nose were responsible for the sensual curve of his lips, but not for the irony she saw there. Masculine appreciation of what he saw flitted across his face before he tamped it down.

Stormy recognized that brief look. He thought he had some kind of power over her. Her defense mechanisms, never far from the surface, snapped into place, but before she could find a voice, he continued.

"Yeah, I'd say prison didn't do you any harm."

His ominous reference to prison crawled all over her. Until she could clear the air with her sister, she had to tolerate her family's abuse, but she'd be damned if she would take it from a stranger on her own turf—regardless of how attractive he might be.

"You flashed some I.D. at my sister and she allowed you in, but I'm not so easily conned," Stormy said frigidly. "Who are you and what do you want?" If the man was her new parole officer, Stormy knew she'd just started their relationship off on the wrong foot.

"Bit of a tiger, aren't you? But not to worry, I won't let that get in the way."

"In the way? Look, mister, just tell me who you are and get out of here."

"Tyler Mangus."

When he said nothing more, Stormy shot him a measuring look and forced a laugh. "I'm afraid your reputation has not preceded you, Mr. Mangus. Your name doesn't ring a single bell. Were you voted man of the year, perhaps? Or maybe you're selling encyclopedias door to door?"

He grinned lazily. "Ex-cons are often mouthy, but I'll say this for you, you're mouthy with style. We'll get along fine."

Stormy didn't miss the dimpling of his cheeks, the flash of the enviably even, white teeth, the unabashed male magnetism he exuded. She could feel it flowing toward her, touching some wellspring deep within her.

At once she erected her barriers. Smiles, dimples and smooth talk had done her in before—not only once, but twice. She wasn't going to be taken in by handsome looks or a silver tongue ever again.

"Don't bet on it," she insisted. "I'll do what's required of me, but nothing more. So let's get to the point of your visit, shall we?"

"Sure thing," he said, seemingly not the least perturbed by her outburst. "I'm an asset-recovery agent."

Stormy was taken aback. He wasn't from the parole office? "You'll have to explain what that means."

"Sure. The company that insured Beach Coast Savings and Loan wants its money back. I'm the one they hired to find it for them. Is that explanation enough for you?"

Stormy's mouth went dry. Shaken, she quickly looked beyond him out to the sand dunes, where stalks of sea oats flailed in the wind.

The dunes were higher this year than last, she noted distractedly. A marine-science program had encouraged St. Augustine residents to bury their used Christmas trees on the beachfront, which helped avoid erosion, giving coastal grasses time and space to take root. Dammit, she fumed, she, too, needed time and space to take root again. She shifted her eyes back to Tyler Mangus and met his gaze with a fierceness she had not displayed in months.

"I testified at my trial and that of Hadley Wilson that I did *not* steal the money. I never even saw that money. I can't return what I never had."

"My client begs to differ with you...in the matter of about one hundred and two thousand dollars, less the few bucks you had the chance to spend, of course. The problem with your testimony, Ms. Elliott, is that it wasn't true. Both you and Hadley Wilson were convicted. The jury found you guilty."

Recalled pain weakened Stormy's knees. She sat down abruptly on the arm of the sofa and glanced away.

No! she chastised herself. *Look the arrogant creep in the eye.* She made the contact. "I was not a good witness for myself," she said, voicing this truth aloud for the first time. "I was—am—innocent. I believed justice would prevail. It didn't."

Tyler Mangus gave her a look of pity, as if embarrassed for her. "Doesn't every convicted felon say he's innocent?"

"I don't expect you to believe me. All I'm saying to you is that I don't have that money. I never had that money."

His smile implied the patience of a saint, that nothing she could say or do would shatter his infuriating composure. "And I don't expect you to come right out and tell me where you hid it."

His words and manner were nettling her more than she cared to admit. "If you're so certain the money has been hidden, go see Hadley Wilson. He's the one who robbed the bank—not me."

"You drove the getaway car."

Fear squeezed Stormy's heart. She camouflaged it with anger. "Get out, Mr. Mangus. Find yourself a copy of the trial transcript and read it. I'm not reliving my testimony for you or anyone. And I'll tell you something else. Whether I committed a crime or not, society has punished me. I've paid my dues. It's over. I don't have to talk to you."

"With that kind of attitude, it's a wonder they let you out so soon."

She tilted her chin. "As it happens," she said, parrying his thrust, "I was a model prisoner. I *earned* my early release."

His eyes twinkled. "Must've been hard—keeping your mouth shut."

In spite of herself, Stormy smiled. Holding her tongue in the face of taunts and goading by guards and other inmates *had* been almost unbearable. "It was awful," she admitted. "Outside of being separated from my daughter, it was the hardest thing I've ever done in my life."

The glow drained from her mood. "On the other hand, the separation, the need to end it, was what drove me to keep out of trouble."

"Mom?" came a little voice from the foyer.

Stormy moved swiftly across the room and put her hands protectively on her daughter's shoulders. Liane had suffered, too. The seven-year-old was even more an innocent victim than Stormy herself had been. And Stormy meant to make amends in any way she could. Sadly, she sensed a rift with Liane, as if her daughter no longer trusted her—or life.

"Liane, this is Mr. Mangus. My daughter, Liane. Mr. Mangus was just leaving," she added, giving him notice.

Liane looked at Tyler with hollow-eyed curiosity, then up at her mother. "Is he a boyfriend of yours? Is he going to get us into trouble?"

The catch in Stormy's heart made her see red. She looked pointedly at Tyler. "No, poppet. Mr. Mangus isn't going to cause any trouble at all."

"Of course, I'm not," he said soothingly. He avoided the mother's glare by focusing on the child. And almost at once, he wished he hadn't. With her waist-length brown hair and soulful eyes, she reminded him of Priscilla.

The familiar pain sliced through his gut as the vision of his daughter floating facedown in the swimming pool veered across his mind's eye. He blinked to erase the agonizing scene, to bring himself back to the living child. "But I'm hoping your mother can help me solve a puzzle. Do you like puzzles, Liane?"

The girl shrugged. "Sometimes."

Giving Tyler a smile with nothing behind it but teeth, Stormy quickly ushered her daughter to the foot of the stairs. "Run up and get your jacket on, sweetheart. We've got a date for the beach, remember?"

"Are you going to help the man solve his puzzle?"

"No, I'm not."

"We don't have to go on the beach if you don't want."

Stormy bent to kiss Liane's brow. "I want to. I've missed it—and you—terribly. Now, scoot. And put on a cap—the wind is nippy."

Stormy watched her daughter climb to the top landing before she turned to discover Tyler Mangus at her elbow. He, too, had watched Liane mount the stairs, and there was a flicker of wistfulness in his expression. A second later, though, it was gone, and Stormy wondered if she had imagined it.

She moved around him to the front door and yanked it open. "I'm requesting you to get off these premises. If you don't you'll be trespassing, and that's against the law."

He sauntered past her onto the small, covered porch. "You spent a bit of time in the law library at Lowell?"

"That bit of legalese I was familiar with before I went to jail. Good day." She began to close the door. He stopped it with the palm of his hand.

"I'll be watching you. My clients want their money."

"Watch all you want. You'll be wasting your time."

"I don't think so." He made a point of assessing her again, from neck to knee, and did not attempt to conceal his admiration. "By the way, I've never been man of the year, but I make an excellent man of the moment."

Unamused and, worse, unnerved, Stormy closed the door in his face. Releasing a taut breath, she stood in the foyer, unmoving, minute after minute, all her reserves drained.

Throughout the whole disastrous affair—the arrest, the trial, her incarceration—she had held back one bit of information. No one had asked it of her, and she had not volunteered it. She held it dear and secret.

Far more experienced in criminal law upon his arrest, Hadley Wilson would not speak to the police without counsel present. If he had later mentioned to his lawyer that little Liane had been in the car when he robbed the bank, the attorney apparently had not regarded the information as pertinent to Hadley's defense; it was not mentioned at Hadley's trial, either.

Stormy didn't want the information to come out, and certainly not while she was on parole. In prison, she had learned enough from other inmates' horror stories to know how insensitive the juvenile court system could be. She'd also learned how easy it was for a parolee to lose custody of a child or children.

And now Tyler Mangus, asset-recovery agent, was looking for the stolen money. That meant he was bound to do a thorough investigation. Would he be less scrupled— and therefore possibly more thorough—than the police, who had focused only on Hadley and herself?

If so, he could put Liane at risk.

That made him dangerous.

He was not easily put off.

That made him treacherous.

He was very good-looking and activated a physical response that had lain dormant within Stormy for many long and lonely months.

That made him a positive menace.

As she went slowly up the stairs to collect Liane, her eyes fell upon her reflection in the antique mirror that graced the foyer. She barely recognized the image of her twenty-nine-year-old self. Poor diet and high anxiety had caused a thinness that made her breasts and hips overly prominent. Eyes that had once sparkled with life now looked at the world with suspicion. Her mouth was too wide, but at least she used to smile. The only smiling she had done of late, though, had been camouflage to avoid exposing her fears and uncertainties.

Liane met her at the top of the stairs. "Are we going to the beach now?"

"Yes, we are," Stormy said, and as she tugged Liane's hat more securely around her daughter's ears, she recalled the peculiar, almost plaintive expression that had transformed Tyler Mangus's handsome features as he observed the child, almost as if he had been reaching out for the girl.

A sudden urgency came upon Stormy, telling her that she must not tempt providence, forget the odds or defy the danger green-eyed Tyler Mangus represented.

TYLER STROLLED DOWN the paved drive and rounded a wild array of unkempt palmetto. He had parked his car a half block away, on the sandy verge of Route A1A, so as not to alert his quarry.

The damp March wind played havoc with his hair, tugged at his coat and whipped his tie over his shoulder, but he was too deep in thought to care.

Though loathe to admit it, he was impressed by the Elliott woman. She had been wary, and with good reason, but not coy. He found her articulate and intelligent. She was prison pale, but that in no way detracted from her willowy good looks.

His first instinct had been to believe her every word.

Luckily, he had caught himself. Women were the most complicated creatures on the face of the earth; he had discovered early on that feminine psychology was nearly impenetrable to the male mind. They lied through their teeth, telling a man everything he wanted to hear. But start to rely on what they said and—wham—you were up to your neck in their crazy, contradictory emotional storms. No way—not for him. Up front and no-strings-attached was the only way to go.

Of course, that was these days.

There once had been a time when he was married. There once had been a time when he was a father.

But that was another life, so distant now that all he recalled was the pain and loss. Especially the loss. "Sweet Priss," he murmured, and he wondered if he'd ever get beyond just marking emotional time.

He slid into the car and turned the key in the ignition. Chilly air blew out of the heater vents, puncturing his mood.

So there was a kid involved here. The main thing was not to let it affect him.

It didn't matter one whit that a thief was a mother, that she was personable and attractive.

On second thought, it did matter. He was as susceptible as the next guy to the opposite sex. Especially a woman as well turned out as Elliott. Okay. He'd keep his guard up. He'd keep his edge. He'd keep his wits about him.

In his mind he reviewed her every gesture, weighed her every word. And instinct told him she was hiding something.

Somewhere, somehow, Stormy Elliott was bound to reveal herself—and the money. It was his job to be there when she did.

As he made a U-turn to head back into St. Augustine proper, Tyler glanced out at the gray-weathered beach house and sent a mental warning to the woman he meant to outmaneuver. *Better keep a low profile, sugar, and stay on the straight and narrow. One misstep—that's all it'll take—and I'll have you.*

Chapter Two

Stormy sat in the dark, sipping hot chocolate. The dim light from the overhead stove vent in the kitchen did not penetrate the breakfast alcove.

The alcove was windowed on three sides, revealing the eerily white dunes and suggesting the ebb and flow of the mighty Atlantic. Now and again the clouds shifted, allowing a scant moon to skim the waves with a glimmer of lacy whitecaps.

After eleven months of bunking in an inmate dormitory with eighty other restless women, Stormy could not get used to the quiet of her sister and brother-in-law's house at night.

She had been home four days and nights, and so far the longed-for freedom was producing not exhilaration but feelings she had yet to put a name to. Anxiety? Confusion, perhaps. Depression? Fear?

She had been mortified when she was sentenced to prison. Even more ashamed and panicked at how powerless she found herself in that rigidly controlled environment. The Department of Corrections had issued her a number. She became that number, nothing more. And eventually she discovered that if she remained nothing, no one could truly hurt her. Ultimately only her body had been present in prison; she was not.

Emotionally she had been dead, coming alive only during the weekly ten-minute phone call she was allowed. She had used those precious minutes to attempt to relate to Liane, to try to keep up with what was happening on the outside, to maintain a thread of sanity.

Upon her release, the weight of humiliation had fallen away, leaving her feeling physically lighter and temporarily exultant. But here she was, days later, all her ebullience draining away.

She was an outsider—a member of her family, but somehow not. She was tainted, she guessed. And she knew in her heart that even when she and Nina made up, things would never be the same again.

She stirred the melting marshmallows into the hot chocolate, took another sip and savored the taste.

It was the first hot chocolate she'd had in a year.

Standing in front of the fridge, deciding what she wanted, pouring the milk, stirring in the chocolate, rummaging for the marshmallows, popping the cup into the microwave—all were ordinary activities that had been denied her for eleven months. Even being up at two in the morning was a luxury she would never again take for granted.

She wanted to forget prison, to erase the humiliation she had suffered. But her brain rolled the memories before her mind's eye, and she was helpless to stop them.

There had been rules, and harsh penalties when the rules were broken. Every single moment of an inmate's day and night had to be accounted for. One rose early, made one's bed to precise specifications, then stood in line to be counted for bed checks, for meals, for showers.

Then there were the strip searches. The ultimate in abasement. And when her period came, she had to ask a guard for each and every sanitary napkin. Since prisons were equal-opportunity employers, the sneers and smirks of male guards often had to be endured in docile silence.

Rewards were few—an extra cup of instant coffee, the occasional orange.

Her chocolate had grown cold, skimmed over. Stormy stared into the cup unseeing as she toted up what she had lost: a thriving sandwich shop on the beach, and her little but lovely carriage house. Both business and house had been sold while she was on bail awaiting trial—sold at a loss to pay attorney fees. All for naught; she had been convicted.

She closed her eyes. While in prison she had felt left out of life, forgotten. She wanted everything restored. Job. House. Money. Love. She was starving for everything in the world. Everything.

A tear rolled down her cheek and splashed into her cup. "No!" she told herself softly. "I won't give in to self-pity. I won't."

"Won't do what?"

Stormy turned and saw her sister. "I was just talking to myself. Couldn't you sleep?"

"How can I, with you wandering the house all night?" Nina plopped down on a stool. "Tully is furious. He needs his rest."

Stormy shook her head. "Nina," she said gently, "this is a big house, and it does belong to both of us."

"What does that mean? That it's Tully who's here on sufferance?"

"I only meant that Liane and I are obliged to live here until I can get on my feet again." Stormy tried to take her sister's hand. Nina jerked it away. Hurt, Stormy was silent as she tried to fathom her sister's attitude.

"Look," she began, "I know it's hard having two families under the same roof. We each need our privacy. But I'm having a bit of trouble adjusting, Nina. My whole life has crashed, and down—"

"Yours! What about ours? I can't go anywhere without someone asking about you, reminding me of what you did. Tully is sure he lost that big plumbing contract because of you."

Stormy stiffened. "Wait a minute! I didn't rob any bank, and you know it. I simply got caught up in the wheels of the justice system when they weren't rolling very smoothly."

"Who believes that!"

"Someday I'm going to clear my name if I can, Nina. Meanwhile, I'd appreciate it if you'd stop blaming me for Tully's—" Stormy stopped. The long and the short of it was that Nina's husband was fond of hatching grandiose schemes with other people's money. He often had good ideas, but he didn't have the patience for careful planning. He wanted to be at the top without having to work to get there.

Stormy suspected her parents had been afraid Tully Dawson would squander Nina's inheritance; thus, they'd placed their carefully saved lifetime earnings in trust. The house was left to both sisters, with the stipulation that it not be sold until Nina was at least thirty-five. Meanwhile, either one or both of them could live there. The trust, which included other investments, took care of upkeep and paid each sister a small stipend each month. Stormy had signed over her stipend to Nina during her incarceration to help Nina care for Liane.

"Blame Tully for what?" Nina spewed. "The reason we can't liquidate the estate is you. Mom and Dad were concerned you'd fritter it away. You were nothing but trouble to them. It broke their hearts when you had Liane out of wedlock. I'm just glad they weren't around to see how you really did turn out."

Every muscle in Stormy's body quivered; her heart contracted in her chest and her breath choked in her throat. "You must be turned inside out by all this to say something so cruel," she gasped. "Nina, I can understand your being bitter—going to prison turned all our lives topsy-turvy. But don't you *ever* make slurs about Liane. Mom and Dad adored her. I won't let you take that away from her. Or me." Stormy stood, holding onto the tabletop for much-needed balance. "We'll be out of this house as soon as I can find a job and an apartment."

"Or a man?" Nina said with a sneer.

Stormy felt her stomach tighten. She wanted so much for her life to return to normal. She especially wished she could experience some sense of closeness with her younger sister. Nina must have been waiting a long time for an opportunity to erupt so viciously. And that was simply too much emotional baggage for Stormy to cope with atop all her other problems.

"One day perhaps there will be a man in my life, but for now, a job will do."

"No one hired you today, did they?" Nina's expression was one of self-satisfaction, as if affirming Stormy's worthlessness to family and society.

Stormy winced. "No, but I'll keep looking." Brave words, Stormy thought, especially since she had discovered that finding work was not going to be as easy as she had thought. Her interviews thus far were disasters. What she wanted most right this minute was to lick her wounds in private. "I'm going for a walk on the beach."

"I suppose you'll want to leave the door unlatched so anybody can come in and murder us in our beds."

"No," Stormy said evenly, "I'll take my key."

A few minutes later, she was on the deserted shoreline, taking long strides in the wet sand while the sharp breeze whipped open her parka. It was never pitch-dark on the beach, the golden sands seeming to cast a glow of their own.

As the salty wind rushed over her body, Stormy felt her humiliation and anger begin to fade. She walked a mile, then two, allowing her mind to empty itself. She swung her arms, taking pleasure in the rhythm of free movement, the give of the sand beneath her shoes, the susurrous waves as they rushed ashore.

Somewhat calmer and renewed in spirit, she turned back, stopping at the foot of the dune walk that gave access to the beach from the house. Stormy stared at the homestead. While her parents were alive, these rooms had been filled with warmth and laughter.

Memories of that warmth and laughter, the knowledge that Liane was safe there in her absence, had sustained Stormy in Lowell. Now the house seemed to hold only gloom and anger and defeat. The lovely, warm aura was gone.

Surely, Stormy thought suddenly, Nina had not been taking out her vitriol on Liane. It was a thought too horrible to bear.

Once inside, as she undressed and crept quietly into the old four-poster she shared with Liane, her earlier exchange with Tyler Mangus flashed into her mind.

She saw again his clear, bright, inquisitive eyes, his lips tilted with irony. Along with his devilish good looks, her memory also logged his peremptory manner, the sharp edge to his charm, the shrewdness he couldn't quite hide. No doubt about it—the man was tough. Implacable.

Still, he had an infectious smile. Man of the moment, indeed.

Beneath all the anxiety, she had felt entirely female in his presence. Felt like a woman, not just a number.

And that spelled danger.

Not to worry, Stormy told herself. She fiercely resented Tyler Mangus's intrusion on their lives, and that alone would keep her from going gaga just because the man seemed to find her attractive.

She turned over and placed an arm lightly about her sleeping daughter. Liane's emotions were fragile. She had not taken the deaths of her grandparents well, and Stormy suspected the child had suffered a confusing sense of betrayal at her mother's long absence. Liane had to be protected, no matter what the cost.

STORMY DID NOT WANT TO GO down to breakfast while Tully and Nina were in the kitchen, but the aroma of freshly perked coffee wafting up the stairs lured her. She slid out of bed without waking Liane and shrugged into her robe.

"Well, well, look who deigns to join us this bright, sunshiny morning," crowed Tully. "My sister-in-law, the jailbird."

Stormy looked to Nina to see if she would curb her husband's ridicule, but Nina just said, "Sit down, I'll pour your coffee. Do you want breakfast?"

"No, thanks. I'll make Liane a cup of cocoa and take my coffee upstairs."

"Too good for the likes of us, eh?" Tully injected.

Stormy hesitated. Tully was slouched at the breakfast bar, unshaven, bleary-eyed. He had come home late last night and gone straight to bed. She suspected he'd loitered at a local bar after work. Still, if Nina was tolerant of such behavior, she didn't think it was her place to comment. On the other hand, she wasn't going to put up with insults.

"Tully," she said with restraint, "please don't get into the habit of calling me a jailbird. You might let it slip in front of Liane. She's been hurt enough. And so have I."

He rolled his eyes. "Listen to your sister there, Nina. She's gone from sinner to saint."

Nina banged his breakfast down in front of him so hard, the toast flew off the plate. "Shut up and eat."

Stormy moved out of their line of fire to the kitchen counter, busying herself making cocoa and toast for Liane, pouring coffee for herself. She put it all on a wicker tray and left the kitchen without a backward glance.

On the staircase landing, she met her nephews. "Hi, boys."

She held up the tray so they could scoot beneath it.

Davie, the five-year-old, stopped. "Look, Aunt Stormy, I dressed myself for school."

"You sure did. You look very handsome."

Tommy, four, was hugging a blanket that had long ago seen better days. "I'm goin' to school, too."

"No, you're not," Davie informed him. "You're still a baby."

"I am not."

"Are, too."

"Am not."

"Give me your blanket, then."

Tommy bunched the rag under his arm and hurried down the steps. Davie grinned up at Stormy. "He's a big sissy."

Stormy smiled. "Maybe not."

"He takes that blanket everywhere. It's disgusting."

His tone was so like Tully's, Stormy knew at once he was mimicking his father. She was glad she had spoken up to her brother-in-law about name-calling.

Liane was sitting up in bed. Stormy set the tray aside and gave the child a hug. Liane did not turn away, but she didn't reciprocate, either.

"It's so wonderful to wake up and have you right here with me every morning," Stormy told her. "I missed you so much."

Liane plucked at the sheet. "Will you ever have to go away again?"

Stormy plumped up Liane's pillows and put the tray across the child's knees.

"Not if I can help it."

Liane's eyes grew wide with doubt. "You said you couldn't help it last time."

Stormy sipped the coffee, using the moment to form her answer. Above all, she knew she must be truthful with Liane; she must somehow convey a sense of reality to her without enlarging on her daughter's feelings of betrayal and abandonment.

"I wish," she said, "that we lived in a world where bad things never happened. It hurt both of us when I had to go to prison. But I didn't abandon you, poppet. The courts said I had to serve—"

"We could have run away together."

Stormy smiled. "Did you think that, too?" Liane nodded, and Stormy went on. "But we would've been scared all the time. At least, I would've been. And if the police had found us, we would've been separated, anyway. Probably longer. The way it worked out, you got to live with Aunt Nina, so I knew you'd be safe. That's what I wanted for you. To be safe."

"I don't like living here, Mom. Aunt Nina fusses all the time."

"Well, we'll be out on our own again soon. Now, eat, then get dressed. I'm driving you to school today."

While Stormy dressed, Liane munched her toast. "Mom, what does *illegitimate* mean?"

Stormy was brushing her hair; her hand stopped in midair. "Where did you hear that word?"

Liane shrugged. "I just heard it."

She's testing me, Stormy decided, *finding out how far I'll go for honesty, how much truth I'll share with her.* Somehow, she had to act as if the conversation were ordinary, and take care not to allow her any negative ideas about her birth, about herself. She sighed inwardly. It was going to be a heavy morning.

"*Illegitimate* is often used to refer to a person born outside of marriage," she began carefully. "But it's not a very useful word. It doesn't—"

Liane had kept her eyes on the toast she was tearing into small bits. Now she burst out with, "Then I'm illegitimate."

Stormy almost choked. How did you tell a seven-year-old about society's thoughtless ways of labeling nonconformist behavior without prejudicing the child totally against the world she must live in. "You know, poppet, that doesn't mean you were born without love," she said. "And love is what's important. I adored your father."

"Why didn't you marry him?"

"He—he changed his mind."

"Just like that?"

Stormy took up the brush again and began working tangles out of her hair. "It seemed so at the time. Looking back, though, I think he was scared of responsibility. Some men are."

"You mean he was scared of me."

"Oh, poppet, it wasn't you. He didn't even know you. Sometimes men get to feeling closed in. That's how your father put it to me."

"What was his name?"

"Truman Witney," Stormy said hollowly.

"Will I ever meet him?"

Stormy's arm dropped like a leaden weight. "I don't know. I doubt he'll ever come back to St. Augustine. His daddy died soon after you were born, and his mother moved up north to live with a widowed sister. I haven't heard from her in years." In truth, Mrs. Witney had accused her of being fast and loose and of trying to trap her son. But surely no seven-year-old needed *that* much truth.

"But if I wanted to meet my daddy, I could?"

"Maybe when you're older," Stormy said lamely. "If the opportunity presents itself."

Nina poked her head around the door. "Stormy, Liane is going to be late for school."

"We'll be down in ten minutes."

Stormy was glad of the interruption, but she knew from the look on Liane's face that the child meant to get a lot more mileage out of the topic. She rushed her through her ablutions and getting dressed.

In the car, Liane sat primly in the front seat, quietly hugging her book bag all the way to school. Digesting their earlier conversation, Stormy surmised. "I'll pick you up at two-thirty, okay?"

"I can ride the bus home."

"I want to pick you up, poppet. I love doing it."

She needed to immerse herself in motherhood. It somehow anchored her, gave her a pivot from which to make all other decisions. Being "Mom" gave her an identity other than inmate number DC 153026.

Liane hesitated before she closed the car door. "He's been following us," she said, nodding toward the street.

Stormy looked over her shoulder, registering that Tyler Mangus was, indeed, in the BMW behind her and that school buses and other parents' cars were lined up waiting to discharge students.

"Go on inside," she told her daughter.

"But...Mom...will you be okay?"

"I'll be fine, and I'll be here at two-thirty. Scoot. There's the first bell."

Once Liane was safely through the schoolhouse doors, Stormy drove to the nearest convenience store. Tyler Mangus pulled up next to her. Temper rising, she hurriedly exited her car, skirted his hood and stood at his window.

"What kind of game do you think you're playing?" she said, her voice lofty and indignant.

He gazed up at her. "No game. Just doing my job."

"If you follow me anywhere near school property again, I'll report you to the principal and have you arrested...as a pervert!"

"Oh, now, would that be nice?" he taunted, enjoying his view of her fine-boned face with its gracefully winged eyebrows and long, thick lashes that did little to shutter the sudden fire in her eyes.

"Slug!" she spat, shaking with inner turmoil, and she returned to her car. She sat behind the steering wheel, her heart racing. Then, collecting her composure, she started the car and drove off.

All the way to her first appointment with her parole officer, she watched the rearview mirror. Tyler Mangus didn't attempt to follow. Or if he did, he had rendered himself invisible.

As she made her way up to the third floor of the courthouse, where the probation offices were, Stormy didn't meet anyone she knew, for which she was everlastingly grateful.

Ironically, one of her best friends had been the court reporter assigned to record her trial. That event had precluded continuing their friendship. Job integrity, Suzanne had insisted. Stormy felt the friendship had died of embarrassment.

She signed in at the probation office and waited in the tiny cubicle of a reception area for her name to be called. She felt jittery and cautioned herself that she need not be demeaned anymore. Though her record said otherwise, she had always been a law-abiding citizen. If she kept that uppermost in her mind, she could manage the meeting.

Still, recalling fellow inmates' tales about parole officers made her shudder. "The men are the worst, always wantin' sumthin'—if you know what I mean."

Stormy knew what the girl had meant.

When her name was called and she realized her case had been assigned to a woman, she sighed with relief.

Nonetheless, Mrs. Lowery, though in her late fifties, was not the grandmotherly sort. She was trim, tough and thorough. After reviewing countless rules and regulations, she leaned back in the chair, giving Stormy fair warning. "Work with me, and I'll work with you. If you don't, I'll recommend your parole be yanked. You know what that means?"

Stormy assured her she did.

"Good. How's the job hunt going?"

"Not as well as I expected," Stormy admitted.

"If you feel you need it, there's a new program called Project Independence. I can recommend you for it."

Stormy declined. "I'll find something. I'm not destitute or homeless—yet."

"Let me know when you start work. I'll visit you on the job and have a word with your supervisor."

Stormy blanched. "Is that necessary?"

The older woman's expression was not unsympathetic. "I'm afraid so. You're a convicted felon, Stormy. Your employers have a right to know that." She gave Stormy her business card. "If you have any problems, call."

Dismissed, Stormy fled the office, chafed. She was out of prison yet still in one.

The late-March sun felt so good on her face, she bypassed her parked car and walked across the old market square to the bayfront.

St. Augustine was the oldest city in the United States. It was also a family town. There were no porno shops, no nude-dancing clubs, no all-night bars. During the day, the historic district was clogged with tourists, beachgoers and the locals who ran the shops and kept the city pulsating.

Tourists scuttled past on their way to hiring horse-drawn carriages or to ride the sightseeing boat that toured Salt Run and Matansas Bay.

Stormy found a vacant bench on the seawall and sat down. The bay was cluttered with craft of every description, driven to safe harbor, perhaps, by the storm that had finally blown itself out to sea last night. Sailboats and sleek sloops, yachts and catamarans were anchored serenely, with dinghies bobbing behind them to get sailors to and from shore.

For a moment Stormy entertained the thought of sailing to a faraway island and leaving her troubles behind. She'd grab up Liane—

"Coffee?" he asked, holding out a paper cup.

The coffee smelled wonderful, but she refused it, wondering how much her expression revealed. "Do you really mean to plague me day in and day out?"

"Yep." Tyler Mangus sat down beside her, put the unaccepted coffee on the bench between them and took a sip of his own. "Nice view," he said.

"Goodbye," she answered, and in a fluid movement was on her feet.

He grabbed her arm. "Hey! Hold it. A man's life is at stake here."

Stormy drew up short. "Whose?"

"Mine. If you don't talk to me, I'll die of a broken heart."

Tyler saw beautiful bemusement on a face that seemed to hide no secrets. But of course, it did, he thought. Waiting for her reply to his silly volley, he gave her his best smile.

"That is too adolescent," she told him. She tried to shake his hand loose, but he continued to hold her tightly.

"Adolescent? How old do you think I am?"

"Listen, you obviously don't need me to feed your vanity. Turn me loose."

"I'm forty-two—long past adolescence. However, I'm told I can pass for thirty-five."

"For all I care, you could pass for dead. Turn me loose or I'll scream."

"You would, wouldn't you?"

"Absolutely." She inhaled a deep breath.

"Please," he said, "sit down for a few minutes. I wasn't even going to approach you, but you looked so damned forlorn when you came out of the courthouse." He released her arm and silently offered her the coffee once more.

"You...you noticed?" Stormy felt conflicting emotions leap and whirl, and her perception of Tyler shifted slightly. He was a danger to her on more than one front, and yet here he was, offering her empathy...as if he somehow cared. Of course, she could be reading him wrong. Probably was. The show of sympathy was doubtless just another tactic to break down her defenses, to render her trusting...careless.

"Let's put it this way—I identify with pain. Of course, that means I'm easily suckered by a sob story."

"You don't look the type to be suckered by anything," she countered. She accepted the proffered coffee and sat down with a sigh. "I don't know if I'm being incredibly stupid or not," she muttered.

"Oh, you're not stupid." Idly, he leaned back on the bench, gazing admirably at her profile and felt an irrational urge to reach out and smooth the tiny frown on her brow. "If I had to put a label on you, it'd be stubborn. Maybe even mind-boggling."

Stormy didn't rise to the bait.

A group of students from nearby Flagler College strolled past. The girls smiled with approval at Tyler. He smiled back. Stormy caught the exchange. "You get a lot of mileage out of your looks, don't you?"

Tyler started. He didn't think himself ugly, but neither did he consider himself overly handsome. "Do my ears deceive me, or is that a compliment?"

"Merely an observation. Besides, I'm not about to be swayed by someone's looks again," she added quietly.

He looked at her sharply but said only, "Yeah, I say that, too. But I'm just lying to myself."

His admission resonated in Stormy's mind. When Hadley Wilson had been introduced to her, she had taken him at his very attractive face value. She had not searched far beneath his looks or charm, and that oversight had landed her a prison sentence.

"Let's just say I look beyond the surface for motive now, Mr. Mangus."

"Tyler, please."

"I know your motive," she added conversationally. "It's money." He looked startled. "Money I don't have, never did have." She turned to face him and was met by the scent of his after-shave. It was woodsy and masculine, and Stormy found herself leaning into his space. Oh, no! she thought. Was she so in need of affection that she'd consider consorting with the enemy? She straightened, stiffening her back. "Why don't you hound Hadley Wilson?"

Tyler frowned. Her slight shift in posture had tightened her blouse against the swell of her breasts. He forced his eyes up, taking in the ivory column of her throat, the shape of her mouth. It was a very nice mouth. Deep inside, he felt the prick of desire.

Whoa! he told himself. No way was he ready to pitch himself headlong into woman trouble. And even if he were, Stormy Elliott was not on his dance card.

Recovering his composure, he answered her question. "Wilson won't talk to me. So, if you want me off your back, maybe you could convince—"

"No!" Stormy clutched her purse, which held the list of rules and regulations that were to guide her life for the next two years. "You know I'm on parole. I'm not allowed to associate with felons, much less visit one in prison—especially my so-called partner in crime." She handed Tyler the half-empty paper cup. "Thanks for the coffee."

Before he could stop her, Stormy was off and running. He merely stared after her, contemplative.

As if she sensed his eyes on her back, she stopped at the curb and pivoted.

"Are you from St. Augustine?" she asked.

"No, I'm—"

"I have a job interview in fifteen minutes at Shoney's—that's on U.S. 1 South. After that, I'm seeing our family attorney. His office is in the three-story pink house on the corner of Spanish and Treasury streets." Her smile was deadly. "Do keep your distance."

When she moved away, it was with long, determined strides and no looking back.

Tyler groaned. He hauled himself off the bench and made his way to his car. The woman was proud and valiant and gutsy. She hadn't asked any quarter...and he dare not give it.

Chapter Three

Stormy looked out the law office's windows to see if she could spot Tyler in the parking lot. No sign of him. Oddly let down, she turned away from the view.

Paradoxically, she had been looking forward to his popping up, even though his presence at every turn was keeping her on edge.

Midinterview at the restaurant, she'd happened to glance up and discovered him sipping coffee in a nearby booth.

Like a coconspirator, he'd winked at her, his mouth lifting in one of his crooked smiles. She'd rapidly returned her concentration to the restaurant manager.

The interview had died when she'd mentioned she was on parole.

Fortunately, Tyler had not been able to overhear the interview, and when she noticed him slip into the men's room, she used the moment to make a hasty departure. All the way back to the historical district and her appointment with the trust attorney, she had reveled in her ability to give Tyler the slip.

Chagrined at the thought that staying a step ahead of him was becoming a game to her, she veered away from thinking any more about him.

Benjamin Flaherty appeared and motioned her into his inner office.

She couldn't remember a time when the pink-faced, rotund, avuncular estate manager had not been involved with the Elliotts. A quiet, self-effacing bachelor, he had often taken his holiday meals with them.

He had studied law, but economics and international money brokering had always fascinated him. While still in college he'd begun buying up pounds, deutschmarks and rands when the dollar exchange rate was low, selling when high. He had an uncanny knack with currency.

Once his fraternity brothers realized his ability, they began depositing their allowances and part-time salaries with Ben. So successful had he been that many of his fraternity brothers continued business with him long after graduation. Those frat brothers became the nucleus of his client roster, Stormy's own father among them.

Ben and her father had also shared an obsessive interest in philately. When Dave Elliott had died, he'd left his stamp collection to Ben and a plea for Ben to act as trustee and manager of the property left to his daughters.

Ben was now long past retirement age. He accepted no new clients or new money.

"Stormy, it's good to have you home," he said in his melodious voice.

"It's wonderful to be home, Ben."

He waved her into an overstuffed club chair beside his desk, then opened a file. "You said on the phone that you wanted to withdraw the power of attorney you'd given Nina."

"Yes, and I thought I'd pick up my trust allowance for this month. If you don't mind."

The old gentleman looked at her, flustered. Apprehension zipped down Stormy's spine. "There isn't a problem with the trust, is there, Ben?'' All sorts of scenarios flashed through her mind: the principal lost through bad investments, or swallowed up in the savings-and-loan collapse. Maybe Ben had lost his touch with exchange rates.

"The principal is intact," he assured her. "But, my dear, you gave Nina access while you . . . in your absence."

Stormy detected disapproval in his voice. "I felt it was the right thing to do, Ben. Nina has two children of her own, and she couldn't absorb the expense of taking care of Liane, too. It wouldn't have been fair to ask that of her."

"In the future," he reprimanded softly, "do check with me before you hand over your trust income to anyone— family members included."

Stormy paled. Lest she had misunderstood his drift, she wanted to hear his innuendo spelled out. "What exactly are you saying?"

His face went a deeper shade of pink. "Nina came in soon after you . . . left and drew an advance on the income. You know I've always accommodated you girls as long as the principal didn't dip below the levels your father insisted be available at the trust's maturity."

Stormy's mouth went dry. "How much of an advance?"

"Fifty-four hundred dollars."

"Fifty-four?" Her stomach seized up. "But—" She did some quick mental calculations. "That's for eighteen months!"

"Nina told me you left some legal bills you wanted cleared up, that you wanted your car put in storage and that you required cash in your draw account in . . . at Lowell."

"It's okay to say it, Ben. Prison. Jail." Dejected, she slumped back in the chair. "I didn't leave any unfinished business behind. I sold my sandwich shop and my house to pay for everything. My car was not put in storage. Nina used it.''

The old family retainer and friend looked grim. ''You're telling me that Nina abused the power of attorney?''

''Yes! She was to take what she needed to feed and clothe Liane. To have money in case Liane broke an arm or got sick.''

Ben shook his head. ''Rest assured I'll have a talk with Nina. I'm compelled to advise you that you have a legal right to pursue recovery, you know.''

''You mean file a civil suit against my own sister? Take her to court?'' Stormy shuddered. That sort of painful breach between herself and Nina could never be healed. ''I don't want to do that. I won't.''

''I feel badly about this, Stormy. I wish you'd consulted me before you gave Nina your power of attorney. I honored it because, frankly, I thought, perhaps, you were too embarrassed to come in and make arrangements yourself.''

Stormy sighed. ''I thought I was being efficient, taking care of loose ends. Everything had to be done so hurriedly. I didn't think I was going to be convicted. Once I was, there was no time for anything!'' Though she knew the answer, she had to ask. ''So there's no cash at all available?''

He shook his head. ''There isn't. Truthfully, I stripped every certificate of deposit of interest and every utility stock of dividends in order to give Nina the cash I thought you needed. Your dad left specific instructions. He placed an ironclad ceiling on the amount of money that could be withdrawn from the trust on an annual basis. I'm afraid the fifty-four hundred pushed it to the ceiling, wiping out even the small reserves I hold back against either of you having an emergency.''

Stormy was shaking her head in an effort to keep tears at bay. "I'm having an awful time finding work, Ben. I was really counting on—"

He opened a drawer and pulled out his personal check-book. "I feel worse about this than you do, my dear. I've let you down, and I feel like I've betrayed the trust your father placed in me. Let me write you a check to tide you over, and when you get on your feet . . ."

Stormy had a thought. "What about Nina's share of the trust? Has she taken an advance on that income, too?"

Ben cleared his throat. "One could make that assumption," he said with tact and delicacy.

Moments later, on the way to pick up Liane from school, Stormy was tangled in anger, fear and panic.

Up until now her brain had been offering practical solutions to every obstacle she thought she might encounter once out of prison. She had never considered that one of the obstacles would be her own sister!

She cringed at the thought of having to ask Nina about the trust money. She was doubtful that she could keep her temper in check, and losing it would only put more strain on their deteriorating relationship.

But, dear God. All she had between herself and disaster was seven dollars and change.

She arrived at the school a few minutes early and found a parking spot at the curb. Behind her, the car-pool brigade began to line up. Feeling claustrophobic, she emerged from the Ford and leaned against the fender. Her eyes darted fore and aft, looking for Tyler. Again, no sign of him. Perhaps her earlier warning had had its effect.

The dismissal bell rang and students began pouring out of the building. When she spied her daughter, Stormy put on a smile.

"How was school?" she asked as she settled the child in the car.

"Same as always. Can we go get a pizza? I'm starved."

Stormy's mouth tasted like ash. "I don't have enough money with me, poppet. Let's eat at home tonight."

Liane flounced. "We're poor, aren't we? Aunt Nina is always complaining there's not enough money."

"Let's just say we're suffering a temporary setback. I'll have a job soon, and with my very first paycheck, we'll go out and eat a mountain of pizza." She glanced at Liane, discovering the child's old-young eyes hard on her. "That's a promise."

"Are you having a hard time finding work because people are afraid you'll steal their money?"

Obviously Liane had been keeping up with Stormy's job-hunt and had hit upon the truth as Stormy herself had. "I'm beginning to think so," she answered honestly.

"Does that hurt your feelings?"

"Actually, it does," she said, amazed at her daughter's perceptiveness. She had a scary thought and voiced it. "Has . . . has anyone been hurting your feelings?"

"Sometimes, but I just pretend they haven't."

Stormy felt as if her heart would break. "That's what I do, too. But if someone is being unkind to you, talk it over with me, okay?"

Liane nodded. "Are we going to get our own house like we had before?"

"We sure are. That's tops on my agenda."

"Then can my best friend come spend the night?"

"Absolutely. Anytime, sweetie. You don't even have to wait for us to get our own place."

"Yes, I do. Aunt Nina says it's selfish of me to want my friends to myself. She says I have to share them with Davie and Tommy. And Uncle Tully doesn't like other kids in the house. He says we make too much noise.''

"I see,'' Stormy said, understanding more than she wanted to. Remorse overwhelmed her. In her absence, her daughter had been treated like an unwanted stepchild—and on her own five thousand dollars, to boot! Stormy had more than one bone to pick with Nina and Tully.

"Red light!'' Liane cried.

Stormy hit the brakes. "Thanks, sweetie. I guess I was daydreaming. Tell me about your best friend, poppet. Is she as smart as you?''

"She's *like* me. She doesn't have a daddy because her mom's divorced, and her mother once went to jail for writing bad checks. But it wasn't Mrs. Byers's fault, because Janelle's daddy took all their money out of the bank without telling anybody.''

It took Stormy until they were parked in the drive at the beach house to compose a reply, and once she did, she had no idea whether Liane would understand it. She brushed stray wisps of hair off her daughter's brow. "I'm going to make it up to you, Liane. Somehow. I'm beginning to see that living with Aunt Nina and Uncle Tully was as much a prison for you as a real one was for me. Will you remember that I love you more than life itself?''

Liane seemed to think that over. "Does that mean you won't fuss at me—ever?''

Stormy laughed. "Not quite, but I might be able to hold off until you get to be a snooty teenager.''

"Oh, I don't want to be a teenager. Then I might have to have a period. Yuk!''

Alarmed motherhood flared in Stormy. "Who told you about that?'' she asked with what she hoped was a semblance of calm.

"Janelle. She has a sister who's almost fifteen, and she's the one with the period, and she has to get it ev-er-y month. Mrs. Byers is always making sure that she does, so they fuss about it a lot. Janelle and I made a pact. We're not going to get periods, even if they're cheap."

"Periods...cheap?" Stormy repeated, beginning to worry about what other misguided ideas Liane might have acquired in her absence.

Liane shrugged. "I guess. Janelle says her mother is always telling her sister that periods are cheaper than alter natives."

"Alter...natives? Oh," Stormy said, grasping the child's mispronunciation.

Liane looked at her mother. "You're not mad, are you?"

Stormy was lost. "About what?"

"Me and Janelle making a pact."

"Oh, no. I think it's a wonderful idea."

Liane beamed. "I knew you would. I told Janelle you wouldn't get me a period if I didn't want one, even if it was on sale at K mart."

"That's...true, poppet." Stormy didn't know whether to laugh or cry. She opened the car door and swung her legs out.

"Mom?"

Stormy stopped, looked back.

"Did anything really, really awful happen to you while you were in jail?"

Standing naked before the guards during strip searches flashed through Stormy's mind. "No, nothing really awful. Why?"

"Aunt Nina said you'd be different when you came home because terrible things had happened to you."

Stormy shifted back onto the seat. "The only truly awful thing was being away from you."

Liane picked at the strap of her book bag. "I was mad at you for going away. But now I'm not. You couldn't help it. Janelle's mother couldn't help it, either. And that's what happened to us. Hadley took that money and didn't tell us."

Stormy felt as if some unbearable burden was slipping away.

"Thank you," she said, softly joyful. She reached over and hugged Liane until the child squirmed. "We're a team again, poppet. Nobody is going to beat us at life ever again. What say we go pig out on baloney sandwiches?"

Liane rolled her eyes. "I *despise* baloney."

Stormy laughed. "Me, too."

"YOU LOOK HAPPY," Nina said by way of greeting to Stormy. She was shrugging into a sweater. David and Tommy, jackets on, hair slicked down and wearing hangdog expressions, were hovering near their mother. "You got the job."

Stormy vacillated. She could see no reason to open herself up to more of Nina's ill-disposed remarks. She fudged the truth. "They'll call me. Are you going out?"

"I'm taking the boys to the dentist. You don't mind if I use the car?"

"I was hoping we'd have time for a talk."

"Later, okay? I'm running behind as it is." Nina turned to go. "Oh, Tully and I are invited over to some friends tonight to play cards. I said we'd go. You'll watch the boys, won't you?"

"I will tonight, but in the future I wish you'd ask me first. I might've had to start work or had other plans."

Nina's expression whipped into a grimace of incensed umbrage. "You have the gall to have that attitude after I've taken care of Liane day and night for almost a solid year?"

It was on the tip of Stormy's tongue to blurt out how costly had been Liane's care, to disclose the conversation she'd had with Benjamin Flaherty, but she bit back the outburst. A shouting match in front of the children would be terrible form. "I only meant I'd hate for you to have to change your plans if I happened not to be available." She handed Nina the car keys. "You'll have to put in some gas."

"I figured that," Nina snapped. She ushered the boys out ahead of her, then stalked away, trailing virtuous indignation like confetti.

Trembling, Stormy sat down on the foyer bench, thinking back to when times were different. When she and Nina had shared the upstairs bedroom. Shared closets and clothes and secrets. But that was all gone now. She had to force herself to remember that. She was not going to get those times back. Mom and Dad, Nina's love. All gone. An awful pessimism descended slowly into her mind.

Liane came and perched beside her and threw an arm around her. "Sometimes I'd like to smack Aunt Nina on the butt."

"Hey! Watch your language."

"Can I say two billy goats butted heads?"

"I know that's a trick question, but, yes, you can say that. It's how you meant—"

"Is it okay if I make a wish?"

"Am I going to be in sheep dip up to my knees if I say yes?"

Liane gave her a brilliant smile. "Then I wish Aunt Nina would get stuck between two billy goats buttin' heads."

"No comment," Stormy said, managing to suppress her smile, but only just.

Undaunted, Liane grabbed her book bag and skipped up the stairs. At the landing she stopped briefly to observe, "When I told Miss Evans I was in sheep dip up to my knees in homework, *she* made me write ten times on the blackboard that I wouldn't say bad words."

Stormy leaned her head back on the wall and closed her eyes. Some role model she was turning out to be.

AFTER SHE AND LIANE ATE sandwiches, Stormy cut and trimmed vegetables to start a pot of soup simmering. Again it struck her how wonderful it was to have the freedom to choose what she wanted to eat, to prepare the meal, to pad back and forth from pantry to sink to fridge. There was no count time, no guards, no clamor. Never in a million years could she explain to anyone how good such ordinary tasks felt.

Liane sat in the alcove, doing her homework. The afternoon sun poured in, tinting her light brown hair gold. Stormy smiled at the child's concentration on gripping the pencil properly to form each letter just so. No matter what, Stormy thought, Liane needed her. Periods for sale— heavens!

She pulled up a stool and sat opposite her daughter. "The tide is going out. Want to walk on the beach and watch the sun go down?"

"Nah. May I call Janelle? We hardly ever get to talk on the phone."

"Sure. If you like, you can invite her to spend the weekend with you."

"Mom! For real?"

"Well, with her mother's permission. Ask if Janelle can ride here on the bus with you tomorrow, and we'll take her home Sunday."

Liane's enthusiasm ebbed. "What about Aunt Nina and Uncle Tully?"

It was Stormy's moment to impart some confidence. "Not to worry. I'll handle them. This house belongs to us as much as it does to your Aunt Nina. It's our home for as long as we need it to be."

Liane slid off the stool. "I'll call Janelle right now! Boy, will she be excited. We can do our science projects together."

"While you're on the phone, I'm going for a quick walk on the beach. I'll latch the front door. Don't let anyone in."

"Oh, Mom, I'm not a baby anymore. I *know* that stuff."

Stormy turned down the heat beneath the soup and waited until she heard Liane giggling into the phone before she slipped into her jacket and stepped outside.

The sun moved on its westerly course, coloring the sky an ever deeper mauve. Only a slight breeze soughed across the Atlantic. Walking along the water's edge, she kept her gaze out to sea, idly watching brown pelicans skim the water in search of schools of mullet.

Inwardly, however, she, too, was searching—solutions to her problems. Finding work was of the utmost importance. Yet her floundering relationship with Nina kept rising to the surface. Nina's contempt for everything Stormy did or said. It was all so out of proportion to reality. And Tully was no help. Her brother-in-law was self-absorbed and, Stormy suspected, rather a bully.

Perhaps before prison, Stormy mused, she had been so enmeshed in taking care of Liane and running the sandwich shop that she had not noticed their behavior. Or when she had, she had attributed Nina's unhappiness and occasional snide remarks to grief over their parents' deaths.

Neither of them had had time to absorb the suddenness of Mom and Dad dying within a year of each other. Their mother had complained of being tired all the time. Believing she was possibly anemic, she finally went to the doctor. He diagnosed advanced leukemia, and within weeks, Corrine Elliott was dead. Ten months later, it had been Nina who found their father slumped over his stamp collection at his desk in the den, dead at sixty-eight of a massive heart attack.

Naively, Stormy had expected that their mutual losses would make Nina and her grow closer, not apart. But, beginning with foolish arguing over the choice of their father's gravestone, Nina's antagonism had blossomed and thrived.

"Spectacular sunset, don't you think?"

Stormy started from her reverie, but did not miss a step. "Go away."

"C'mon. We had a good day today." Tyler glanced at her face, saw dismay of the highest order and sighed. "I take that back. We did *not* have a good day. You didn't get the job."

"Gee, why don't you hire yourself out as super sleuth?"

He chuckled. "I already have. And the business you had with the attorney didn't go to your liking."

"Where were you? Bivouacked beneath a window, eavesdropping?"

"You're broke, aren't you?"

Stormy remained silent, but the look on her face said it all. Tyler wanted to reach into his wallet and give her every cent he had, just to see her smile. Unfortunately, that would be courting every last one of his unlucky stars. "So," he said. "Your back is against the wall."

Her pride forced her to lift her chin and calmly meet Tyler's gaze. "I suppose that gives you immense satisfaction."

"Where is it? In a bank? A safety deposit box? Under your mattress?"

Stormy groaned. "Don't you understand English?"

"Sure, lay some on me." His lopsided smile began to form, crooking up the corner of his mouth.

Clad in a tan Windbreaker, tight, faded jeans and well-worn sneakers, he exuded a seemingly uncomplicated beachcomber magnetism. Stormy felt her heart beat faster, and she abruptly looked away.

"How much do you get paid to plague a person like me?"

He laughed. "A lot. Plus thirty-three percent of recovered funds, property, whatever."

"Keep following me and you'll collect thirty-three percent of zero."

"That's my problem."

Stormy found herself enjoying their fencing and promptly warned herself against it. Vexed at her own emotions, she pivoted and aimed her footsteps back up the beach. Tyler moved in tandem with her.

"I do have my back up against it," she admitted. "What I need is a friend—not you."

"I'm a terrific listener."

"You're also the enemy."

Tyler pursed his lips. "True. But that doesn't detract from my ability to offer a sympathetic ear to a beautiful woman."

"Forget I said anything," she said, suspicious of this sudden friendly flirtation.

"I don't think I want to do that."

Stormy looked at him. The last, faint colors of the day streaked across sharp cheekbones, making him appear harsh, dangerous. He was keeping pace with her, elbowing into her space, radiating a maleness that was impossible to ignore. His arm brushed hers. The contact disturbed her, engaging all her senses.

At Lowell, the main topic of inmate conversation had been men and sex. She had not joined the crude gossip, but she understood the inmates' fantasies. Lacking the man, they had substituted words and images.

She was becoming captivated by Tyler's mesmerizing green eyes and throaty voice. Being near him was hazardous. She liked it too much. She lengthened her stride.

Tyler regarded her in a half-amused, sardonic way as she put distance between them. "I love the way you walk," he called softly. "You're liquid. You seem to pour from step to step."

Stormy stopped in her tracks and turned to glower at him. All her frustrations boiled up inside her until she could no longer contain them.

"Do you honestly believe that paying me compliments is going to get you somewhere? Do you think because I've been in prison that I'm so starved for—for a man that I'm going to throw myself at your feet?

"You don't know what it's like to lose everything you own, lose everything you've ever dreamed of. I don't even have any friends anymore. When you've been in prison, people become suspicious of you. You're not ordinary anymore. People don't want to get close because they think I'm tainted and maybe I'll cause them trouble. They'd rather not be involved. They can't trust me, so they won't give me a job. Even my own sister would prefer me on the other side of the earth! And now here you are—playing games with my life. I won't have it. I just won't!''

At the end of her breathless, nonstop litany, she spun away and raced for the dune walk.

Tyler did know what it was like to have it all—then lose it. He ran after her. She had stopped at the railing and bent over it, gasping.

"Go away...please...just go away. I don't have your damned money. I don't want you in my life!''

A merry-go-round of swirling emotions was making Tyler dizzy. What the hell. He couldn't just walk away from her. Her bitterness and agony mirrored his own. It was moving. It touched him. "Listen, sugar, if you were acting, that was the best damned piece of drama I've seen in years. If not...well, we've got ourselves a whole other ball game.''

She brushed away her tears and lifted her head. Could he mean that he was beginning to believe her? "Don't call me 'sugar.'''

"Sweetie?"

"You're a condescending wretch.''

"I've been called worse.''

"I'm *thinking* worse.''

He laughed, the tension broken. "I guessed as much.'' He sat on the top step and patted the boards, gesturing her to sit down. "Look, let's discuss this from my point of view.''

"Haven't *all* our conversations been from your point of view?''

"Dammit, will you quit sparring and hear me out?''

Stormy refused to sit, but she did lean on the railing, one foot on the lower step. "I'm listening.''

"Suppose I went to my clients and said, 'Hey, folks, the Elliott woman doesn't have your money.' 'How do you know?' they'll ask. 'Because she *told* me she didn't,' I'll say. Know what would happen then? I'd be laughed right out of my reputation, that's what. My clients think you have the money or at least you know where it is. You say you're innocent, but you were found guilty. You didn't file an appeal. If you were innocent, why didn't you file an appeal? Why didn't you keep fighting? My clients looked at that."

Stormy sniffed. "I wanted to, but my lawyer explained to me that while the appeal was pending, I wouldn't be eligible for early release. And if I lost, I'd have that much more time to spend in prison. I couldn't take that chance. I just wanted to get the whole mess over with. Besides, appeals cost money, and I had none left." Her eyes glistened. "Liane is so young. Each day away from her was—"

"Okay, okay," he said soothingly. If she broke down and started sobbing again, he knew he wouldn't be able to keep his hands off her. "Your attorney filed a motion for a speedy trial. Why didn't you wait until after Hadley Wilson had been tried?"

"Robbing banks can be a federal offense. And federal sentences are stiffer than state guidelines. So my attorney filed for the speedy trial. Had I been found guilty under federal law, I'd still be in jail. The feds couldn't get their case ready under the speedy-trial act because they wanted to prosecute Hadley and me together. We petitioned the state for a separate trial and got it. I didn't want to be tried with Hadley because we'd found out he made his living robbing banks. I-it was a nightmare."

It was fully dark now, the crescent moon casting only gleaming slivers on the ocean. Floodlights began snapping on at homes up and down the beach.

Stormy was waiting for Tyler to make some reply. He didn't, but she could feel herself flush hotly at the look in his eyes. Uncomfortable at his smoldering perusal, she straightened. "I've got to go. Liane is in the house by herself."

Tyler gave her one of his crooked smiles. "Feel any better?"

"I made a fool of myself, I guess."

"My turn next time."

She uttered a tiny laugh. "I may just hold you to that."

He stayed at the foot of the walk until she reached the kitchen door. Before she slipped inside, she turned. He thought he saw her lift her hand, but in the dimness, he couldn't be sure.

"Stormy," he murmured into the night. "You're blowing all my circuits."

As he walked back along the beach to his car, a pair of gulls followed him, swooping and squawking as if to reprimand him for invading their territory.

He cocked his head up. "Sorry, fellas. But we all gotta play the game."

Chapter Four

Liane bustled about the kitchen like a little mother, putting cereal in bowls, pouring milk and buttering toast.

"You've got this down pretty good," an observant Stormy told her. "Do you fix breakfast often?"

"Only when Aunt Nina doesn't get up. But I can never make the boys brush their teeth."

"I do, too, brush my teeth," said Davie. "Tommy's the one who eats the toothpaste."

The younger boy laughed. "I like toothpaste. It's zingy."

"Chill out and eat," ordered Liane. The boys accepted their cousin's authority and began to spoon up their cereal.

After breakfast Stormy stood at the foot of the drive and waited with the children until their school buses came, wondering how often Nina and Tully had abandoned their parental responsibilities and left Liane to cope. It was just one more issue atop the others that would have to be addressed.

Tommy's nursery school van collected him first. Before Liane and Davie climbed aboard their bus, Liane reminded her mother. "Don't forget to call Mrs. Byers."

Back inside, Stormy made the call. Mrs. Byers's voice was bubbly with infectious laughter.

"Pooh! Call me Noreen," she told Stormy. "Janelle's got her overnight bag with her. I'm thrilled you want her. I'm having a garage sale this weekend, and Janelle would have been underfoot. Too helpful, if you know what I mean."

They chatted pleasantly about their girls, then Noreen said, "Janelle mentioned your troubles. If you ever want to talk..."

Stormy hesitated. "I'm trying to forget it ever happened."

"I know the feeling, but sometimes things build up. Actually, a group of us meets once a week—you're welcome to join us."

"Group?"

"Women who've been in jail. We talk and listen, help one another get mainstreamed, pass on job tips and so forth. We share what works, what doesn't." Noreen paused. "We're not habitual criminals. If you come and listen, you'll learn that most of us got into trouble because of the man in our lives at the time."

"I can relate to that," Stormy said with feeling.

"In that case, keep my number handy."

"I will, thanks."

Being able to talk with other women who shared the same frustrations appealed to Stormy, but at the moment, her deplorable finances needed her attention. And talking with Noreen had given her an idea.

Garage sales produced income, but were hit or miss, only as successful as the traffic they drew. One place drew lots of foot traffic, rain or shine, and that was the flea market.

The more Stormy thought about having a table at a flea market, the more excited she became. St. Augustine, Jacksonville and nearby Daytona Beach had permanent weekend marts.

She didn't report to the parole office again for thirty days. If she spent a week getting up the products she wanted to sell, that would leave her three weekends for marketing. With a fait accompli, she could prove to Mrs. Lowery that she was earning her keep. Then she wouldn't have to suffer the humiliation of having the parole officer approach her supervisor on a job. She'd be her own boss. She'd have her self-esteem back.

The problem was seed money. Instant cash. Not a lot— two hundred dollars, perhaps. And she knew just how to get it.

She pulled her hair into a ponytail, changed into jeans and a flannel shirt and went into the garage. She raised the double doors to allow in daylight.

Stored atop plywood sheets in the rafters were all the belongings she had carefully packed away against the day when she'd be out of prison and have her own life again: a television, a VCR, a microwave, a typewriter, a stereo system, a computer, binoculars, a few good pieces of crystal and her share of her mother's jewelry, which she would never part with. But the rest she would pawn! And after she'd made some money, she'd retrieve her things from the pawnshop. It was like investing in herself, giving herself a loan. She couldn't imagine why she hadn't thought of it before.

She took the aluminum extension ladder off its hooks on the wall and wrestled it upright against a rafter beam.

She'd go through all the boxes, sort everything out and move those things she wanted to pawn to the edge of the plywood platforms. When Tully got up, he could help her load them into her car.

She was five rungs up when the ladder began to slide out from under her. She froze, too far up to jump and too far down to grab a beam. It flashed through her mind she was going to fall and probably break her neck.

Then the ladder rattled, jerked and stopped sliding.

"I'm a sucker for a damsel in distress," said Tyler. "What fairy tale are we playing? 'Rapunzel'? The one where the princess lowers her hair out the window of the locked tower so the prince can climb up and seduce her?"

Stormy did not loosen her death grip on the ladder as she looked down at Tyler. His sneaker-clad feet were braced against the legs of the ladder, his hands holding each side of the extension to keep it from sliding farther. Though breathless with arrested fear, she managed to observe, "Awfully quick to the rescue, weren't you? Were you, perhaps, spying on me from the bushes?"

"Nope, I was walking up the driveway like an ordinary human being. I was waiting out on the highway for you to leave this morning—you usually head out right after the kids get on the bus. Since you didn't, I came to beg a cup of coffee. If I'd known you weren't going out at the crack of dawn, I could've slept in."

"So sorry I've inconvenienced you."

Tyler was enjoying the view of her backside fitted nicely inside her jeans. "You going up or coming down? I didn't eat my Wheaties this morning, so I don't know how much longer I can keep this extension in place."

Stormy began a careful descent. Once her feet were on the concrete floor, she realized, too late, that she was snugged between Tyler and the ladder, her back against his chest. "I'm on the ground. You can move now."

"Can't," he said mischievously. He inhaled deeply, his nerve endings aflame. The scent she wore had an Oriental note that came so close to triggering an arousal, he was caught off guard. "I think my muscles have seized up," he explained, somehow making the possibility sound provocative.

Stormy felt his breath warm on her neck. A blush rose to her face. Every inch of him rested against her, and she didn't dare move. "Okay, you've had your little joke."

"Are you inviting me for coffee?"

"I'll get you a cup and bring it out here. Nina and Tully are sleeping."

He moved his left arm away. To escape, she was obliged to step over a foot that still braced the ladder.

"One sugar, no cream," he said.

She put two mugs of that morning's coffee into the microwave to reheat, then dashed to the downstairs bathroom to freshen up. She told herself she wasn't doing it for Tyler, but she knew that, if this were war, she'd be court-martialed and hanged for fraternizing with the enemy.

But Tyler was an amicable enemy, she told herself.

It was terrible logic, and she knew it. She abruptly shut down the inner debate.

Carrying the coffee, she reentered the garage.

Tyler was standing in a far corner, the better to get a glimpse into the rafters. "What's up there?" he asked as he accepted the proffered mug.

"My things."

He sipped the coffee, keeping his eyes on her over the rim of the cup. "Would your 'things' add up to one hundred and two thousand dollars by any chance?"

Her dark eyes gleamed with quick amusement, and Tyler was enchanted.

"Since you can't take my word for anything, why don't you help me go through them and see for yourself?"

"Well, shoot! Why didn't I think of that?"

"Your brain cells are dead?"

"I love a woman with wit and charm." He drained his cup and set it aside. "Let's have at it."

Stormy found an old rubber welcome mat, which Tyler placed under the foot of the ladder to keep it from sliding. Next he demonstrated how to lock the ladder extensions into place. "Lead the way," he said.

The first three boxes opened were filled with stuffed toys Liane had outgrown. Stormy shoved them aside. "These aren't what I'm looking for."

"Really?" Tyler rummaged in the boxes anyway, surreptitiously but carefully squeezing and poking each animal. Nothing there.

The next box contained only shredded paper. Perplexed, Stormy swirled the paper with her hands. Then she looked at the side of the box. It was clearly marked in her own hand, CRYSTAL.

She directed Tyler to a box marked T.V. "Drag that one over here."

He tossed it. It was empty. Growing more perplexed and apprehensive, Stormy quickly checked others, working her way through boxes until she was on her knees in the eaves. Each and every box had been rifled. Even her clothes and linens and albums had been ransacked.

Panicked, she moved around on her hands and knees, looking for the boxes labeled BLANKETS. She hauled them from beneath the dimly lit eaves and began quickly sorting through them. No use. Her jewelry box was gone, too.

She leaned back on her heels amid the paper and stared at Tyler, her expression a mixture of confusion and suspicion. "Did you do this?" she choked. "Have you already been up here looking for the money?"

Tyler was taken aback. "I haven't set foot in this garage until this morning. And I wouldn't have then, but for seeing that you were about to fall flat on your beautiful butt. Anyway, why would I take your stuff? The cash those things would generate wouldn't begin to cover the amount I'm looking for."

"But my television, my typewriter, my jewelry—everything is gone!"

"Did Hadley Wilson have access to this garage?"

Stormy shook her head. "No. He was arrested at the same time I was, and he never even raised bail. He went straight from the county jail to state prison once he was convicted. If you're thinking he hid the money among my things, the answer is, he didn't. Besides, I wasn't living here when I knew him."

"Maybe your sister stored your stuff elsewhere for safekeeping."

"I'll ask. But that doesn't seem logical. Anyway, there isn't any other place to store them."

Tyler wondered how long it would take for Stormy to hit on the truth—that her sister had searched the boxes for the stolen money. Stormy's family had probably come to the same conclusion he had: Wherever the money was, it had not yet been touched. Stormy had made certain that all and sundry knew she'd raised her attorney's fees by selling her business and house. While out on bail, she had been conservative, splurging not so much as an extra penny.

That didn't prove she had no knowledge of where the money was, as she claimed. It simply meant she wasn't stupid enough to go around spending ill-gotten gains while under surveillance.

Perhaps, Tyler chastised himself, he had alerted her to his presence too soon.

"Does this house have an attic?" he ventured.

Stormy moved as if in a trance to gather up shredded paper and stuff it into the empty boxes. "There's an attic, but it's packed to the rafters with things Mom and Dad put up there." Stormy paused, managing a smile. "Mom never threw away anything."

Tyler became thoughtful. If the money *had* been hidden among Stormy's boxes, it was gone now. He could attest to that. But what, if anything, had Stormy had to do with the situation? Inviting him to help her go through her possessions had either been a gesture of her innocence . . . or a monumental *ruse de guerre*.

It was time to finagle an interview with her family members. He coaxed her down the ladder.

"Do you suppose you could spare another cup of coffee? That was dry work."

She led him from the garage through the catch-all room lined with hooks holding fishing poles, swimsuits, and deflated inner tubes and into the kitchen.

Nina and Tully were in the breakfast alcove. They looked up in unison as Stormy entered, and they frowned when Tyler appeared behind her.

"I thought you told her, no boyfriends," Tully said to his wife.

The discourtesy angered Stormy. "Mr. Mangus is an asset-recovery agent," she announced stiffly.

Tully smirked. "Oh, yeah? Whose assets?"

"Those of the Beach Coast Savings and Loan," Tyler answered, calmly returning the rude volley lobbed his way.

"My brother-in-law, Tully Dawson," Stormy put in. "I believe you've met my sister, Nina."

Tyler nodded and leaned against the counter near Stormy while she poured coffee into their mugs. The moment was awkward, but he'd dealt with worse. And his response had had the effect of shifting Tully's interest from Stormy to himself.

"You're looking for Stormy's loot," Tully said. "It isn't here, buddy. We've checked."

Stormy pivoted away from the counter. "Checked?" Her eyes shot sparks. "You mean it was you who went through my things?"

"You got it. We're not interested in being charged as accessories to a crime. Had to look, didn't I, to see if you were pulling a fast one on us."

Stormy was speechless. Tully and Nina had believed her capable of stealing? Still did?

Something was rotten in Denmark, Tyler thought. Tully Dawson did not give off honest vibes. Clearly, the man had pawed through Stormy's possessions for his own benefit. The idea made Tyler's adrenaline gush as from an uncapped oil well.

Then he saw the shock and devastation lurching across Stormy's face. He wanted to jump in front of her, protect her from hurt, make her battle his own.

Good sense intervened. Reluctantly he stoppered his anger. Stormy had the passion to handle this situation on her own. Best he merely observe and gather as much perspective as he could. It was obvious the Dawsons believed Stormy guilty of the theft—and they were piqued that she had not shared the windfall with them.

The coffee was forgotten.

"Where's my television, my typewriter, my computer, my jewelry box?" Stormy was asking in a seemingly unemotional monotone.

Tully pushed away from the table. "Hell, I don't have to put up with this. I'm not on trial." He turned to leave the room. "Nina, find me a clean shirt."

His face set in fury, he stalked out.

Stormy was trembling but holding herself rigid. From two feet away Tyler could feel inner rage.

Nina made as if to follow her husband. Stormy barred her way. "No, you don't, Nina. I want an explanation."

"In front of a stranger?"

"In front of the world, if need be!"

"Tully thought we ought to have a look, is all. It's no big deal."

"You helped him." Flat again. Then, "You did more than look."

Nina dropped her gaze. "We didn't think you'd mind. Tully borrowed the typewriter and computer for his office. We put the television in our bedroom. Tully said the tubes would go bad if it wasn't used."

"My jewelry?"

"I have it. I'll get it for you."

"Just a minute. I saw Ben Flaherty yesterday."

Nina paled.

"You abused the power of attorney. You lied to Ben. You owe me an explanation, Nina."

Nina seemed to hitch herself taller. "In the first place, we didn't expect you to be released so soon. In the second, Tully won the bid on this fantastic contract. The money was slow coming in and he needed cash to meet payroll."

"So you used up all the cash available in our trust fund for that? Nina, I gave you control of my share of the trust so that you could take care of Liane—her clothes, lunch money, if she got sick or something. That was our agreement."

"Tully needed the money!"

"Why didn't you put it back into the trust once the job paid out?"

Nina looked out the window.

Stormy followed her gaze. Sunlight splashed bright and golden over the dunes; the ocean was blue and sparkling. A poignant contrast with the doom and gloom here inside.

Nina spoke. "Tully was fired as the plumbing contractor. But it wasn't his fault. The crew he had was inexperienced, and—"

"Nothing is ever Tully's fault," Stormy said, disgusted.

"He tries," Nina insisted. "Things don't always go the way he plans."

"Have you ever noticed that all his plans are made with other people's money? Couldn't you have drawn the line? Couldn't you just once have said no?"

"He threatened to leave me!" Nina shouted. "And all because of you! We were doing fine until you got into trouble. Nobody wants to hire him now. And having Liane here was a reminder every single day of where you were and what you had done." Cords stood out in Nina's neck. "You owe us, Stormy! We want our respectability back! We want our life back. And another thing. If you want to go around having bastards, fine! Mom and Dad may have been forgiving, but they're dead. I'm not. I'm tired of you shaming our family."

Stormy took a step back, pain flaring in her chest, taking her breath away. "Nina…" she whispered. "When did this happen? When did you stop being my sister? How can you say something like that about Liane?"

"Oh, that's rich," Nina rasped. "Pretend you're the injured party. Well, you might fake him out," she said, gesturing toward Tyler, "but it won't work on me."

Stormy had forgotten Tyler. She looked at him now, not speaking, her face stark, a naked beacon of confusion and pain.

He couldn't sidestep it. Discovered that he didn't want to. She was right: She needed a friend. He moved to her and put his arm around her waist. When she offered no resistance, he guided her out of the house and down the drive to his car.

He took her a few blocks down the highway to a local watering hole that boasted five tables and friendly service. When a waitress appeared, he ordered a pizza to get rid of her. Then he kept silent, waiting.

Stormy still looked shell-shocked. Eventually, she said, "I'm sorry you had to witness that."

"Don't be. You handled a difficult situation with far more skill than I could've. Had it been my brother, we'd have come to blows."

"I felt like it," she said, managing the barest hint of a smile. "It didn't used to be this way," she mused sadly. "Or if it did, I didn't notice. Maybe I've had my head in the sand."

"People change," he offered.

"Nina hates me."

He was not about to dispute it, but he felt sure he had seen more in the confrontation than Stormy had. "She probably has to. If she didn't focus on you, she'd have to look at herself. I have a feeling she wouldn't like what she saw. I suspect her marriage is in trouble, and as long as she and Dawson stand united against you, the focus is off them and they don't have to deal with their own problems."

"What are you now, a psychiatrist?"

His gaze was piercing. "For the moment, why don't you just think of me as a friend?"

"You heard everything Nina said?" Stormy asked, her voice pensive.

"Couldn't miss."

"I've never been married," she put before him, waiting to see if he understood the import.

Tyler felt an urge to reach for her hand, then argued himself out of it. "I got the message about your daughter. That's what you're driving at, isn't it?" When she nodded, he added, "Accidents happen, but I get the impression you're not sorry about that one."

"I'm not."

"I like a woman who takes responsibility for her actions. You won't get a put-down from me on that score. Not that my opinion counts one way or the other."

"Maybe it does."

That surprised him. Then he surprised himself by saying, "I had a daughter once myself."

"Once?"

"She drowned."

Stormy shuddered. "I—I couldn't bear it if anything happened to Liane."

"Priss looked a bit like Liane."

So that explained the curious way he had looked at Liane that first day, Stormy thought. She was silent a moment, absorbing his simply spoken tragedy. "You're married, then?"

He shook his head. "Once Priss was gone, the marriage was doomed. Neither of us could live with the guilt. At first we blamed each other, then we blamed ourselves. I had the pool filled in, but..."

Just as Stormy was composing a sympathetic comment, the waitress placed a bubbling double-cheese pizza before them.

Stormy stared at it, her eyes haunted. Pizza was Liane's favorite. Only yesterday Stormy had had to refuse her daughter the treat for lack of money.

"What's wrong?" Tyler asked. "Would you prefer a salad? We'll order—"

"I have to go." She stood up, her face bleak, and began to hurry out.

Tyler was baffled, but he wasn't about to let her dash headlong down the highway in her condition. "Wait, I'll drive you back," he said, already on his feet and dumping cash onto the table.

"No, please, you stay. I'll walk home along the beach. It isn't far. Anyway, I need to think, and I think best when I'm alone."

He opened his mouth to argue, then closed it, bedeviled by a frustrating sense of powerlessness. He wanted to reach inside her world of hurt and yank her out of it. At least comfort her. But neither of those options was included in his job description.

The waitress came over and indicated the uneaten pizza. "Something wrong?"

He sighed. "Nope. Everything is just hunky-dory."

Chapter Five

The ocean breeze dried the tear tracks on her cheeks as Stormy plodded through the damp sand toward home.

Darn it! How could she keep allowing Tyler Mangus to sucker her? *Friend, my foot!* she thought. She was behaving like a charter member of Stupid Women Anonymous. Confiding in Tyler could only lead to exposing Liane.

She had survived eleven months among women toughened by life and circumstances. She'd had to dig deep to find the strength to withstand serving her time. By now, she ought to know one thing at the very least—she ought to know better than to trust *anyone.* Especially a man.

That she now had to include her family among those less than trustworthy made her heart ache. She suspected Tyler's observations were correct. Nina and Tully *were* focusing on her rather than delving into their own relationship to find out why their marriage wasn't working. Perhaps once she and Liane were out from underfoot, Nina and Tully would resolve their differences.

However, acknowledging Tyler's perceptiveness made it difficult to discount his sensitivity to her, especially in the face of her own family's callousness. And the sad tale about his daughter's death and his failed marriage was certainly not a deception. His pain had been palpable.

His sensuality was palpable, too. But was that a calculated feint to distract her, to keep her off balance?

As Stormy continued to walk along the beach, the waves lapping at her feet, loneliness surfaced and cast its mantle over her.

She longed for someone to share her fears, her hopes and, yes, she admitted, her body. It had been two years since she had even been kissed. She needed someone to touch, to snuggle up with each night. Someone to share with. Wasn't that what life was all about?

So that's what it was. She felt herself responding to Tyler out of some primitive biological quirk. Simple as that. It wasn't that he touched her emotionally where no man ever had before—thank goodness.

Still, during those long, horrible months in prison, with so much time for soul-searching, she had realized something: she had never really committed herself to the men she had known—perhaps not even to Liane's father. Truman Witney had been a delightful, comfortable habit; they had dated all through high school and college. She had loved him, yes, and she had given him her body, but had she ever really trusted him with her soul? Would he have known what to do with it if she had? They had both been so young. So unformed, really.

Nor had she committed any significant part of herself to Hadley Wilson. He had been fun, exciting, and he had not minded that Liane tagged along on their very first date. That had appealed to the mother in Stormy. Of course, in retrospect, he'd probably had an ulterior motive in cultivating Liane's company.

A wave rushed ashore and swamped her to the knees. Cold, it jolted her from her reverie. What was she even thinking about? A man was certainly not on her list of priorities right now. Creating a new life for herself, and regaining her independence were infinitely more important.

AT HOME, she found her jewelry box on the kitchen counter. The only thing missing was a pair of amethyst earrings.

Nina was in the master bedroom, making the bed. Stormy knocked on the door frame. Nina looked up, revealing tear-swollen eyes. "What do you want now?"

Reluctantly, Stormy squelched the rush of love she felt, the urge to hurry across the room and take her baby sister into her arms and tell her everything would work out.

"For a start, my amethyst earrings," she said, noticing her television and VCR on a stand near the foot of the bed.

Nina avoided her eyes. "I wore them New Year's Eve. I lost one."

"I've got to raise some cash, Nina."

"Well, don't look to me. We don't have any."

"I hate to have to do it, but I'm going to take my TV and VCR to a pawnshop. Then I'm going up to the attic to see if there's anything there worth selling."

Nina's mouth almost disappeared into her face with disapproval. "That's Mom and Dad's stuff! You don't have the right. Anyway, half of it's mine."

"I have the right to live decently," Stormy said softly. "Is Tully going to repay the part of my trust income you gave him?"

Nina moved around the bed, jerking on the sheet. "I just told you, we don't have it."

"But you do consider it owed?"

"We don't, but I guess *you* do."

"You're welcome to go up to the attic with me and put dibs on anything you want to keep."

"Oh, take what you want. You will, anyway. You always do."

Stormy hesitated. "Shall I disconnect the TV, or will you?"

Nina went to the wall, grabbed the wires and yanked the plugs from the sockets. "Satisfied?"

"Thank you," Stormy said civilly. She rolled the equipment into the hall. "By the way," she called over her shoulder, "Liane is having a friend over for the weekend."

Nina came to the bedroom threshold. "Tully doesn't like the house full of noisy kids."

Stormy captured her sister's gaze and held it. "Well, it isn't Tully's house, is it?"

Nina slammed the bedroom door. The sound reverberated throughout the old homestead.

For one brief moment, Stormy considered apologizing for her comment. She decided against it. No amount of discussion or apology was going to change facts or Nina's attitude.

She rolled the television and VCR out the front door and manhandled them into the back seat of her car.

Going into the pawnshop was not as easy as she had anticipated. Parked out front, looking at the grungy windows, she had serious second thoughts. *My life has bottomed out, and they'll know it,* she thought.

While she pondered whether to go into the shop or leave, a shadow fell across her. She looked up. Tyler put his hands on the roof of the car and leaned down. His expression circumspect, he eyed the back seat.

"Out for a drive or a little ready cash?"

Stormy felt the blood creep up her neck and inflame her cheeks. "What's it to you?"

"Just taking notes, dear heart, that's all."

"You're hassling me, Tyler. That has to be against the law. You're driving me crazy."

"I understand," he said easily. "But you know I think you're something special, don't you?"

Stormy ignored the fluttery sensation in her stomach. "Special, but not innocent?"

He sidestepped the question. "Here's what I've got so far. You haven't been near a bank or safety deposit box. You haven't been digging in the sand dunes for hidden treasure. The boxes you had stored in your garage held nothing of interest to my clients. You haven't been on a spending spree with money no one can account for. Those things are in your favor."

"Then why don't you go away and leave me alone?"

"Oh, two or three things." His voice flowed like silk. "Maybe I like your smile. Or could be I'm being paid a tidy sum by my clients—per diem, expenses, et cetera—and I want to max that out. Don't want to get a reputation for being cheap. Three, I've never visited St. Augustine before. It's a nice, friendly little town. I'm enjoying myself."

Stormy couldn't help it. She smiled. "You're smooth, you know that?"

"I'll try anything once."

"You know what I think? I think you practice in front of a mirror."

"Now that hurts."

"So take an aspirin."

His gravelly laughter brought Stormy up short. Damn! She'd done it again. Fallen under his charm as if it were manna sprinkled from heaven.

A bearded, disreputable-looking creature shuffling out of the pawnshop counting his money drew her attention. Stormy cringed. She couldn't do it. She put the car key into the ignition. Then, frowning, she dropped her hand into her lap.

She *had* to do it. She was every bit as needy as the old reprobate now peddling away on a bicycle nearly as scruffy as he was.

Tyler watched her, reading the indecisiveness waffling over her lovely face. She needed help. *So what? So Tyler Mangus to the rescue?* he thought, undecided himself.

"You ever sell anything to a pawnshop before?" he asked.

Mortified at having an audience for her predicament— especially because that audience was Tyler Mangus— Stormy shook her head.

"Nothing to it," he said gently. "The first two years I was in the army, I hocked my watch the day before every payday. I got so regular, the pawnbroker just put the watch on his wrist and handed me twenty bucks. When I shipped out to Nam, he cried, he liked that watch so damned much."

She gave him a baleful look. "You're making that up."

"Part of it," he admitted, opening the car door. "I'll carry the stuff in for you."

"Don't rush me."

"This'll look good on my report. 'Subject of investigation pawned valuables to raise cash.'"

Stormy capitulated and stepped out of the car. "Honestly?"

"Unless it's a subterfuge to foil my investigation."

"If those weren't my things you're holding, I'd stomp on your instep," Stormy assured him.

But once inside the pawnshop, she was glad of Tyler's presence. The pawnbroker looked positively Machiavellian.

"A hundred and ten dollars for both," he said. "You bring in the remote controls, and I'll give you another fifteen."

Stormy stood there, appalled at the low offer. "But—"

"Take it or leave it, lady. I got TVs and VCRs up the—"

Tyler coughed.

"Up to the rafters."

She looked to Tyler for advice. He shrugged. "I'll take it," she said.

It wasn't much, but once the cash was tucked safely into her wallet, she felt wonderfully affluent. It was more money than she'd had in hand in a year.

"What now?" Tyler asked as he ushered her outside. "A shopping spree?"

"Nope. I'm going into business for myself."

"On a hundred and ten bucks?"

"If I can manage it." She paused. "Thank you for helping me in there."

"All part of the service."

There was enough innuendo attached to his words for Stormy to guess he was offering more. Much more. The thought was like an electric shock. "I have to be going now."

"You know," Tyler said before she turned away, "I'm almost to the point of conceding that you don't have the money."

Stormy gaped. "Really?"

"However, it's somewhere. Perhaps if we sat down and went over the events, minute by minute—say, over dinner..."

"Oh."

"Is that a yes or a no?"

"No. I'm entertaining my daughter and her friend for the weekend."

"I'll take them to dinner, too." She raised her eyebrows at that. "We'll talk business after dinner," he clarified hopefully.

She made no reply.

"Think about it," he insisted. "I'm good with kids. Or at least I used to be." Pain momentarily shadowed his eyes.

"I'm sure you are," she said softly. "And Tyler?" He looked at her. "I'm sorry about your daughter. But... no thanks."

He frowned. "Why do I get the feeling you're deliberately keeping your daughter out of the picture?"

"Because she's not involved in this!" Stormy said hotly, panicking.

Tyler looked thoughtful for a moment, then said lightly, "I'd still like to take you to dinner. You know, during World War II, no general on either side planned battle strategy until he had a complete biography of his enemy. Over dinner, I can tell you the story of my life. Then you'd be well armed, maybe learn how to outsmart me."

Stormy gave him a look of utter innocence. "But that would be a double-edged sword, wouldn't it. And how smart would I be to fall on it?"

Tyler groaned. "Ouch."

"Now, if you'll excuse me..."

He bowed. "Oh, by all means, madam. Where are we off to next?"

"I'm going home." Then she added impishly, "to clean out the attic."

He straightened, his radar flashing a red alert. "Need any help?"

"Nope. But I'll be sure to let you know if I come across anything resembling a hundred and two thousand dollars.

I'll wave a white flag. Where will you be lurking? On the highway or in the dunes?''

His smile was laced with sardonic amusement. "Sorry, unless you're willing to hear my bio, I'm not revealing any war strategy.''

Giving him a small smile and a wide berth, Stormy strolled to her car. When she pulled out into traffic, Tyler was still standing at the curb, staring after her.

After Stormy disappeared from sight, Tyler focused his mind on his investigation in an effort to dispel other, unwanted thoughts. Thoughts about how stimulated he was by her give-and-take. Thoughts about how her eyes gleamed with such intensity when she thought he wasn't watching. Thoughts about the lovely curve of her breasts.

Objective thinking told him it was time to close in. He decided to move from town to an efficiency motel on the beach less than two miles from Stormy's house.

He told himself it was good business to stay as close as he could get, lest she slip the money past him while he was elsewhere.

SEVERAL HOURS LATER, he was lounging in a lawn chair on the damp sand, his binoculars trained on Stormy and two little girls as they beachcombed.

He spun the lens to magnify Stormy. She filled his vision. Could she fill the emptiness inside him?

He wanted her, yet he sensed the primal stirrings within him were not all sexual. Sex played a part, of course. But she had attributes a man could be proud of outside the bedroom, too. Considering how loosely some people parented these days, it was refreshing to watch her with Liane, to note the fierceness, the seriousness with which she tackled her responsibilities to her child.

He liked her eyes, too. They lacked innocence, but she had a direct gaze that radiated intelligence and honesty.

Honesty? Did he think her honest? he wondered.

If he answered yes, that meant he ought to close the investigation on Stormy Elliott. "No way," he said aloud. He wasn't about to milk his clients, as he'd jokingly implied to Stormy. He had his honor, after all. And that honor demanded that, no matter what his emotions said, he had to deliver, if not the goods, at least a complete, thorough, totally dispassionate report on a complete, thorough, totally dispassionate investigation.

A gust of wind caught at Stormy's hat and sent it tumbling down the beach. Laughing, she and the girls raced after it.

Tyler caught himself laughing with them. Then he sighed in self-disgust. Dispassionate? Ha! He was becoming involved up to his neck. Not only was that dangerous to his emotional well-being, it was unprofessional as hell. And Stormy Elliott wasn't even the kind of woman he got involved with. The others knew what they wanted and got it with no strings attached.

No strings, he mused. Now there was a bit of gallows humor for you. He was weaving the noose for his own damned neck.

The hat retrieved and clamped again firmly on her head, Stormy and the girls wandered back up the beach. Tyler found himself watching her lips, enjoying the flashes of her smile. The trio moved onto the dune walk. He watched until they disappeared into the house and only then lowered the binoculars.

He folded up the chair and began the trek back to his motel, vowing that Stormy Elliott would get no more logic-distorting compassion from him.

"I TOLD YOU I would watch the boys, Nina, and I will. I'm happy to."

"No, you have that man coming around. Tully thinks it's best we take them to the baby-sitter."

"I don't have *that man* coming around. I did not invite him. He's investigating the whereabouts of the stolen money. I can't stop him from doing that. What you're really saying is that you don't think I'm a fit parent. You're just trying to make me feel guilty."

"Guilty is as guilty does," Nina said archly.

Tommy and Davie hovered. "We want to stay with Aunt Stormy," they cried in unison.

Nina gave them a look. They quieted.

Stormy knelt down and hugged her nephews. "Next time, okay, boys?"

"Are you still going to bake cookies?"

"Yes, and I'll bake two giant ones for the two of you."

"You won't let the girls eat 'em up?" Davie asked, eyeing his cousin and her friend, who were in the breakfast alcove bent over their homework.

"Nope. We'll put your names on them."

After Nina ushered the boys out, Liane slid off her stool and put her arms around her mother. "Don't feel bad. You can help Janelle and me with our science project."

"Maybe for a few minutes," Stormy acquiesced, thinking that refusing the gesture might dampen the thoughtfulness her daughter was exhibiting.

She was instructed to carefully dismantle azalea buds that had been plucked from the bushes that grew alongside the garage. The dismembered parts were then to be pasted onto construction paper.

"You can help paste, too," Liane volunteered.

"Only you have to leave enough room for us to write down what the part is," Janelle said. "If the writing isn't our own, Miss Evans will know, and, boy, will she be mad. Last time my homework was too neat, Miss Evans called my mom and told her second grade was for kids.''

"I'll keep that in mind," Stormy assured them both. "What are we studying? How plants grow?"

Liane hesitated. "Sort of. We're learning about the difference between plants and animals."

"That's interesting," Stormy supplied.

Janelle smiled. "It sure is. And even if plants and animals are different, they all have sex."

"Rocks don't," put in Liane.

Janelle rolled her eyes. "That's because rocks are minerals, silly."

Stormy made a strangled sound. "Miss Evans talks about sex?"

"Not exactly. We get to start sex education in the fifth grade, but see…" Janelle pointed to a shredded flower part "That's the pistil. It's the female part of the flower. And that part over there, that's the stamen—the man part. It has the pollen, and when a bee comes along, it takes the pollen from the stamen to the pistil, so pretty soon you get a baby plant. Of course, in humans, the girl has an egg and the boy has a sperm. That's what makes a human baby. A sperm is extra, extra tiny, but it looks like a tadpole." The seven-year-old mistook Stormy's appalled expression for confusion. "It's okay if you don't understand. I know all this 'cause I'm scientific. Miss Evans thinks I'm gifted. I might even get to skip third grade."

In order to keep from clamping her hands over Liane's ears, Stormy had to remind herself that this was the pair that had made a pact not to have periods.

It was Liane who was confused. "How does a bee get the pollen from the sperm to the egg? Everybody I know runs from bees."

"I don't know yet," Janelle admitted. "We'll probably learn that part next year."

"I bet Mom can tell us," Liane volunteered.

Stormy wiped paste from her fingers. "Listen, girls, why don't you finish your homework while I start the cookie dough? And afterward, you two can help me finish up in the attic."

The seven-year-olds exchanged looks.

"Is that a stall?" Liane asked her friend.

Janelle nodded. "I told you—mothers are all alike."

"And after that," Stormy continued, ignoring the fact that she was being discussed sotto voce by the imps, "I'll treat us to banana splits at the Dairy Queen."

"Then can we stay up late and watch *Tales from the Crypt?*" Liane asked.

Stormy smiled. "Sure, if the program is all about giant plants who eat up impertinent little girls."

Liane turned to her friend. "That means no."

TYLER FELT LOUSY, even though he'd just had a delightful, if lonely, meal at an oceanfront restaurant and the soft March evening was perfect for the stroll back to his motel.

Usually when he had what he called "the miseries," he could retire to the comfort of his cabin tucked away on the edge of the Ocala National Forest. And somehow, after a few days of fishing in the creek outside his back door, a good adventure novel read in front of the fireplace or some puttering about in the as yet unfinished loft, he'd feel restored. Misery, he decided, was best suffered in the warmth of the predictable and familiar.

He stopped at the beach road, waiting for a break in traffic to cross, and gave himself up to what he'd been avoiding all evening—daydreaming about Stormy. In his fantasy he brushed a lock of hair from her cheek, the gesture a prelude to the slow and delicious discovery of her mouth, her neck, her breasts, her legs, her...

When the oncoming headlights swept beyond him, he saw Stormy whiz around the curb in her old Ford.

For a moment he stood on the roadside, stunned. Then he sprinted through the traffic and ran the half block to his car. Damn! He'd thought her in for the night. *See?* he told himself. *You let yourself get soft on the woman, and what does she do? Pulls a fast one on you.*

He fumbled with his keys, cursed, finally got them into the ignition and jockeyed his way into the slow-moving line of traffic. Hell and damnation! He'd never catch up to her now.

The traffic came to a full stop. Tyler groaned. The May Street drawbridge had gone up.

Then, beneath the bridge lights, he spied the Ford—first in line to get across. He leaned back in his seat with a sigh. For once the gods were favoring him.

On the other hand, he thought sourly, maybe they weren't.

LIANE AND JANELLE ORDERED their banana splits but, uncharacteristically, skipped the nuts. Both had loose baby teeth and worried that a tooth would come out, get swallowed and they'd miss an opportunity to collect from the Tooth Fairy.

Stormy stood behind the girls and smiled at the counterman's reaction. Both girls were costumed in outfits they'd acquired in the attic. They trailed about in long dresses complemented with ancient fox-fur wraps, cloches, beaded purses, and silver shoes, all circa the 1940s. Topped with Maybelline makeup. After being assured they'd get extra whipped cream in lieu of nuts, they click-clacked across the tile floor to a booth like a pair of prissy matrons out for Sunday tea.

Stormy rounded out the order with a third banana split.

"Make that four," Tyler said, leaning past Stormy's shoulder.

She pivoted and drew a deep breath. His face was only inches from hers. His eyes looked strained, weary, as if his usual guardedness had lost its sentry, allowing her a glimpse of something vulnerable and restless. "When are you going to stop following me?" came out a whisper.

"Oh, sometime in the next millenium," he whispered back, and brushed against her to toss money onto the counter.

Gooseflesh erupted down her arms at his touch. She could not avoid noticing the way his shirt was partially unbuttoned, revealing sculpted muscles and a dark mat of hair. He fairly oozed sensual energy. She could feel herself succumbing, sense the secret spring inside her leaping at his masculinity. She moved down the counter to await her order, away from him. She had to.

Tyler followed, lured, he told himself, by her woebegone expression.

"Do you really think it's necessary to follow me when I have the children with me?"

"Since when does having a kid in tow make somebody honest?"

She inwardly winced at his casual proximity to the very truth she was trying to conceal. "You're not only mean and hard-hearted, you're also small spirited."

"Not me. I count myself among that honorable group of men who believe in God, like animals and tolerate mother-in-laws." Because it lurked in the back of his mind that she was capable of using female tricks to disarm him, because he *was* feeling disarmed, and because he was

floundering in a confused morass of jealousy and unwanted desire, he said suddenly, accusingly, "You must
have twisted poor Hadley Wilson into knots, didn't you?
He probably didn't know which end was up."

Stormy gaped at him, open-mouthed, and her reply,
when she could finally manage one, was coated with
astonishment. "You're a pathological idiot!"

"You mean he resisted your charms?" Tyler said archly.

The look she gave him would have crippled a lesser man.
"I didn't offer him my charms."

Tyler drank in that fascinating tidbit, and he suddenly
felt exhilarated.

The banana splits were ready, pushed toward Stormy on
a tray. She grabbed one off, shoved it at Tyler, took the
tray and stormed off to join the girls.

Tyler took his sundae and wandered into the dining
area, looking for a place to sit. He eyed Stormy, who was
acting wholly preoccupied with the little girls. Total pretense, he told himself and sat in the booth behind them. If
she felt him staring at the back of her head, she gave no
sign.

He watched Liane, the way she tilted her head toward
her friend and giggled. He smiled at the cloche drooping
down to her neck, the rouge and lipstick so unartfully applied to round baby cheeks and lips. Priscilla had loved to
play dress up. He remembered once when she had—

Tyler felt a sudden ache behind his breastbone so pro-
nounced that he couldn't make it go away. He closed his
eyes and sat utterly still, suspended in time and memories.
He thought for an instant he was about to weep. Abruptly
abandoning any idea of further observation of Stormy for
the evening—she had her hands full with those two and
would hardly be up to anything illegal, despite his jibes to
the contrary—he got up and left the restaurant.

Liane pointed him out to Janelle as Tyler passed their table. "That's the man who wants us to help him solve a puzzle."

Stormy's mind was racked with Tyler; she didn't want her conversation to be filled with him, too. "Eat up, girls. It's already past your bedtime."

Still, it surprised her that he had not hung about and made more of a nuisance of himself. Out the corner of her eye, she watched him cross the lighted parking lot, get into his car and drive away.

Good, she thought. Perhaps at last she was free of Tyler Mangus.

The odd thing was, a wave of disappointment washed over her at the thought.

Chapter Six

The following morning Nina and Tully were cranky and argumentative. Their raised voices roused Stormy from the sofa in the living room. To keep Liane and Janelle and herself from being the target of stray barbs, Stormy fixed toast and milk and coffee and made a game of serving the little girls breakfast in bed.

Still enamoured with playing dress up and behaving the grand dames, which breakfast in bed enhanced, they insisted upon wearing all their antiquated finery again. Before Stormy could discourage them, they began pulling on the dresses over jeans and shirts.

Stormy bit her lip. There was a small secondhand shop on Charlotte Street called The Way We Were, and she had hoped to include some of what the girls wore in her offering to the shop owners. Still, she protested only mildly. "Easter is three weeks away," she told her daughter. "If we can sell the cloche and the furs, that'll buy you a new Easter dress."

"I'll just wear this," Liane said, eyeing her mother with stubborn aplomb.

"Can we wear makeup again today, too?" Janelle asked, all hope.

Stormy gave in. "All right. But don't pack it on like you did last night."

While the girls primped in front of the dresser mirror, Stormy applied her own cosmetics in the bathroom.

Her mind, though, was not on appearances, but on plotting immediate financial strategy.

Thirty dollars of what she had received from the pawnshop had to be set aside to pay her monthly probation fee, and about the same amount for Liane's school lunch money. Plus, she'd have to allow for extra auto expenses—gas and oil—against all the miles she'd be putting on the car.

She reviewed what she knew about flea markets. They resembled Far Eastern bazaars and were popular with those hunting bargains. She hadn't yet hit upon the perfect product to sell, but she knew it would have to be whatever she could buy the most of with the least amount of money. And then there were the fees to rent a vendor space. Preferably in a high-traffic aisle, which, no doubt, would cost extra.

St. Augustine had a sizable flea market, but the foot traffic depended quite a lot on tourists. That made it unreliable. The Jacksonville area had several gargantuan marts, as well, but she discounted hiring a table in any of them. The best slots were already taken up by regulars, mostly professional vendors. That meant stiff competition for the smaller enterprise, not to mention expenses. The gasoline alone would put a deep gouge in her precious cash reserves.

She had often been to the Daytona Beach flea market, and that was the one that most appealed to her now. It was a large, covered market, an easy hour's drive from St. Augustine. Years ago she had purchased her used computer there from a man who had a stall on Sundays.

The money from the pawnshop had put some immediate cash into her hands, but not enough. She could only cross her fingers and hope Lady Luck had her in view when she took the loot from the attic into the secondhand shop.

If that didn't garner her enough seed money, then, by damn, she'd pick up discarded aluminum cans and glass bottles and cart them to the recycling station.

Thus determined, she took herself off to the kitchen to make sandwiches. She would not spend cash for anything more than soft drinks while on her scouting expeditions.

Her nephews were in the den, eating cereal and watching Saturday morning cartoons. In the kitchen she found Nina loading the dishwasher. She offered a "good morning" and left it at that as she opened cupboards and took down a can of tuna and a jar of peanut butter.

She felt Nina's wary, hostile gaze on her, and it was almost like being in prison again. She shivered, trying to shake off the sensation.

Nina sniffed and said, "That man was on the beach this morning, lingering in front of the house." She made the statement an accusation.

Stormy admitted to the tiniest prick of pleasure. So Tyler had not abandoned his pursuit, after all. His pursuit of the money, that is, she reminded herself. She glanced out the kitchen window, to no avail. He was not in sight. "We don't own the beach, Nina. I can't tell him to stay off it."

"I think you're leading him on."

"He's here to do a job. It's just bad luck that I'm involved."

"You don't seem too unhappy that he's paying attention to you."

Stormy stopped spreading peanut butter on bread slices and gave her sister a forthright look. "Maybe I'm not. You know, I haven't had a man's arms around me in almost two years. I miss that."

"You're less than two weeks out of prison and already you're planning an affair with the first man to come along? That's disgusting."

Nina's censure wafted over Stormy. A retort came to her lips, but she swallowed it back. Tyler's assessment of Nina and Tully's marriage, that perhaps Nina herself was unhappy, gave Stormy pause. "The only thing I'm planning right now is how to make a living. Tell me," she added, "what is it that's making you so angry? Are you miserable in your marriage, with life in general?" She paused. "Are you pregnant again?"

Nina's chin went up, very much like Stormy's own when pressed. "I'm not pregnant. And I'm not miserable. I have a fine husband and two great kids. Whatever provoked you to say such a thing?"

Stormy opened the tuna and forked it into a bowl. "You seldom smile, and I haven't heard you laugh since I've been home. I only hear you arguing with Tully. Maybe you ought to talk to somebody."

"Oh? Like who?"

"A therapist."

"What a stupid thing to say! You're the one who needs therapy. You're the one who's always getting into trouble."

Stormy gave a sad little smile. "I guess it seems that way to you." She stuffed the sandwiches into plastic bags. "We won't be home until late. After I take those clothes by The Way We Were, I'm checking out the flea market in Daytona. I'm thinking about opening a stall."

Nina crossed her arms. "Oh? First you frequent pawnshops, now you're going to become a shill? Why can't you do something respectable, like have your own restaurant again?''

"Nina, you may not consider flea marketing chic, but having a stall is just as respectable as owning a sandwich shop. Besides, I'm a felon, remember? I can't have a beer or liquor license anymore, so even if I had the wherewithal, a restaurant is out. I have to find something else to do that will support Liane and me. And at the market, Liane can be with me every step of the way—no baby-sitters. It'll be exciting for her, and we can spend more time together.''

"Oh, sure, you're such a good little mother. Maybe you should've thought about Liane before you took up with Hadley Wilson and got us all into this mess.''

It took several heartbeats for Stormy to marshal enough prudence to deflect Nina's emotional bullet. "I'm trying to be a good mother, Nina. And I'm trying to do what is right. Believe me, a little support from you would be welcome.''

Nina's face colored. "What do you call what I've been doing for the past year?''

Taking advantage of me, Stormy thought. Instead of speaking in the heat of anger, she stepped into the hall, and a moment later she heard the dishwasher door being slammed, china rattling.

Gloomy but unflinching, Stormy nodded. The sounds were a fitting exclamation point to both Nina's acrimony and her own determination.

THE OWNER OF THE SHOP, Barbara, fingered the clothes spread out over the counter. "I'll give you eighty dollars for the lot.''

"That's all?'' Stormy could not keep the dismay from her voice.

The woman gestured toward the beaded bag Liane held. "Thirty-five dollars for the purse."

Liane tucked the bag beneath her arm. "Mom!"

Stormy turned back to the shop owner. "Why so much for the purse?"

"Those aren't ersatz beads, they're real seed pearls."

Stormy took Liane aside. "We need the money, poppet, or I wouldn't ask you to give it up."

Liane clutched the purse and gazed at her mother with wide, solemn eyes. A cocoon of guilt enclosed Stormy.

Up until that moment, Janelle had been hanging back. Now she came over and put her arm around Liane's shoulder. "When my dad took all our money, we had to sell *everything* in our house to help Mom."

Oh, these old, old children, Stormy thought, weeping inside. "Never mind," she said, and she turned to Barbara. "Eighty dollars it is, then. And thank you."

She called to the children, but they were whispering. Then Liane put the purse on the counter. The shop owner looked at Stormy. She paused, thinking, then looked at Liane's determined little face. Finally she nodded at Barbara. The woman counted out the money into Liane's hand, and the child held it out to her mother.

While they were buckling seat belts, an idea pierced Stormy's remorse. She twisted to face the girls in the back seat. "Poppet, suppose we consider the thirty-five dollars your part of the investment in our new business together?"

"What kind of business? Aren't I too little to be in business?"

"No, you're not. Not in this one."

Liane brightened instantly at the prospect of being involved in something so adult as "investing" in a business, and all the way to Daytona, Stormy entertained the girls with her ideas and what she hoped to accomplish. She found she enjoyed sharing with the girls, and Liane came back with intelligent ideas of her own. "I could sell the toys I don't play with anymore."

"You certainly could," Stormy agreed. So involved was she in their spirited discussion that it wasn't until they'd found a spot in the acres and acres of parking lot that she glanced into the rearview mirror to search Tyler Mangus out.

STORMY HESITATED just inside the entrance to the flea market. There seemed to be only one decibel level—loud.

Having been shut away for so long, she had forgotten how chaotic were people's movements en masse, forgotten the bustle and dissonance a crowd created. Which was why, she realized now, prison guards never allowed inmates to gather into groups. Inmates were always shunted into columns, counted and controlled. She exhaled in an effort to release her anxiety.

They walked in the aisles, stopping to admire stacks of hand-woven baskets, racks of earrings, glass cases of watches and rings, clothes of every imaginable kind—from hand-painted T-shirts to lacy lingerie—pottery, china, scarves, plants and shrubs.

Stormy felt overwhelmed. As each possibility of what to sell came to her, she happened upon a vendor selling it. She began to think this wasn't such a good idea after all.

The children were happily, obliviously enthralled with everything.

In their glittery dresses, hems held up daintily, and shiny shoes, they click-clacked over the concrete walkways, chattering, admiring and being admired, accepting as their due the comments of passersby. "Oh, aren't they darling…'' ''Gee, I used to own a dress like that…'' ''How sweet. Remember grandma's fox fur?''

Others chuckled at the incongruity of the trio: Liane and Janelle costumed to the nines in feather boa and moth-eaten fur, while Stormy trailed behind dressed in jeans, her brown hair tucked beneath a baseball cap, looking ready to play shortstop in a sandlot game.

Finally they came upon the vendor office. Stormy took a pamphlet that laid out the rules of the market, the fees and how to book a space.

''I'm starved,'' announced Liane. ''My stomach wants me to invest some of my money in curly fries and an orange drink.''

Thinking of the sandwiches in the car, Stormy hesitated. But, wanting to reward Liane's recent maturity and generosity, she gave in gracefully.

At the top of each aisle was a food concession. The smells of hot dogs and French fries seemed to permeate the entire market.

While the girls claimed a vacant table, Stormy stood in line to order their food.

Knowing now the way Tyler operated, she kept glancing over her shoulder until the man behind her in line gave her a beefy smile. ''I ain't had a good-lookin' woman starin' at me like you're doing in better'n twenty years,'' he said. ''Is my cologne *really* working?''

Stormy blushed furiously and mumbled an apology.

Relief mingled with disappointment when Tyler did not appear, and for the remainder of the day Stormy tried to relegate him to a far corner of her mind.

To Liane and Janelle's delight, she decided they should walk the market once more. She took notes, recording the variety of merchandise, which vendors seemed to be the busiest, which aisles bustled with shoppers, and those that did not. She made a leisurely pass at the foot of each long, covered corridor into the open grassy lots, where all manner of things, from seedlings to sofas, were being hawked. And before they left, she went back to the market office and reserved a table for the following two weekends.

As she put the receipt into her purse, she felt good, pleased that the aisle she had chosen had an opening. It was awash with vendors of watches, leather goods, socks, perfume, earrings, sunglasses, towels and T-shirts, and most of them had been doing a brisk business each time she passed.

Once back in St. Augustine, she stopped to buy soft drinks and drove to a playground near the county library where they could picnic on their now slightly limp sandwiches. For the first time in two days, the girls were willing to part with their costumes so they could play on swings and monkey bars.

As Stormy sat at the picnic table and pored over her notes until dusk, she fully realized the challenge she had set herself. Specializing in one particular item seemed to be the key to success. If she could just hit on the right product....

SUNDAY MORNING UNFOLDED with relative calm. Puffy white clouds hung in an azure sky; waves lapped lazily at the shore. The breeze was so gentle, it barely rippled the newspaper Stormy was scanning.

She put down the pen with which she'd been circling advertisements for garage sales, closed her eyes and raised her face to the heavens. It was early yet, and the sun had not yet warmed the deck beyond comfort. Dear God, the times she had dreamed of days like this while in prison.

Beneath the deck floor, which formed the roof over a small patio below, she could hear Liane and Janelle in earnest discussion about how best to catch a lizard.

Behind her, the house was quiet. Tully had gone out early to play golf with a contractor with whom he hoped to do business. Angry at Tully for abandoning her, Nina took herself and the boys to spend the day with another golf widow.

The sun created a kaleidoscope of bursting colors beneath Stormy's eyelids. She felt deliciously lazy, her mind empty of everything. Everything except Tyler, she realized. It was busy sprouting questions about him.

What had caused him to rush from the Dairy Queen without so much as a parting shot? Why hadn't he followed her yesterday? Had he broken his pattern in an attempt to keep her off balance?

Maybe he'd had a date.

Of course.

The thought was oddly disturbing, but she clutched at it to keep her interest at bay.

She opened her eyes and groped for her pen. And her heart gave a tiny lurch. There was Tyler, sitting balanced on the railing that surrounded the deck. The next thing she noticed was that beneath his strong, broad forehead, his eyebrows yoked bloodshot eyes, and his cheeks were unshaven.

"What were you thinking about?" he asked. "You had an almost beatific smile on your face."

"Am I smiling now?"

"Decidedly not."

"Well, now I'm thinking about you."

"Oh?"

"You look awful."

"Want to know why?"

She realized she wanted to know everything about him: where he was born; who his friends were; how he had lived up until the very moment he had stepped into her life.

"Not particularly," she said.

"Could we get in out of this sun? The glare off the sand is blinding me."

Stormy hesitated. Why not? She called down to the girls that she was going inside. Tyler followed her to the breakfast alcove, his attention captured by her erect carriage, her new sense of purposefulness. Had she somehow gotten her hands on the money without his knowing? he wondered. He turned the thought over in his mind.

Sensing the intensity in his gaze and unsure whether it boded good or bad, Stormy ambushed him with a smile. "I was thinking about having a second cup of coffee. You look like you could use a cup."

"Coffee would be nice." Then he observed, "The house is quiet."

"Nina and Tully are out for the day." She lifted the percolator, discovered it empty. "I'll have to make a fresh pot."

"I have time." Tyler inspected her profile as she worked at the counter. He liked it. He noticed the way her knit shirt and cotton slacks revealed her shape. He remembered her feistiness and decided her name fit her as well as her clothing did. She was born to enchant, and with her a man would never know a dull moment, he thought as he watched her insert the coffee filter and measure out the rich, dark grounds. "I know it's ludicrous to even ask this," he threw out casually, "but had we met under different circumstances, don't you think we might've been . . . receptive to one another?"

Stormy took down a mug and blindly fastened her eyes on its empty depths. "What difference does it make? We're... adversaries."

"Maybe not."

They regarded each other in a complicated silence. The chemistry was there, vibrating and alive, and Stormy became aware that, whatever their peculiar relationship, it was rapidly accelerating.

"Have you decided I don't have the money?"

He crossed the room to her and braced his hands on either side of her on the counter. Their faces were only inches apart, his green eyes dark and probing, as if he, too, was trying to read the message in those few moments of silence.

Stormy held her breath. She wanted to caress away the frown lines on his brow, kiss away the haunted look in his remarkable eyes. She wanted to rub her cheek against the bristles of his day-old beard and put her arms around his neck and pull him close so that their bodies and hearts and souls enmeshed.

She willed her arms to stay at her side while his voice wove itself around her in tight, raw threads of sound.

"I knew you were trouble the minute I laid eyes on you. For five years I haven't felt anything, couldn't feel anything, didn't want to feel—until now."

Stormy couldn't think of anything sensible to say.

"When Priss died, a part of me died with her. I don't know if all seven-year-olds look alike, but Liane is Priscilla all over again—the eyes, the giggles, the pigtails, the tilt of the head. I want to walk away from this job, from her, from you." He laid his palm against her flushed cheek, his thumb softly tracing her cheekbone. He bent his head toward hers. "But, you see, I can't...."

His lips brushed hers. A mere butterfly touch.

No! Stormy thought. *I'm too needy, too vulnerable.*

He kissed her eyes and feathered kisses down to her neck, running his tongue lightly over her earlobe. No other part of their bodies touched, yet Stormy was certain she could feel the tempo of his heart pounding against her own, hear the blood coursing through his veins.

The screened door slammed, followed by the mingled voices of Liane and Janelle.

Tyler raised his head and smiled, and when he withdrew, Stormy felt as if he were taking with him everything that was vital to her survival.

Liane bustled into the kitchen to get soft drinks from the fridge, then climbed up onto a stool and faced Tyler, who had retreated to the alcove. Her eyes searched him for a moment. "Did you solve your puzzle?"

"Nope, not yet. But I'm working on it."

Stormy called up reality to counteract the bewildering present. She could not, would not, offer up Liane to Tyler's investigation.

She put a mug of coffee in front of Tyler. To the girls she said, "You two better go wash up and—"

"Let them stay a moment," Tyler said.

Stormy understood he was holding her up for emotional ransom. "All right, but just for a few minutes. We're going to some garage sales, and afterward, I've got to take Janelle home."

"Mom and I are in business together," Liane informed Tyler.

"That's terrific. Tell me about it."

Thus prompted, Liane did just that.

Stormy struggled to disengage the sensations set in motion by Tyler's kisses in order to monitor his conversation with Liane. Standing by, ready to attack, ready to challenge, she did not sit, but leaned against the counter, sipping her coffee.

His interest keen but not overdone, Tyler questioned Liane as an equal, not a lesser, being. And Liane, the minx, was wholly bewitched by his attention.

Stormy reacted with guilt. While her grandfather was alive, Liane had had a surrogate father. Since Tully had not taken up that role, Stormy saw now that Liane missed having a man in her life as much as she did.

She snapped from her reverie when Liane was midsentence.

"Boxes and boxes of stuffed animals in the attic. Maybe people would buy them for their kids for Easter."

"Oh!" Stormy cried. "That's it! I've been racking my brain for what we could sell. And it was right in front of our noses. We can buy up ones we find at garage sales, too. Wash them, repair them..."

"That's what I was just about to suggest," said Liane, exasperation coating her every syllable.

Stormy put her hand on her daughter's shoulder. "You and Janelle go get washed up, okay? I want to shop at as many sales as we can today."

Her face pink with elation, Stormy slid onto one of the stools vacated by the girls. "I got a table right in the middle of the aisle. I know how I can make it appealing—there's an old high chair in the attic. I can—" She stopped, noticing that Tyler was watching her with a guarded expression. "I'm sorry, I got carried away. I'm sure how I earn a living doesn't interest you at all."

"Everything about you interests me."

Then she understood. His tone said he wanted to pick up where they'd left off before being interrupted by the children. Stormy told herself she could not afford to pursue an affair. Particularly not with this man.

No matter how tempting his kisses? she asked herself. No matter how good they made her feel? Her heart begged her to chance it, to reach for the happiness that seemed now to be within her grasp.

"You'd better go," she told him, but her voice held little conviction.

He reached for her hand and turned it over. With a fingertip he began to trace the lines in her palm, causing treacherous sensations to skitter up her spine. "Let's hit those garage sales together," he said.

"No." She reclaimed possession of her hand and placed it in her lap.

"What do you expect me to do?" he said, enjoying the interesting play of light and shadow over her features, even though his growing need for her made him feel vulnerable and uneasy. "Sit on my duff while you make up your mind? Do you have any idea what's happening between us? Do you have any idea of the—"

"Sure," she said, not allowing him to finish, taking refuge in the obvious and evading the implied. "You're looking for the bank's money."

He made a sound of disgust, then looked away, and fell silent.

Stormy managed not to leap into the quiet.

"The ground rules are changing," he said softly. "Are you certain that's the way you want it?"

"I haven't the slightest notion what you're talking about."

"You have never in your life been that dumb." When she made no reply, he moved away from the table. "Okay, have it your way. The money was stolen. I aim to find it. Tell me where it is, I'll collect it, turn it over to its rightful owners and that will be that. End. *Fini.*" He regarded her. "Of course, you've kept something back from me, held it in reserve. I've spent hours trying to figure it. I've pored over the transcripts of your hearing, your trial, and Wilson's. No luck. So I guess the only way I'll find out what it is and be able to leave you in peace, is if you tell me.''

She met his gaze head on. ''Well, I'm not going to, so don't hold your breath.''

His eyebrows went up. ''Aha,'' he said victoriously. ''I was right.''

Stormy felt the blood drain from her face. ''That was a trick,'' she accused.

''Nope. We're playing for high stakes, and you aren't paying proper attention.''

So angry, her voice barely rose above a whisper, she said, ''You made me think—''

''If there's any single thing I know about you, my love, it's that you do your own thinking.''

''Get out. Get away from me and stay away, or I'll call the police.'' She wouldn't, of course. She didn't trust them any more than she trusted Nina or Tully. Or Tyler Mangus. She felt betrayed on every front.

Tyler rubbed his hand over his jaw. ''Guess I'd better get along home and shave, it being Sunday and all.''

He stopped at the table on the deck and peered at the newspaper, making a mental note of the garage sales Stormy had circled.

''Snooping won't do you any good,'' she called with disdain.

''Can't hurt,'' he tossed over his shoulder.

But he knew it could. The question was, *who* would be hurt?

Dammit, he thought. How in hell had he let this happen?

Chapter Seven

He arrived back at Stormy's home with less than seconds to spare; she was just backing out of the drive. While she waited for a break in traffic in order to pull onto the highway, he gave a short blast on his horn. She acknowledged him with the best of her repertoire of acerbic glares, which did not detract one whit from the attractiveness of her features.

He reciprocated with a smile. If she were that seductive in anger, what a wonder she must be in passion. The idea generated notable heat . . . and some incredible fantasies. But while he entertained a fleeting daydream, she managed to slip into the traffic and leave him behind. Damn!

Once in the housing subdivisions, traffic was lighter, and he had no problem staying within a car length or two of her. He observed her buying up all manner of stuffed toys.

Though he often parked right behind her at the sales, not once did she acknowledge his presence by word or gesture.

But Liane and Janelle did. Between stops, the little girls were on their knees in the back seat, making all manner of faces at him out of the rear window. He joined in the game, giving, he thought, as good as he got. At a stop sign, he offered his pièce de résistance—thumbs in ears, fingers flapping and tongue drooping out the side of his mouth. This sent the girls into such a spasm of giggling; Stormy caught them at it. After working the next sale, she put the girls in the front seat with her, and Tyler had to find another way to amuse himself.

Which he did by doing a postmortem on the events of the past week. And he still hadn't a clue where the money might be. Sitting in some old trunk somewhere, gathering dust instead of interest, perhaps. Of course, he wanted to find it. He had a reputation for closing cases from Atlanta to Miami. He did not want to jeopardize that reputation.

However, it was the matter of Stormy Elliott that now took priority in his mind.

Though loathe to admit it, he was experiencing a constant, imperative impulse to touch her, to hold her, to explore every inch of her, down to counting her lush eyelashes.

If he closed his eyes, he could, with the utmost clarity, recapture the texture of her skin against his lips, the taste of her mouth on his tongue.

That he was going to bed alone at night with only the *thought* of her to keep him warm was deprivation of the worst sort.

The question was how to make Stormy see eye to eye with him on this.

Subtle persuasion was probably the ticket. But what form?

Then it came to him. Stormy was a single parent with a deep attachment to her daughter. Therein lay the key. He'd win Liane over. Hell, he liked her already, and the kid didn't seem to mind him, either. Stormy was bound to notice if Liane was on his side. He was a little bit out of practice with children, but everything would come back to him.

The main thing was not to be pushy. Kids got ticked off at pushy, know-it-all adults. His best bet was to be alert for opportunities to win Liane over, not contrive them.

Strategy plotted, he felt a rush of pleasure that stayed with him all afternoon. Oddly, even the pain he suffered at comparing Liane with Priscilla began to abate.

He was trailing only a car length behind when Stormy stopped in front of a modest house that had obviously been the site of a successful yard sale.

Several women were busy folding tables and packing scattered remnants of clothes and toys into cardboard boxes. One woman went to remove the Yard Sale sign propped against the mailbox post.

Tyler watched Stormy and the girls approach the woman. They chatted a moment, then the woman waved to her friends on the lawn and escorted her visitors into the house.

He settled down to await Stormy's reappearance.

NOREEN BYERS WAS BLOND, buxom and bubbly, yet there was something in her carriage that spoke of steel and substance. Stormy liked her at once.

"I can't tell you how much I appreciate your taking Janelle this weekend," Noreen said. "It's been a madhouse around here. You'll stay for dinner, won't you?"

"Can we, Mom?" Liane pleaded. "Janelle wants to show me her New Kids on the Block collection."

"It's just black beans and rice and cornbread," Noreen put in. "The beans have been in the slow cooker all day."

"I love black beans and rice," said Liane.

Stormy laughed. "Since when?"

Janelle grabbed Liane's hand, and they disappeared into the depths of the house.

Three other women soon made an appearance in the kitchen, introducing themselves as Sandy, Thelma and Janice.

Two of them sat down at the scarred old table with Stormy. Small and birdlike, Sandy moved serenely about the kitchen, removing dishes from cupboards, laying out condiments and pouring iced tea with solitary deliberation. Stormy grasped the familiarity in those ordinary but cherished tasks, recognizing that Sandy, too, had recently been released from jail.

Thelma caught Stormy's eye. "We all went through that phase."

"You're the . . . the *group,*" Stormy said.

"Support group," Janice emphasized. "We're all ex-cons of one sort or another."

Stormy panicked. "I don't think I ought to be here. I'm on parole."

"Aren't we all? Or probation, anyway," said Noreen. "You don't have to be concerned about association, though. We're a self-help group. It's allowed."

Embarrassed, Stormy shifted in her chair. "I'm sorry. I didn't mean to imply. . ."

Noreen smiled. "It's okay. We know exactly what you meant—that's why we meet. We *do* know what each of us faces. We know the hardships, the suffering, the fears."

"I had a panic attack yesterday," said Thelma. "A police cruiser came up behind me with sirens blaring. I thought my heart would bust right out of my chest."

Noreen laughed. "Didn't have far to burst, did it? Thin as you are."

"We can't all be as blessed as you, Noreen. At least I don't have to spend thirty bucks for underwiring in a bra.

Anyway, the cop went around me to a fender-bender at the intersection. But I was so shaky, I had to pull over and catch my breath.''

Noreen put an arm around the woman. "Nothing happened, and you're safe. That's the thought to hang on to." Noreen looked over Thelma's head to Stormy.

"Thelma let her boyfriend use her car while she was at work one day. Two days later, she was stopped for having a headlight out, and when she had trouble finding the registration, the cops 'helped.' In the process, they found a bag of marijuana under the seat. She was arrested for possession. Her stud disappeared and let her take the rap."

"I don't use drugs," Thelma put in, "but I couldn't convince the court."

Stormy related to that.

The food was served. Sandy sat down. "How did we do on the sale?"

Janice smiled. "Six hundred thirty-seven dollars and change."

Sandy burst into tears.

Thelma looked fondly at the sobbing young woman. "Sandy needed four hundred dollars to pay a lawyer to go into court with her tomorrow. Now she has it. She has a hearing in family court. She's trying to get her children back from her ex-husband."

Stormy's heart turned over. "I couldn't bear it if someone tried to take Liane away from me."

"The courts know that, society knows that, the men in our lives know that—so what emotional bullet do you think they use to keep us in line?"

"Point taken," Stormy said softly.

Sandy blew her nose and began to spoon up tiny bites of rice and beans. "Bennie is going to be shocked as hell when I show up in court tomorrow with a lawyer." She leaned toward Stormy. "He walked out on me and the kids, left us with the mortgage payments and never paid a dime of child support. Eventually I lost everything, and we were reduced to living out of the car. By that time Bennie had found someone else—someone more 'moral,' at least for appearance's sake. She couldn't have a husband who didn't 'do' for his children, so Bennie had me investigated, and I ended up being charged with neglect." Her shoulders slumped. "I was just trying to hold it together."

Noreen got up and made hot dogs for the kids, adding potato chips, pickles and glasses of iced tea to the tray. "This will occupy them for another half hour," she said, and went to deliver the food. When she returned she wore a concerned expression.

"Does one of us have any trouble the rest of us don't know about?"

The women around the table looked at her.

"What do you mean?" asked Sandy in alarm.

"There's a dusty BMW parked near the drive. A man wearing a *GQ* wardrobe is leaning against it. Not the type to shop garage sales, I assure you. He looks ready to storm a Viking hideaway singlehandedly."

Stormy's face flamed. The description fit Tyler. "He's my trouble, I'm afraid. I'll go get rid of him."

Noreen stayed her with a gesture. "Is he dangerous?"

Stormy shook her head. "Not in the way you mean. He's more an... irritation."

"Oh, well, then, leave him be," Noreen counseled. "Sometimes a confrontation is what a man is after. It has to do with control, manipulation. Let him sit out there and twiddle his thumbs. Might do him some good."

Noreen refilled tea glasses, then hesitated. "Listen, we don't want you to get the idea that we're against men in general—we're not. It's just that each of us was betrayed by the man in her life. If we could find an honest, caring man who doesn't have a hidden agenda—"

"The first one we find is mine!" yelled a laughing Thelma. "I've been looking the longest."

After the giggles ebbed, Noreen continued explaining the group. "We try to support one another, lend a hand where we can, share job information, referral services. Since even parents and friends look at us funny and businesspeople are suspicious of us, we try to help mainstream ourselves in small ways that count. We work hard at keeping frustration at bay and our dignity intact."

Janice leaned forward. "I'll give you a 'for instance.' I needed a job with hours the same as school because I couldn't afford a full-time baby-sitter. What we came up with was that I could volunteer to help in my daughter's classroom a couple of afternoons a week. When a position came open in the school cafeteria, I knew about it right away, applied and got it. I had to explain my arrest record, but because of my excellent 'record' on the premises, the school was willing to listen. And they believed me when I explained that I didn't *know* my husband was fencing stolen televisions."

At Stormy's raised eyebrows, Janice sighed and explained, "Jasper was an electronics wizard. He had a shop set up in the garage to repair televisions and VCRs. It didn't seem so out of the ordinary for someone to drop off a TV for repair and never return for it. When Jasper had four or five unclaimed TVs, he'd have me put an ad in the paper to sell them. I did. I didn't know he was buying stolen TVs and having me resell them. I think the judge gave me sixty days just for being stupid." Janice shook her head. "They were the worst two months of my life."

"Where's your husband now?" Stormy asked.

"In prison. He blames me. Said I was an idiot not to recognize a sting operation when I saw it. I write to him . . . but I don't think we'll stay married." Her face drooped. "Unless he starts accepting responsibility for his behavior." Her blue eyes glowed with sudden intensity. "Before I got into this group, I thought I had to stay married to him no matter what—that I couldn't possibly take care of myself and my kid. Now I'm learning about options."

Noreen set out a chocolate cheesecake, which made all the women moan about calories—and later ask for seconds. Over cake, Noreen addressed Stormy. "I know something of your plight because Liane and Janelle are friends. Would you like to share it with us? You don't have to, but if you do, we'd like you to know we don't discuss anything anyone says outside these walls—ever."

Noreen's words were as much a warning as an invitation. Stormy wavered. She liked Noreen. She liked the others. But she also felt that she was far more fortunate than they. Different. Wasn't she? Then she looked around again, and she realized these women's fears as parents, as citizens, *were* the same as her own. Like it not, she was one of them, and their camaraderie was inviting. "I didn't come over here with the idea of dumping my problems on your doorstep."

Noreen laughed. "Of course, you didn't. You came to return one of mine!"

"We adore dissecting somebody else's problems," said Thelma. "It gives us something to think about other than ourselves. Besides, we might learn something from you."

It was the right thing to say. Stormy relaxed. Briefly, she described the events that lead to her incarceration, Nina's recent anger and resentment, her concerns about Liane—all of which brought forth knowing nods. She received enthusiastic support for becoming a flea-market merchant.

"We've got two boxes of stuffed animals left over from the yard sale," announced Thelma. "Take them, too."

"I'll buy them from you," Stormy countered.

"No," said Noreen. "Accept them as a gift. If they sell, it'll be your turn next to provide the cheesecake."

Next time? Stormy vacillated, uncertain.

"Of course, you'll come back. We'll want to hear all about your success."

Stormy gave a smile. "I'll give it a try, but I'll be working weekends. I can't say what my hours—"

"Oh, we usually meet on Monday evenings. We're only here tonight because of the sale."

"Uh, Stormy," Thelma said, "you somehow left out the part about the *GQ* Viking stalking you in his BMW."

Stormy twiddled with her fork. "His name is Tyler Mangus, and he's an asset-recovery agent looking for the stolen money."

"Uh-oh," said Janice, discerning the careful editing of emotion from Stormy's voice. "You're sweet on him, aren't you?"

"I'm *confused* about him," Stormy insisted.

At that instant, just as Noreen was glancing at her watch, her teenaged daughter, Elise, made a breathless entrance. "I'm not late, am I, Mom?"

Stormy was glad for the interruption, and her attention went to the teen, as did everyone else's. Elise was a few inches taller than her mother, with the ripe slenderness of youth. Long, dark lashes fanned out against her tanned cheeks, which enhanced the emerald green of her eyes. Shoulder-length hair, soft and loose, framed a face that carried a pert nose and a pouty lower lip—yet her mouth seemed ready to smile. Stormy at once understood Noreen's consternation about this daughter. If Liane grew to young adulthood looking like Elise, Stormy determined then and there she'd lock her away until she was thirty.

Noreen pursed her lips. "You're not late, darling daughter. But it boggles the mind that your date-of-the-day wound his watch, didn't run out of gas, didn't have a flat tire, didn't misplace his wallet—"

Elise laughed and hugged her mother. "You're just showing off in front of your friends. Anyway, I have good news for you."

"You've decided to become a nun?"

"Almost." Elise's eyes gleamed with devilment. "I'm just as virginal now as when I left this morning."

Before her mother could form a comment, the telephone rang. Elise shot out of the kitchen to answer it. Noreen sighed. "To think I have to go through this *twice!* When I got pregnant with that girl, God did not have his eye on me. He had it on the sparrow."

"Well, at least you talk about sex with Elise," said Janice. "That's more than my mother ever did with me. If she had just explained to me about an erection and what a man expected to *do* with it, I'd never have even *considered . . .*"

The women laughed, and Stormy used the moment to update Noreen about Liane and Janelle's scientific discussion. Noreen winced.

"I'm trying my damnedest to hold off on the actual technical explanation until Janelle is at least in third grade, but I may have to speed it up. Why can't they just get into dissecting frogs or something?"

"Well, I kinda like the idea of getting pollinated by a bee," said Thelma. "It shows imagination. Which reminds me, I gotta go. I promised my mom I'd pick the kids up before *Sixty Minutes*. If I don't, I won't hear the end of it. I'm not exactly her fair-haired girl as it is.''

Amid hugs and good cheer, the group broke. Sandy and Noreen helped Stormy drag the boxes of stuffed toys out to her car.

Twilight had slipped like a soft shawl over the neighborhood. Tyler was a mere silhouette inside his car. Stormy glanced his way. He didn't move. ''Something's wrong,'' she said quietly, carefully stifling her alarm. ''He wouldn't pass up an opportunity to check out who you are and what we've been doing.''

Followed by Noreen and Sandy, Stormy led the way and peeked into the car window. Tyler was sound asleep, his head thrown back, his Adam's apple prominent.

''They look so harmless when they're asleep, don't they?'' Noreen observed in a whisper.

''This one would be a rogue asleep or awake,'' Stormy insisted, backing away.

Janice sighed. ''He's gorgeous.''

''How do you resist it?'' Noreen asked, eyeing Stormy with awe.

''I remind myself why he's in my life. Will he be okay here until he wakes up?''

''Sure. This is a quiet, dead-end street.''

''Then I'll just collect Liane and be on my way.'' She smiled at the other woman. ''And thanks. I'm glad I finally got to meet you.''

''Same here. Next Monday, okay? About seven-thirty. If the weather's nice, we put the kids out in the backyard. Otherwise, we just live with the interruptions.''

''I'm really not sure I can contribute anything....''

''Yes, you can. You're smart. And don't forget the cheesecake.''

Stormy grinned at her new friend. "May I say, for a woman, you're not too shabby at manipulation yourself."

Noreen grinned back. "Well, thank you. That's the nicest thing anyone has said about me in months. For that, you can just stay put. I'll go roust Liane for you."

OVER THE NEXT FEW DAYS, the beach house was a zoo.

Stormy commandeered the garage to sort all the stuffed animals by color, fabric and size. Those that needed repair before washing she stored in the family room, where she repacked stuffing and sewed seams until her fingertips were raw from pushing a needle.

The laundry room stayed hot and steamy, the washer and dryer in constant motion. When the *thump-thump* of the wet toys turning in the dryer sent Nina into fits of vituperation, Stormy put them out on the deck to finish drying in the sun.

When he was home, Tully stalked the house like a wounded elephant, angry and complaining. Nothing Nina said or did or cooked pleased him. He behaved as if the lack of a television in his bedroom was a deprivation of the highest order. He squawked when the kids even hinted at watching a cartoon.

Stormy wrapped herself in a cocoon of enthusiasm to help deflect the bellyaching and barbs sent her way.

She had one disaster. The red felt tongue in one teddy bear bled pink onto an entire washerload of animals. She also learned that those toys stuffed with cotton batting instead of foam had to be reshaped immediately they came out of the washer or they dried into lumpy, misshapen, unrecognizable creatures.

She had to scour the washer and dryer after each load to locate eyes and ornaments that had worked loose, and she had to find a local hobby shop that could provide replacements.

Meanwhile, she read the ads in the local *Penny Saver*, watching for moving sales, discovering that families who were relocating were most likely to sell toys by the boxload at a single, low price.

Liane sorted out the best of the cars, trucks, games and children's books for ''her'' end of the business.

Davie and Tommy happily explored and ''tested out'' the purchases for hours on end every evening. Their time thus occupied freed up the television for Tully, so that by the end of the week, grudging calm had fallen over the house.

Stormy went to bed each night with a sense of accomplishment.

But she dreamed of Tyler and often awoke with a fluttering heart and a tightness in her midsection. Awake, she replayed in her mind the taste of his gossamer-light kiss, the feathery trail of his lips on her neck, her eyelids. She was plagued with thoughts of *if only....*

Daily, she expected him to appear on the beach.

She expected to find him sauntering up the dune walk or to surprise her in the grocery store. She expected to discover him in her rearview mirror as she took Liane to school or scouted yard sales.

Tyler knew almost everything about her, she reasoned, so why not her phone number? When the phone rang, she bolted to answer it. The caller was never Tyler.

Countless scenarios floated through her mind, but there was only one answer that made sense. She had convinced Tyler of her honesty. He no longer believed she had the stolen money. He had other leads and had gone off to pursue them.

In all those months of trial and incarceration, she had been denied her sensuality for so long that she had stupidly misread the chemistry between them. Nina was right. She'd gone ga-ga over the first man to pay attention to her after prison.

Anyway, his interest in Liane was dubious, too. Liane could not take the place of his daughter, and even though Liane could probably use a father figure, it was better that she not get too attached to a man who was clearly moving on as quickly as he could.

And the man *was* easy to get attached to. If there was one thing Stormy had learned about Tyler Mangus, it was that he was very good at psyching people out. He knew precisely which emotional buttons to push.

It was better that he was gone, out of her life.

If that's true, said a sagacious interior voice, *why are you so miserable?*

Chapter Eight

Stormy stepped back to admire her handiwork. Two pink sheets, neatly pinned and draped, covered the six-foot-long table. Stored beneath the table were boxes of inventory to replace what sold. And if fortune favored her, there were still more boxes in the trunk of her car.

Piled every which way atop the table in what she hoped was an eye-catching display were stuffed animals of every description. Whiskered cats, fluffy dogs, teddy bears large and small, floppy-eared rabbits, gray whales and two long-necked giraffes competed for space. A herd of baby elephants with droopy trunks and pink ears were lined up trunk to tail. Scattered among the larger animals were terry-cloth dolls and little white mice, fuzzy green snakes and dappled horses with tails and manes of brand-new yarn. Toys that could be enhanced with colorful ribbons wore them.

The result was a riot of color, and the high chair she'd had trouble making room for in the car was worth the effort. Placed at the end of the table, it made her selling area seem more substantial. Perched in the chair was a big furry bear dressed in a plaid waistcoat and a red bow tie. She'd added a pair of old eyeglasses and had priced him at four dollars—her most expensive item. Flea-market shoppers wanted bargains, and Stormy was determined to provide them.

At the other end of the table, Liane held forth at her own "table"—an upturned cardboard box on which she displayed all manner of small toys, from trucks and yo-yos to tiny wooden dolls. She, too, had extra inventory beneath her display.

She held up a small shiny red car. "What price do you think I ought to put on this one, Mom?"

"Try twenty-five cents. If it hasn't sold by afternoon, take off a nickel."

Liane frowned. "What would that be?"

"Two dimes."

The child brightened. "I think I'll sell everything in dimes. I know dimes." She glanced around at the still-empty aisles. "Now, if customers would just come!"

"They will," Stormy replied with more hope than certainty in her voice.

Up and down the aisles, other vendors were setting up displays. Nearby a radio played a lively country-western tune.

The early-morning fog had dissipated, revealing a clear blue sky that promised a soft spring day—not too hot, not too cold—just right for a trip to the flea market.

The food kiosks were gearing up. The aroma of freshly brewed coffee wafted in the air.

Stormy felt a thread of anticipation coiling deep within her. *This has got to work,* she prayed silently. *It has got to!*

The smell of coffee lured her. In the bustle of loading the car, she'd forgotten their bagged lunches and thermos. "Listen, poppet, I'm going to get us something to drink. You stay put."

"Suppose somebody wants to buy something?"

"Sell it to them. Everything is marked...see?" She lifted the floppy ear of a rabbit and pointed out the gummed tag. "This one is two dollars. You'll be all right, sweetie." She pointed to the food kiosk. "I'm just going over there. I won't be out of sight. Back in a flash."

She was as good as her word. On the return down the aisle, she could not keep from admiring her table as she approached it. Shoppers, she decided, would not be able to pass it by. And once they noted the prices, surely they'd make a purchase.

Two heads bobbed at the end of the table. Stormy grinned. Liane was making her first sale!

But then the shopper rose up off bended knee.

Tyler!

A sudden weakness in her knees sideswiped Stormy's balance. She hesitated a moment. Joy and dismay collided within her, the contradictory feelings seeming to declare war inside her.

As if he had antennae tuned to her arrival, Tyler lifted his gaze and stared at her gravely, feasting his eyes on her as a sailor long at sea might gaze at land on the horizon.

It seemed to him that every second away from her had been wasted. He wished he could embrace her, smother her with kisses.

He took pleasure simply in the way she moved, head held high, back straight, her long, shapely legs scissoring with perfect rhythm. There was no longer even a scant hint of prison pallor. Her skin glowed with a healthy tan, making her deep-set brown eyes appear almost black.

Stormy couldn't keep from smiling. Not a single ornery epithet found its way to her mind or tongue.

Carefully, so as not to spill her coffee, she gestured toward the display, reaching for composure in her most nonchalant voice. "Well, what do you think?"

"That was a mean thing you did."

Stormy was nonplussed. "What?"

"Going off and leaving me sleeping in my car on a strange road. You could've had the courtesy to wake me."

"Oh. I do feel bad about that."

Tyler's pseudoirritation was his only defense against the emotions coursing through him. Some live thing had broken free and begun to pound violently in his rib cage. "Inconsiderate behavior like that is never without its day of reckoning, you know."

"Oh? And what do you call your behavior? You went away without so much as a by-your-leave."

His eyes narrowed. "Are you saying you missed having me around?"

"Goodness, no. But if your investigation is finished, I'd like to know it." She opened the carton of milk and gave it to Liane.

"Tyler thinks I ought to sell my stuff for *five* dimes," Liane said.

Stormy glanced at her daughter. "Did Tyler buy anything from you?"

"No. He doesn't have any kids to buy things for. He used to have a *darling* daughter like me, but she died and went to kid's heaven." She looked up at Tyler. "That's right, isn't it?"

"Exactly right," he said.

Stormy frowned. She had mixed emotions about someone discussing death with Liane. But the child seemed to be handling it just fine. "Five dimes might be a bit overpriced. People want bargains."

Liane looked from her mother to Tyler, and with that sixth sense that children often have of an adult storm brewing, she retreated to her end of the table and began rearranging the display of toys.

Tyler closed in on Stormy. "That wasn't nice. Did you have to contradict me in front of the child?"

"I'm her mother. I know what's best. I want her to grow up with good sense."

"Fat chance, with you as a role model."

"You can try baiting me all day long. It won't do you a bit of good."

"So don't you want to know where I've been all week?" he said grumpily.

She smiled archly. "Slumming?"

He ignored the sarcasm. "You could call it that. I reviewed your trial transcript and Hadley Wilson's testimony and compared them. Then I followed the route you took from your front door to the bank, on to Epcot Center and Disney World... That was a nice touch, by the way—separate hotel rooms."

He had also made a two-day detour and spent some time at his cabin, rationalizing that he wasn't really walking off the job. On the slim chance that Stormy *did* have access to his client's money and was to retrieve it in his absence, he'd find out soon enough. After all, how easily could an ex-con with her seven-year-old daughter in tow vanish into thin air? And he'd needed the calm and serenity being at the cabin always gave him.

But this time the cabin had felt... empty. He had spent hours imagining Stormy and Liane there, and the images had stayed with him as he tackled the mundane tasks of reviewing phone messages, answering mail and paying bills. He had stalked through the unfinished loft a half dozen times with an eye to how it could be finished to suit a child. It was at that point that he realized how woefully short of logic and reality his images were falling. Stormy hadn't the least inkling of his infatuation—at least of its depth.

"So you reviewed the transcripts again," she said, yanking him back to the present. "What's your point?" A clump of ice had settled around her heart. Fear.

"Well, here we have two consenting adults checking into separate hotel rooms.... I find that peculiar."

Stormy's mind raced. Could Tyler be fishing? Could he be jealous? "That's not so peculiar," she said with a careful absence of expression. "In this day and age. After all, Hadley and I weren't all that well acquainted."

He assessed her as if transfixed. "You know, I half believe that."

While they were thus caught up, the aisles had been filling with a hum of activity. Shoppers seemed to have arrived out of thin air and many stopped to examine Stormy's display. Personal conversation was put on hold as Stormy gave her attention to marketing her wares. Still, she was aware of Tyler's presence. He moved away occasionally, elbowed out by aggressive shoppers, but he was never very distant.

Her first sale was one of the giraffes. She put the three dollars into the cigar box that served as her cash register, then flicked a smile at Tyler. "Now I truly feel like I'm in business."

Liane, too, began to sell her wares. While Stormy was busy with another customer, Liane had to make change for a dollar bill. Tyler helped her.

At noon, Stormy ran out of change. Tyler went to the office to exchange a handful of twenty-dollar bills for ones and fives.

People commented that the animals were perfect for Easter baskets. A grandmother of nine bought a toy for each grandchild. Boyfriends bought for girlfriends. And vice versa. A child of four or so set up a squall when her mother refused her a toy. Stormy was ready to *give* the toddler the animal when the mother finally relented.

Liane complained of hunger. Tyler fetched hot dogs and soft drinks.

After each sale, Stormy pulled replacements from the inventory beneath the table. Sometime after three she discovered she had emptied the boxes. Though she could see her car from her space, she didn't dare leave the table or Liane unattended. Tyler went to her car and retrieved the rest of the toys.

Stormy sold the teddy bear wearing the plaid waistcoat. Then she sold the high chair. Almost an antique, it brought a whopping twenty dollars.

Liane became weary. Tyler borrowed a lawn chair from a nearby merchant and put Liane on his lap, where, hugging her own cash box, she curled into slumber, oblivious to the noise and chatter around her.

By five-thirty, foot traffic was becoming scarce. Stormy looked longingly at Tyler and Liane. Tomorrow, she'd bring her own lawn chair. Her legs ached from standing. Her mouth was dry from chitchat. But, wonder of wonders, her cigar box was filled to overflowing.

Other vendors were beginning to close up shop, and Stormy took her cue from them. Tyler carried Liane to the car and gently placed her on the back seat to finish her nap. Then he helped Stormy pack up.

"I guess I owe you one," she said. "I couldn't have gotten through the day without your help. Thanks a lot."

"No thanks necessary—I enjoyed myself." He hesitated. "But there is one thing you could do for me. I'd like to go over the trial transcripts with you."

Wariness overtook her. "Why? What's the use?"

"Dammit, I don't *know* the use. I only know I'm missing something important. Maybe together we can find it."

Stormy feinted, trying to get a handle on where he was trying to take her. "You think Hadley hid the money somewhere between the time he stole it and we came home?"

"It's a thought."

"I really don't see how I can help you. I told everything I knew in court." She got into her car and put the cigar box beneath the seat.

Tyler closed the door, rested his arm on the roof and bent down to gaze at her, his expression solemn. "If there was any single thing you could have out of the mess you were in, what would it be?"

Stormy didn't even have to think about it. "Vindication."

"Suppose that were possible?"

She gave him a sharp glance. "Do you know something I don't?"

"Let's just say I suspect something you don't. And if we put our heads together..."

"Tyler, don't play games with my life."

He leaned closer and for a moment, Stormy thought he was going to kiss her. To her amazement, her mouth opened slightly and she held her breath.

But his hand snaked through the window and dropped several toy cars into her lap. "I bought these from Liane. They're collector's items—some of the early Matchbox series. Put them away in a safe place—you or Liane may want them one day."

All this he said with his face a scant two inches from hers, his breath warm on her cheek, and when the corner of his mouth turned up, she knew *he* knew she'd been expecting his kiss—had been *anticipating* it.

Mortification washed over her like a tidal wave.

In the next instant, he straightened.

"Worm!" she accused hoarsely, unguardedly indignant.

"I need your cooperation, but I don't want you to come back later and accuse me of undue influence." Still wearing the crooked, knowing smile, he strode away.

Stormy clutched the toy cars in her lap and watched him until he disappeared, silently cursing him out. But even to her own inner ear, she didn't sound convincing.

TYLER'S SMILE WIDENED into a self-satisfied grin. Seeing was believing, wasn't it? Stormy Elliott liked him. More than liked him, he suspected. Knowing that, he told himself, he could wait.

He felt alive again, no longer numb. Perhaps he had finally finished grieving. Perhaps time and distance had healed his ragged scars.

He got behind the wheel of his car. However, emotions aside, he still had a case to resolve.

He was ninety-nine percent certain that Stormy Elliott was telling the truth.

He was ninety-nine percent certain that she did not know what had happened to the stolen money.

Since she'd practically admitted she was still hiding some detail about the crime, he was also ninety-nine percent certain that that detail might help straighten everything out.

And he was ninety-nine percent certain that they could make it as a couple. Nix that. A trio.

Since he had talked to his clients only yesterday, he was one-hundred percent certain of one thing: the insurance company wanted to recover the stolen money. They didn't care *who* had it.

He folded his hands on the steering wheel and rested his chin atop them, brooding.

Ninety-nine percent.

That one lousy leftover one percent was a bitch.

Dusk approached. The flea market emptied itself of vendors and shoppers alike, the stragglers casting long shadows along the grounds. Tyler continued to brood.

Then he sat up suddenly. Holy Hannah! He had it! It was a wild idea, but—

All he needed was Stormy's trust....

STORMY WAS WEARY but euphoric. Spread out before her on the kitchen table were the proceeds of the weekend. Saturday, she had pulled in eight hundred dollars. Today, Sunday, she had done four hundred and twenty-six dollars. And had she not run out of inventory, she would've done even better.

Tyler had not put in an appearance their second day at the flea market, but much to Stormy's dismay, he might as well have. All day long Liane's chatter had begun, "Tyler this...Tyler that...Tyler said..." And, of course, Stormy had to listen to every Tyler-attributed comment—to ascertain that it was harmless.

With cash in hand, though, she somehow felt better able to cope with life—even with Tyler. Dear God, she was solvent! She had enough money to put a new set of tires on the car, to buy Liane a spring outfit or two; enough money to set aside a deposit on an apartment, to redeem her things at the pawnshop and still have cash left over to work yard and moving sales for more inventory.

As she began to put rubber bands around the stacks of bills, a shadow fell across her. She looked up into Nina's astonished face.

"Did you make all that at the flea market?"

Stormy laughed. "Unbelievable, isn't it?"

"You'd better put it in the bank."

Stormy shook her head. "I'm not ready to go anywhere near a bank."

"You can't leave that much cash lying around."

"I'm not going to leave it 'lying around,' Nina. I'm going to put what I don't need right away in Dad's old safe."

"It'd make me nervous having that much cash in the house. Suppose we're burgled?"

"I don't think we will be." Stormy gathered up the money and put it into a paper sack. "It's late. I'm going to bed." The odd, hesitant look on Nina's face stopped her. "Was there something else?" she asked.

Nina tossed her head. "Now that you have money, don't you think you ought to contribute toward household expenses? It's unfair to expect Tully to carry the whole load."

Stormy was beginning to believe that Nina's sense of fair play and reality was completely warped. Her sister had milked her trust-fund income without a hint of a guilty conscience. "I'll pay the water bill, Nina, and help buy groceries," she said with barely restrained impatience. "But that's it, because I expect to be out of here within the month. And please stop invoking Tully's name every time you want something from me."

"I only want what is rightfully mine. If Dad hadn't given you the money to open your sandwich shop, there'd be a lot more money in the trust now."

Stormy's jaw dropped. "Dad *loaned* me that money, and I paid him back. Every penny, with interest."

"So you say."

Stormy scrutinized her younger sister. "Nina, why are you so down on me? What's going on inside your head?"

"You think I'm a pushover, don't you? You've always been arrogant, snubbing your nose at what's respectable, what's moral."

"If you're harping back to Liane..." Stormy said, a soft but audible warning in her voice.

Nina wasn't listening. "You just breeze through life, no matter what. You get everything tossed at your feet. What do you think Mom and Dad would've said if *I* had had a baby out of wedlock?"

Stormy leaned against the kitchen counter. A thought was coming to her, vague at first but crystal clear a moment later. "You were pregnant when you married Tully," she said flatly. "That's what this is all about, isn't it? You feel cheated. Cheated of your independence. It all makes sense now." Stormy watched Nina's face grow pink.

"I haven't been cheated. Tully did right by me. He's always done right by me."

"I wonder how often he reminds you of that?"

Nina stiffened, the question unanswered. Suddenly Stormy wanted to put her arms around her sister, soothe her, tell her that she would make everything okay again. But she knew that was a fantasy. Whatever inner turmoil Nina suffered, Nina would have to work it through.

But Stormy could see now that her homecoming, her presence in the household, was a daily catalyst, a wind that stirred and brought to blaze Nina's long-smoldering embers of shame and, perhaps, jealousy. Still, short of grabbing Liane and leaving that moment, there was little she could do to tamp out Nina's blaze. She tried words.

"I'm not so independent as you may suppose, Nina. I have needs that are going unmet right this minute. Besides, being totally independent is not all it's cracked up to be. You, on the other hand, have two lovely children to my one, you have a husband to my none. You have a kind of sharing with Tully that I have yet to experience with a man. You're a *family.* I envy that."

Confusion skittered across Nina's face. "You don't."

Stormy picked up the paper sack of cash. "I do. You think about it. I know you and Tully argue a lot, but if an outside force threatens, you join together, present a united front. I don't have that luxury. Tully may not be... well... some things, but he loves you."

"I wish somebody had told me love included washing mounds of dirty socks and underwear," Nina said in a rare display of wry humor.

Stormy laughed. Then she sobered. "Maybe we did let you down there, Nina. You were the baby in the family— the adorable baby. We all doted on you. Maybe tried to shelter you too much."

Nina's expression filled with sadness. "I wish Daddy were here to dote on me now."

Stormy sighed. "I do, too."

WHEN SHE LAID HER HEAD on her pillow, Stormy's brain felt crowded. Thoughts and images of Nina, Tully, her parents, Liane and Tyler collided with one another.

Tyler...

She had known from the moment she first laid eyes on him, he was going to make trouble. And he had. He had managed to penetrate her facade of nonchalance, and he threatened to reach her at depths she had not even known existed. Not to mention his sensual pull on her. She had been celibate so long, her response to him was almost frightening.

In addition to which, much as she hated to admit it, she couldn't help but notice how good he was with Liane. Nor could she deny that Liane was smitten with Tyler.

The problem was, falling in love meant putting yourself at someone else's mercy. And look what had happened to her the last time she'd fancied herself in love. She'd been deserted and left to raise a child on her own. How much and how far could she trust Tyler?

Could he be serious about the possibility of vindication at this late date? Or was he holding it out as a tantalizing inducement to capture her cooperation?

Through thick and thin, she had managed to keep concealed Liane's presence in the car at the time of the robbery. The witness who had come forward to identify her had not noticed the girl asleep in the back seat.

Did she now dare allow Tyler to learn of that?

What would be the repercussions?

She was on parole. Her life belonged to the state of Florida. She could not marry without her parole officer's approval. She had to report housing and job changes. She could not hang about in bars or give the impression of being tipsy. She was subject to random urine tests for drugs and alcohol. Even something as minor as a traffic violation could land her back in prison.

And, what would become of Liane? Nina could no longer be depended upon to care for her niece, yet Stormy shuddered at the thought of her daughter being shunted from one foster home to another while she served out her prison term. Or, worse, have Liane taken away from her if it were discovered that she, the ex-con mother, had brought her daughter along on her supposed heist.

But to have the slate wiped clean, to have her conviction overturned . . . Vindication . . .

Stormy spent the night tossing and turning, trying to fathom a solution to her dilemma.

Chapter Nine

"Good grief!" exclaimed Noreen Byers as Stormy unbagged the items she'd brought for the group. "Cheesecake from the best bakery in town, and fresh strawberries—which I happen to know are selling for two dollars a pint at the moment. You must've had a wingding of a weekend."

"If I tell you how well I did, you won't think I'm boasting, will you?"

"When you come to this group," chimed Thelma, "one of your prerogatives is that you're *allowed* to boast."

Stormy told them, and the women gaped.

Noreen was the first to recover. "You're not joking, are you?"

Stormy pulled out a chair from the table and sat down. "No joke. I'm stunned myself. I still have a lot to learn, though. And I have run into a snag."

"What snag?" teased Noreen. "You need help to carry the cash to the bank?"

"No. But *help* is the operative word."

"That's what we're here for. Fire away."

"What I mean is, I could use another pair of hands."

Sandy, who had been sitting quietly, lifted her head. "I need some part-time work."

Stormy scrutinized the other woman. Sandy didn't look as sad and scared as she had last week, but she didn't look exactly happy, either. "You didn't get custody of your children?"

"No," the woman said in a painfully soft voice. "But I can have them every other weekend, every other holiday and four weeks in the summer."

"That's a beginning," Janice said consolingly. "For a first skirmish in court, I'd say it was a victory."

Sandy managed a smile. "It is. I know it is." She looked at Stormy. "Now I need to make more money. The lawyer said if I wanted more time with the kids, I'd have to prove I'm able to provide for them. I can work evenings and the weekends I don't have the kids. I don't care what I'm doing, as long as it's legal."

"What I need is someone to work yard sales to buy up inventory," Stormy told her. "I can't manage to work the sales and the flea market at the same time. And weekends are when people hold the best yard sales. You'll have to have the nerve to bargain prices down, though."

Sandy straightened in her seat and said with spirit, "Just watch me—I'll have people practically giving me the stuff!"

Everyone laughed with delight.

"I can't pay you a salary, though, because I can't guarantee sales."

Sandy looked startled. "I won't be paid by the hour?"

"Nope, you'll be a contract worker. We'll write up a contract that details what expenses I'll reimburse, like gasoline, and, of course, I'll provide the up-front money to buy the toys."

"But how do I make any money?"

"You'll receive a percentage of net sales. Say ten percent. If you wash and repair the things you buy so that all I have to do is market them, I'll pay you twenty percent."

Sandy paled. "Dear God, had I worked for you this past weekend, I'd be sitting here with...with two-hundred and forty dollars in my purse!"

"Not quite. That would be twenty percent of my gross. Don't forget expenses—renting the space, cash to buy the inventory—"

"Well, then, what were your expenses?" Thelma asked.

Stormy smiled. "About a hundred and ten dollars and a heck of a lot of elbow grease."

"Write up a contract!" yelped Sandy. "I'm in."

"See?" said Noreen, laughing. "I told you we learned from one another. Who'd have guessed we had an entrepreneur among us?"

"It could've been a fluke that I made so much money," cautioned Stormy. "Easter is coming up, so people were buying things for Easter baskets. But I'm keeping an ear to the ground for other things to sell, too."

"Like what?" Thelma asked.

Stormy shook her head. "I don't know. Something unique, something people might not expect to find at a flea market. But most of all, inexpensive to acquire."

"I have the feeling that next week we're all going to be hitting garage sales," said Janice. She leaned forward, her expression intense. "Maybe down the road, we could think of forming a business partnership or something. Think of the money that could be made if you had tables at all the other flea markets. There must be more than a dozen within a hundred-mile radius of St. Augustine."

Stormy hesitated. "I like the idea—but for the future. Because what you're suggesting means we'd need a warehouse to store inventory, enough cash to buy what we hope to sell, time to repair—''

"But suppose," put in Thelma," that we each buy a few things as we have the cash to spare. Maybe then we could all go in on a vendor space a couple of times a year. I always need money for the kids' school clothes and Christmas."

"Just listen to us!" exclaimed Janice. "We're talking like real businesswomen."

"It only takes a good idea and the moxie to execute it," said Noreen. "Our problem was defeatism. We always thought we couldn't win."

"Until now," added Sandy, looking admiringly at Stormy.

"Nobody ever said we weren't smart," said Thelma. "Just dumb when it comes to men."

"We shouldn't be laughing," said Janice. "It's true!"

"But we've learned we can make choices," put in Sandy.

"Speaking of choices," said Noreen, "anybody want to *choose* to help dye Easter eggs next weekend? I promised the girls we'd do it the old-fashioned way."

For a few minutes the women compared notes on boiling pine needles, beets and carrots for natural dyes. Noreen got up to refill coffee cups, and she gazed at the cheesecake and strawberries.

"What do you girls say? Do we eat this all by ourselves and suffer the guilt, or do we share it with the kids?"

"Let's offer them ice cream," said Janice. "That way we won't be accused of child abuse." Stormy winced. "Sorry," Janice apologized. "Me and my gallows humor."

"I agree," said Noreen. "Let's talk about something nice—like the hunk Stormy left behind sleeping in his car last week."

Stormy felt the blood rush to her cheeks. "No, let's not."

"Gosh," said Thelma craftily. "Didn't Noreen tell you we don't keep secrets from one another?"

"Tyler Mangus isn't a secret. But..."

"But what?" Noreen raised an eyebrow.

Stormy looked at the women and recognized that she was safe among them. They were willing to listen, to share, not to judge. They understood her inner turmoil; they experienced the same. When she realized she'd been holding her breath, she exhaled. "Tyler may be on to one of my secrets," she said.

While Noreen served the cheesecake, Stormy outlined the robbery and Liane's presence that weekend. "The prosecutors took for granted it was only Hadley and me. My attorney instructed me not to volunteer any information, so I didn't. And Hadley never took the stand. Now Tyler is inferring that there's a possibility my conviction could be overturned."

"Does that mean he's uncovered some new evidence?" someone asked.

"That's just it. I don't know what it means. If it were just me, I'd go all out. But there's Liane to consider."

Sandy, feeling keenly the loss of her own children, said, "I think you were right to keep Liane out of things. What could she have added to the trial? She didn't know anything. When I had to take my kids into court, they were scared to death, and they cried for weeks afterward."

"But suppose, just suppose," Stormy mused, "there is a chance of getting my conviction set aside?"

"And just *suppose* someone complains that you haul your kid around while you rob banks?" Sandy said, putting into words Stormy's deepest fear.

Stormy nodded. "That's my rock and a hard place."

Janice laid her hand on Stormy's arm. "What about this Mangus guy? Can you trust him?"

Stormy propped her chin in her hands. "That's the crux of it, isn't it?"

Noreen sighed. "After all we've been through, why is it that every major decision in our lives continues to revolve around a man?"

"That's easy," said Thelma. "There are so many of them. They're everywhere you turn." She sniffed. "And I *still* wish I had one to call my own."

At that moment the teenage Elise came into the kitchen. She plucked a strawberry from her mother's plate and eyed the half-eaten cheesecake. "All those calories are going straight to your hips," she told all and sundry.

Noreen chased her out of the kitchen.

Everyone had seconds. "Let's just say we need it to fortify us against life," said Janice.

"And pray that Stormy keeps having lucrative weekends," added Thelma. "I could get used to saddlebag hips—easily."

Before they broke for the evening, Stormy and Sandy exchanged telephone numbers, and Noreen convinced Stormy to allow Liane to spend the following Saturday with Janelle to help dye eggs.

On the way home, Liane was beside herself with excitement.

"Since we're gonna use leaves an' things like that, it'll count as another science project. Won't that be great? And I can dye enough eggs for Davie's and Tommy's baskets. They still believe in the Easter Bunny."

"Oh?" Stormy said. "And you don't?"

"Don't be silly, Mom. There's no such thing as a giant rabbit. Anyway, rabbits don't lay eggs. I'll tell you something else. . . ."

"I can't wait to hear," Stormy said, feeling a sense of sadness that Liane was growing out of the magic of childhood into logic and life.

"I don't believe reindeer can fly. They can jump high, but that's not the same as flying. I think Santa has another way he brings presents."

"You're probably right," Stormy assured her, smiling inside once more.

"I thought so. Just how does he do it?"

Oh, dear, thought Stormy. "I don't know, poppet. Santa never tells his secrets."

Liane eyed her mother. "I'll ask Tyler. He'll know."

Stormy opened her mouth to protest, then closed it. Silence, she decided, was more than golden; right now it was salvation.

She sighed inwardly. But a certain silence was weighing on her mind. Could she trust Tyler with her secret?

Vindication.

It was so tempting.

She would listen to what he had to say.

That was all.

Period.

BUT THE PROBLEM that developed during the next few days was that Tyler didn't so much as show his face.

When Stormy had errands to run, she found herself driving slowly past Tyler's motel. His car was seldom there during the day, only late in the evening. She never managed to screw up the courage to stop.

Morning and evening she went for walks on the beach. No Tyler.

Well, he had to eat somewhere. She treated Liane and her nephews to pizza at Pete's, lingering long past dusk. She stopped at a coffee shop he'd mentioned and hung around so long that the waitress regaled her with the story of her life.

Still no Tyler. What was going on?

SANDY CAME TO the beach house on Wednesday evening. Stormy showed her the kinds of toys to search out and buy and explained how best to clean and repair them. Sandy left with a hundred dollars of Stormy's cache and a plan to work the Jacksonville Beach yard sales.

By the middle of the week there was a subtle truce in the household. Stormy had installed her reclaimed television in the den for the children, which left Tully free use of the one in the family room. She had paid the water bill and stocked the larder.

On Thursday, Tully worked late. Nina asked to borrow the car to take the boys for haircuts and to the movies. Offhandedly, she invited Liane.

The child looked to her mother. "You think Tyler might come over today?"

"I doubt it, poppet." *Today or any other day,* she added silently.

Liane sighed heavily. "Then I guess I'll go to the movies."

Nina ushered the children out, and Stormy found herself home alone and at loose ends.

She tried watching a television talk show, but neither her mind nor her body would sit still. She went into the garage to sort toys. The task soon palled. It wasn't that her interest in a livelihood evaporated, but that it got submerged in her curiosity about Tyler. She felt like a pullet wondering where the fox was lurking.

Outside, the sun blazed, drowning the coast in golden warmth. Barefoot, Stormy went for a walk on the beach, hoping that the gentle susurrus of the waves washing ashore would cleanse her mind of Tyler. But the sea was eerily calm. Even the squawking seagulls that swooped and skimmed the air around her were more an irritation than a distraction.

She arrived back at the dune walk just as preoccupied as when she had left and irritably hosed the sand off her feet at the spigot at the edge of the deck.

"Anyone ever tell you that you have magnificent ankles?"

Stormy jerked upright, and the hose in her hand jerked with her. Water spurted in a perfect arc to drench Tyler's jeans. He yelped and leapt away.

"Serves you right for sneaking up on me," she said with a tremor in her voice as light as fluttering moth wings. She turned away, ostensibly to shut off the spigot, but more so that Tyler would not see the joy leap across her features. Her need of him was almost like pain. She didn't want to reveal that, either.

He was busy pulling keys, change and bits of paper out of his soggy pants and putting them on the patio table, the activity accompanied by much muttering and a string of epithets. "The hell I was sneaking. If you hadn't been so engrossed in yourself, you'd have seen me arrive."

"I suppose you should come on inside. We can toss your jeans into the dryer." She couldn't repress a giggle at his sodden dishevelment.

"If this is so funny, how come I'm not laughing," he said grimly.

"Let's wait until you're stripped down. Might be something funny in that."

"Wrong. When I strip in front of a woman, I guarantee you, she isn't laughing."

"Oh?" Stormy managed lightly as she led him into the washroom, yanked a towel from a shelf and held it out to him. "What would this mythical woman be doing? Displaying pity? Faking arousal?"

A gleam settled in his eyes. He began to unzip his jeans. "Tell you what—I'll show you."

With a stalwart display of utter contempt, Stormy dropped the towel at his feet and retreated—quickly. "I'll be in the kitchen."

She needed to put her chaotic emotions into some sort of order and to school her features into a semblance of indifference. Fat chance, when, in a moment or two, she'd be seeing him half-naked—and she *knew* she wouldn't be laughing.

She heard the dryer start. Good. At least he hadn't handed over his pants expecting *her* to dry them.

Then he emerged into the kitchen. She gulped. The towel was wrapped snugly about his waist, leaving a lot of powerful, well-muscled leg revealed. Stormy indulged herself in one stray, lingering glance, then snapped her gaze up and kept it above his waist.

"Want something to drink?" she asked. At his nod, she began opening cans of soda and pouring it over ice.

He sat on a stool in the breakfast nook and watched her. When she finally sat across from him, he took a long swallow of his drink, then put the glass down and eyed her gravely. "I want you to tell me something. And I want the truth."

"You already know everything about me," she complained. "And I don't know a thing about you."

"Oh, hell. I was born. I grew up. I was in the service. I got out of the service. I married, I divorced. I have a brother, a mother, a father."

"Where do you live, usually?"

Tyler told her. "I also keep an answering and mail service in Tallahassee. For the most part, my car is my office. At the cabin, I have a computer, a fax, a modem. That's my life."

She sniffed. "Sounds...mechanical."

"What do you want me to say? That I'm one of the good guys? I am. I pay my bills, I drink in moderation, I treat old people with respect. I like animals. I don't beat up on women."

"Not even verbally?"

"With you, I'm only trying to give as good as I get."

"Why do you...behave as if you're really interested in helping me, then go off for days without a word?"

"I have work to do. But on that score, I'm the injured party. I called. You weren't here. I left a message, and you didn't return my call."

Stormy came alert. "You did not."

"I most certainly did."

Stormy pointed to the refrigerator, its door covered with notes and children's drawings held with decorative magnets. "If you had called, the message would be on the fridge." *And Nina would've said something,* she thought, if only to reprove.

"Well, let's see," Tyler said, getting up to peruse the scribblings. "Aha!" He took a paper down and laid it on the table before her.

"But...but that's one of Davie's drawings."

"Well, it took about ten painful minutes for him to write it out. Fortunately, I'm a patient man." He pointed to the telephone number, written in crayon, and his name trailing down the edge of the paper.

"You could've called back," Stormy accused.

Tyler grappled with his exasperation. "Listen, let's get back to basics. I'm here now. I asked for the truth."

"What truth?" Stormy felt contentious. Tyler's primary interest was his case, his clients, right? True, his cause might be her cause, too, but she was not yet ready to offer up Liane.

"Is something happening between us?" he asked.

The question, totally unexpected, seemed to hover in the air like a cruise missile.

Her gaze met his and held. His face was so carefully devoid of expression, she had no hint of where he meant to take this or what her answer should be. "Are you asking out of curiosity or for verification?"

Had Tyler had on his jeans, he would've stalked out. "Forget I asked, okay? Obviously, what's going on between us is still war!"

"You didn't give me a chance to answer!"

"If you have to think about it—"

"What did you expect? That I'd swoon into your arms?"

He nodded.

"Get your jeans on and get out."

He stood and hitched the loosening towel about his hips. "I'm the kind of man who can accept defeat graciously—"

"Wonderful."

"Once."

He came out of the washroom tucking his wallet into the rear pocket of his damp jeans. "I'd like to take you to lunch tomorrow," he said calmly.

"No, thank you. School's out for Good Friday. I'm taking Liane shopping for an Easter outfit."

"I'll take you both to lunch. I like Liane. She makes me think how sweet you probably were before you grew up to be such a shrew."

"You *are* verbally abusive."

"I can go the other way, if you'd let me. Listen to this. My darling," he crooned audaciously, "your skin is like the finest silk. Inhaling the sweet fragrance of you makes me wild with desire. My heart thunders, my manhood—"

Stormy gasped. "Your *what?*"

"You made me lose my train of thought."

"You didn't have one," she said, laughter in her voice.

"I did. I was asking you and Liane to lunch."

"Oh, all right. We accept. But—"

He put a fingertip to her lips. "No buts." He traced the shape of her mouth, whispering, "My heart thunders...."

The mere touch of his finger on her lips seemed to Stormy more sensuous than even his recent nearnakedness, and it took several heartbeats for her to come to her senses. "Stop that, please," she said, moving away.

He followed her with his eyes. "You know I want you."

Stormy exhaled. "Do you believe I had anything to do with the bank robbery?"

Tyler went silent. He didn't have an easy answer. That one lousy percent still plagued him. "What is this? Some sort of test? If I say I think you were innocent, does that mean I'll find favor with you? If I say I'm not sure or it doesn't matter to me—then what?"

"I don't know! I need somebody to believe me. No one does or did. I was stripped of my life! I want my integrity back. You just want me *on* my back."

Jaw rigid, Tyler glared at her. "You're fascinating, you know that? Somehow, no matter what's going down, you manage to turn the dial to your regularly scheduled program. What the hell are you so scared of?"

You, she thought. *Falling in love. Getting hurt. Staying hurt.* "Pain."

Tyler's jaw softened. He knew about pain. Hell, he was even *in* pain right this minute. The ache in his groin defied comprehension. His lips shaped the barest hint of a smile. "Your parents sure pegged you right when they named you." He turned to go. "I'll pick you and Liane up about noon tomorrow."

"Maybe we shouldn't—"

"Noon, dammit."

Chapter Ten

"Tyler invited me, too, didn't he?"

"Yes, he did."

"Well, then, if you're wearing makeup, why can't I?"

Stormy sighed. "For the tenth time—because you're too young."

"You let me wear it before."

"You were playing dress-up." Stormy capped her mascara. "It was part of the costume. Now is not appropriate."

Liane flounced unhappily onto the bed. "Couldn't I just wear a teensy-weensy bit of lipstick?"

"No."

"Eye shadow?"

"No."

"I'm old enough to be in business with you."

"Smart enough, too," Stormy replied.

"Just this much blush?" Liane begged, holding up thumb and forefinger.

"No."

"You just want to be pretty for Tyler all by yourself. You don't want *me* to be pretty."

Stormy turned away from the mirror to stare at her daughter. "You are pretty. In fact, you're especially pretty.

But we are not competing for Tyler's attention, poppet. We're just going to lunch.''

"Well, he *used* to like me better than you. He said so. He said he wished you were as nice as me."

"Probably he still wishes that."

"Then can you be nice to him instead of fussing?" Liane continued with childish logic. "I could use a stepdad, you know. Other kids at school have them." She lifted her head in an autocratic manner. "They're *very* useful. They pay bills and buy their stepkids clothes and take them to play miniature golf."

For a moment Stormy was speechless. "Liane, one does not acquire a stepfather because he's *useful*."

"I don't see why not."

"The reason you don't see why not is the same reason you can't wear makeup. You're too young. I want you to promise me you won't talk like this while we're out with Tyler."

The child balked. "Miss Evans says everyone has the right to free speech."

"Oh?" Stormy cooed in gentle reminder. "What about sheep dip?"

Liane sniffed. "That's different. And, anyway, I *need* a stepdad so I won't be illegitimate anymore."

Stormy felt as if all the oxygen in her lungs had been sucked out. She should have known this was coming, instead of hoping Liane would forget about it. She glanced at her watch. There was so little time before Tyler arrived. Well, he'd just have to wait. She went to the bed and sat beside Liane.

"Sweetheart, nothing we can do now will change the facts about your birth. But those facts are nothing for you to be ashamed of. You were born of love, poppet, and that is a wonderful thing."

The point Stormy was trying to make went askew. Liane kept on looking glum. "You mean I'll be illegitimate forever? No matter what?"

Stormy felt her throat close up.

"What Aunt Nina said is true! I'm not even as good as Davie and Tommy, and they're *boys!*" Liane scooted off the bed and raced into the hall and down the steps. Within seconds, Stormy heard the front door slam.

She finished dressing quickly, slipping into a blue-and-white-print dress, soft as silk, belted in white to complement white sandals. Her hair was piled atop her head, but strands were already coming loose. She left it. The disarray matched her mood. She felt totally inadequate. In prison she had learned to keep a low profile, to harbor only meager expectations in order to protect herself from disappointment. But she couldn't seem to protect her child. The only way she knew how was to keep on showing Liane how much she loved her. It frightened her to think that that might be too little, too late.

LIANE PLOPPED DOWN on the front stoop. She watched Tyler turn into the drive, park and get out. Smiling, he approached her.

"Why so glum on a beautiful day like today? Did you lose a battle with your cousins?"

Liane allowed a tear to trickle down her cheek. "With Mom."

"Shove over," Tyler said, and he sat down beside her. "I used to have fights with my mom."

"You did? What about?"

"Oh, leaving dirty clothes lying around, missing curfew, saying bad words, fighting with my brother."

"But I bet you weren't illegitimate."

Tyler was taken aback. "Well...no," he answered, wondering that Liane even knew the word.

"Well, I am, and I'm going to be illegitimate the rest of my life, even when I'm grown up. There's nothing that can be done about it—ever."

Tyler took one of Liane's hands from her lap and held it in his own, inspecting it as if it were a jewel of great beauty. "Well, you know, if your mom got married, and the man she married adopted you, you'd be...legitimate."

Liane gasped. "Are you sure?"

"Positive."

Liane let that sink in, then went back to looking grim. "That'll never happen. Mom already said I can't have a stepdad."

"The man who adopted you wouldn't be your stepdad. He'd be your real father."

"I don't think so. I already have a dad. His name is Truman Witney. He left before I was born."

"That would make him your biological father—not necessarily your *real* dad."

Liane's demeanor brightened. "You mean Truman Witney would just be my scientific father?"

"Exactly," Tyler said, impressed as much with Liane's grasp of the concept as he was with his own powers of persuasion. He *was* good with kids. He wished Stormy was witnessing this exchange.

Liane cut her eyes to Tyler. "Do you have any sperm? The kind that look like tadpoles?"

"What?" The word jerked from Tyler's vocal cords like rough gravel; he felt as if a noose had suddenly been yanked around his neck.

"Do you know how a bee gets pollen from the sperm to the egg to make babies?"

Tyler leapt to his feet. "Where's your mother? I told her noon."

"Does that mean you don't know or you just won't tell me?"

"It means, go find your mother. Tell her I'm waiting."

"Will you tell her how I can get adopted?" Liane begged, homing in on the topic that was uppermost in her mind.

"At the proper time."

"Promise?"

"I promise."

Liane at once became contrite. "I think I made Mom cry."

"I'll cheer her up," Tyler replied as the front door opened and Stormy emerged.

Tyler had more sophistication than to gape, but he came close. Stormy looked exquisite.

"Have you been waiting long?" she asked.

"A few minutes. Liane and I were just having one hell of a chat."

Stormy glanced at her daughter. "Perhaps this isn't a good idea," she suggested, looking ready to retreat.

"Mom, I want to go! You said—"

Tyler quickly took Stormy's arm. "Now, look here. I'm in charge today. No bickering or you'll both get spanked."

Liane giggled.

Tyler brushed Stormy's ear with his lips. "Among other things, you look good enough to eat." He got a whiff of her fragrance. It was erotic, heady, the kind of scent that caused a testosterone storm in a man.

He pulled back. Lunch, he reminded himself. But first, there was some business to take care of. He hustled Stormy and Liane into the car.

When he drove past the Clam Shell, Stormy glanced back at the restaurant, puzzled. "I thought that's where—"

"It is," he said. "We have a reservation for one o'clock."

Stormy stiffened. "You've planned a trick of some sort, haven't you?"

"Not a trick, no. Trust me, okay? I just want to prove a point—one that I think has been overlooked. It has to do with the money. Can we leave it at that for the moment?"

Stormy felt her heart speed up. "You found it?"

"It's better if you don't ask any questions."

"You mean just go blindly into my fate?" Stormy debated whether to order him to stop so that she and Liane could exit the car. "I don't like this, Tyler. I'm getting nervous. If you've found the money, I don't want to be anywhere near it. That would make it seem as if I knew where it was all along."

"I'm trying to do this *without* putting you into any jeopardy."

"Can you guarantee that?"

Tyler glanced at her, meeting her rather chilly brown gaze. "How are things at home?"

"We've called a truce. You're trying to change the subject."

"A truce. Now why didn't I think of doing that?"

"Because you're so arrogant, you're always sure you'll win."

His green eyes twinkled. "Remind me never to ask you another rhetorical question."

Liane poked him in the back of the neck. "When are you gonna tell her?"

"Tell me what?" Stormy asked.

"Nothing," Tyler said, issuing a warning frown at Liane in the rearview mirror. "Sit back and buckle your seat belt."

Liane flung herself across the back seat. "I hate grown-ups."

Stormy shook her head. Fate was not in her corner today. She cocked her head at Liane. "I'll tolerate your being in a bad mood, but I won't tolerate your being rude. Turn around and take us home, Tyler."

Tyler clucked. "I didn't take offense. Liane and I will handle our own battles, won't we, kid?"

"I'm sorry," Liane squeaked.

Tyler slowed and turned off the main road into the parking lot of a bank. Stormy's breath caught in her throat. "What's the meaning of bringing us here?"

"You'll see."

"Like déjà vu? No thanks." It was just like with Hadley. Stormy drew deep breaths, closed her eyes and waited for her pulse rate to sink toward normal. It didn't. Tyler was opening her door. Liane was already out, standing on the sidewalk.

"No!" Stormy said, feeling trapped.

"Nothing bad is going to happen," Tyler coaxed.

"It's the same—"

"This is a branch of my bank in Tallahassee. They're doing me a small favor. You don't have to say a word. They have no idea who you are."

"Everybody knows!"

"Not true. Most people live in their own little world. And you're hardly in the headlines." He held out his hand. "C'mon. Don't be a coward."

"I'm not a coward. I'm being sensible. Suppose I see someone I know?"

"Say hello."

She refused to budge.

Tyler kept his frustration in check. "Listen, whether you believe it or not, I'm looking out for your best interests. Besides, the way you're headed with your flea marketing, you'll have knocked down thirty thousand dollars by year's end. What're you gonna do if you can't handle banks? Stuff it in a shoebox and keep it under your bed?"

"Don't appeal to my practical side. I'm not ready. And you don't know how much money I've made."

"You forget. I was there." He grasped her arm and tugged. "Out!"

She wanted to stand on her own, but her legs were so wobbly, she was forced to lean on Tyler or fold up on the asphalt. He put his arm around her and moved her forward, into the bank lobby.

Liane trailed behind them. "I hope I get a lollipop," she said. Stormy turned and grabbed Liane's hand.

"Shh."

Tyler was afraid to turn loose of Stormy lest she bolt. He pulled her along to the receptionist and introduced himself. The woman left, then returned with a guard and the bank manager.

All the tellers were looking at them. Stormy felt on display—matted, framed and hung. She leaned into Tyler. "I'm going to kill you for this," she said without moving her lips. "You wait and see."

They were shown into a small, softly lighted room. The guard closed the door behind them and stood in front of it, his hand on the weapon anchored at his side.

"Oooooo!" exclaimed Liane. "Look at all the money!"

Stormy was looking. There were piles and piles of it—stacks of ones and fives and tens and twenties arrayed across the table.

She didn't know where the next moments went. She remained frozen in unseeing, unthinking panic. As if from a distance, she finally heard Tyler murmur a thank-you to the bank manager. She felt his hand spanning the small of her back, urging her to move. The guard followed them out. She only seemed to come to her senses when she was seated once again in Tyler's BMW and they were on the road. Tyler was cautioning Liane not to eat her lollipop until after they'd had lunch.

At the Clam Shell, they were shown to a table overlooking the harbor, and Stormy felt some color returning to her cheeks.

"Good," Tyler observed. "You're back with us." Then, because she was still somewhat ashen, he said gently, "For more reasons than one, it had to be done. You can't spend your life avoiding banks."

Stormy sought sanctuary in anger. "You could've undone my *life!*"

"Are you sure you want to have this conversation in front of Liane?"

Stormy glared at him. He looked laid-back, the only sign of tension, a vein throbbing in his temple. "Just tell me, what was the meaning of—"

"Let's order first," he said.

"Don't draw out the suspense. I can walk home from here."

"You want a scene? Okay. Let's do it right!" He pushed back his chair and stood up. "Wait here."

Stormy felt extreme discomfort. It was anybody's guess what Tyler had up his sleeve.

"I asked you not to pick a fight with him," Liane piped up, giving immutable evidence of whose side she was on. "Now, we probably will have to walk home."

Stormy reminded herself that being a parent *did* have its good days. She was ready for one.

Tyler announced his return by tossing a bundle onto the table, loudly displacing the salt-and-pepper shakers. Nearby diners looked up, startled. Stormy winced.

Liane suddenly sat up straight. "That looks just like Hadley's."

"It is just like Hadley's," Tyler said of the denim hip pack. "You have a good memory."

"He wore it when he took us to Disney World, didn't he, Mom?"

Stormy felt as if her whole world had just collapsed. "Liane, be quiet!"

Tyler's gaze was riveted on Stormy. "I finally guessed, you know. You barely allow Liane out of your sight. I couldn't fathom your going off to Epcot Center and Disney World without her—yet there wasn't a single line in the trial transcripts that referred to Liane."

"I didn't see the robbery," Liane volunteered. "'Cause I was asleep in the back seat."

Tyler lifted the pack off the table, put it in the vacant chair beside him and signaled the waitress.

"I'm not going to be able to eat," Stormy said.

Tyler ordered white wine and the luncheon special for them both, a kiddie dinner and soft drink for Liane—and all the while Stormy was shaking her head.

"It's good to feed your tension," Tyler said once the waitress left with their order.

"Oh, look!" Liane exclaimed. Outside on the terrace, a busboy was setting out kitchen scraps for a trio of cats. "May I go out and watch?" she asked.

Stormy gave her permission. "Just on the terrace, where I can see you," she cautioned. Liane was up and out the door in a flash.

Stormy returned her attention to Tyler, who held up his hands as if to deflect a blow.

"I *was* going to wait until Liane was out of earshot, but you were in such a hurry..."

Stormy leaned forward, the tendons in her neck taut. "Do you know what could happen if it became common knowledge that Liane was involved? On top of everything else, I'd have to fight charges of being an unfit mother. I could lose my daughter. The state casts a very dim eye on parents who take their children along on—" She abruptly stopped talking while their wine was poured.

"I understand," Tyler said.

"You don't," she said with unmerciful firmness.

"I do," he insisted quietly. "When Priss died, we were subjected to a very thorough investigation. I meant it when I said I have your best interests at heart."

"You have a peculiar way of showing it."

"I had to find out what you were hiding from me."

"And now that you know?"

"It's over and done with."

Confused, Stormy leaned back in her chair. "Then... what was the purpose of going to the bank?"

Tyler indicated the hip pack. "Take a peek."

Stormy reached over, unzipped the bag, looked in and jerked back. "It's full of money!"

"Don't get excited. It's mine."

Stormy eyed Liane and saw that she was safely in view, albeit down on her knees trying to coax a calico cat to take a scrap from her fingers while the busboy looked on. Stormy took a sip of wine to camouflage how overwhelmed she felt. "I'm not usually this dense," she told Tyler. "But I'm missing whatever point it is you're trying to make."

He grinned. "Everybody missed it, love. You see, the bank teller testified that Hadley Wilson handed her his pack and told her to fill it. She did, stuffing it with as many ones as she had on hand and only then going on to larger bills. The next teller he made her pass it to did the same—they're taught this stuff. There's no way on God's green earth that a pack this size will hold one hundred and two thousand dollars unless you stuff it with fifty- and hundred-dollar bills. Even then, it's a tight squeeze.

"You testified that Wilson went into the bank with his hands empty and returned with his hands empty. So where did he put all that money?"

Stormy shook her head. "I don't know."

"What was he wearing that day? Think."

"Bermuda shorts…a polo shirt…sandals. And the hip pack, of course."

Tyler twirled his long-stemmed wineglass, then tilted it toward the pack. "There's eighty-five hundred dollars in there. I couldn't get any more in."

"The conclusion I come to," Tyler said, watching Stormy's face, "is that Hadley Wilson didn't steal one hundred two thousand dollars."

Stormy's jaw dropped. "But that's what he was convicted of… what I—"

"Calm down and hear me out. What it boils down to is that the prosecutor accepted the result of the bank's audit on the amount of money missing. He made the obvious assumption that Hadley Wilson stole *all* the missing funds. And an audit, of course, is going to reveal any missing monies—whatever the reason—even teller shortages. I think the bank, or somebody at the bank, did a number on you and Wilson."

"But Hadley did rob the bank! He admitted it."

"Sure he did. And a lovely four-day weekend at Disney World only costs about a thousand bucks. Unless you did some tall shopping, drank yourselves silly and stayed in five-hundred-dollar-a-night suites."

"We did no such thing."

"I didn't think so. My guess is that Wilson's little escapade at the bank only netted him petty cash—maybe five, six thousand, tops."

Stormy sat back in her chair. Clarity was slow in coming, but when it did, her eyes glowed like amber. "Tyler...are you saying the bank *lied* about how much money Hadley stole?"

"How much Wilson stole? Yes. How much is missing? No. I think the audit is fairly accurate, though it's been my experience that even bank examiners can and do juggle figures. We'll probably never know down to the last dime the exact amount that's gone missing.

"As for the charges against you and Wilson, the amount doesn't really matter. Any amount stolen above seventy-five dollars is a felony. That happened. The greater amount is what my clients are concerned about. After all, they had to cover the loss."

Shock overtook Stormy. "You mean the reason you can't find the money is that most of it was never stolen in the first place? That means I was railroaded!" she cried, dazed.

"Oh, the money was stolen all right. It was really a stroke of luck for somebody that the feds declined to prosecute, leaving it up to the state."

Stormy stiffened. "You mean me? Because we filed a motion for a separate trial and invoked the Speedy Trial Act?"

"Nope. You could've done that regardless of who prosecuted you. But when the feds get on a case, they worry it to bare bone. They investigate down to how many hairs are on your head. There are audits, background checks—''

"All that was done by the state district attorney."

"Not the D.A. himself. By one of his staff, maybe. And just suppose that staffer was young, green and right out of law school. He'd walk right into the bank, ask for their robbery audit to determine how much was missing and call it a day."

Stormy eyed Tyler with new respect. "You've checked that out, haven't you?"

Tyler smiled. "I've been as busy as a bee in heat. Which reminds me, Liane seems—" he cleared his throat "—a bit confused about the birds and bees—scientifically speaking, that is."

Stormy's face went pink. "She didn't ask you about sperm, did she?"

"I'm glad to hear you're on top of it," he said, relieved. He opened his mouth to say more, but was interrupted by their food arriving.

He tapped on the window to claim Liane's attention and signaled her to come inside.

In a daze, Stormy took her daughter to wash her hands, and when they returned to the table, Stormy could barely swallow a bite. So much was at stake. By silent mutual consent, she and Tyler did not continue their discussion in front of Liane.

Once, during the meal, she gazed up at him, looking at him as if seeing him for the first time. He had, without seeming to, earned her respect. He had effectively countered every suspicion she'd had of him. Though she had fought him every step of the way, he had kept his word about helping her. And in the back of her mind, she knew

with all her heart that, had they met under any other circumstances, by now they'd be lovers.

She shook her head at the notion. What he was doing,
she reminded herself, had done, was part and parcel of
how he worked.

Tyler had a forkful of broiled fish near his mouth when
he spied her scrutiny. He lifted an eyebrow. "Do I have
cocktail sauce on my face?"

She shook her head. Her mouth looked soft, as if ready
to be kissed, and he wondered if that was a reflection of
her thoughts. He smiled at the notion.

"What was that for?" Stormy asked.

"Can't a man smile without your giving him the third
degree?"

"Maybe. Any man other than you, that is."

Tyler laughed outright. "I think this whole jigsaw puzzle of an affair is coming together nicely."

"Affair?" she said archly.

But Tyler wasn't to be provoked. He merely gave her his
best crooked smile, complete with dimples, and changed
the subject. "So, where are we taking Liane shopping?"

"Not we, me."

"Let me tag along," he proposed. "I'll behave."

Oddly loathe to dispense with his company when lunch
was over, Stormy directed him to the J.C. Penney store in
the Ponce de Leon Mall, where Liane stubbornly refused
all efforts to interest her in frilly Easter frocks. She wanted
something she "could *wear.*"

"The kid knows what she wants," Tyler observed. "Just
like her mother."

Stormy paid for the simple dress and some shorts and
tank tops Liane chose, but her mind was on Tyler's words.
It was true that she knew most of what she wanted. And
she knew she'd have to work hard to achieve her goals.

And, whatever the outcome of Tyler's investigation, she believed now vindication was possible. And she certainly wanted that.

Tyler himself was another matter. The emotions racking her concerning him were jumbled and chaotic. It was patently absurd to even *consider* the notion that she was in love with him. Wasn't it?

WHILE LIANE RACED into the house to call Janelle and regale her with descriptions of her new clothes, Tyler said goodbye to Stormy on the front porch.

"We have a conversation to finish," he said. "I'd like it to be without interruption. Are you open for a walk on the beach?"

Stormy protested only mildly. "I have to finish getting things ready for the flea market tomorrow."

"Say, nine o'clock tonight at the foot of your walk? I'll meet you there." He turned to go.

"Thank you for lunch...and everything," she called after him.

Later, as she washed and fluffed stuffed animals and packed them into boxes, she realized that she was deep in unfamiliar territory. Whenever she was with Tyler, she felt split in two, part of her on the sidelines waiting to see what would happen and the other part playing out a battle she no longer quite understood.

In her other life, before prison, she had accepted men in her life as a given. Among the inmates, talk of men had been constant and often vulgar. It was odd that now, on the outside, she understood what drove her sister inmates. The desire she had for Tyler was eating away at her. And she couldn't even tell him!

He had kissed her—once! What was a single kiss in the cosmic scheme of things?

Nothing, that's what.

She'd hear him out tonight. On Monday, she'd call the attorney who'd defended her at her trial and see where he could take the information Tyler had unearthed.

And that, she guessed, would be that.

Because if the money wasn't to be found, then Tyler had no reason to stay in St. Augustine.

Stormy felt suddenly that something in her chest had broken under a burden of disappointment and loneliness. She sat down on the concrete floor of the garage amid the cardboard boxes, buried her face in her hands and cried.

Chapter Eleven

After making certain Liane was sound asleep, Stormy went quietly downstairs. Nina and Tully were in the family room, and through the closed door she heard their muffled voices raised in argument. Hand raised to knock, she hesitated, debating whether to alert them that she was going to the beach.

She heard the word *money* clearly. Tully was browbeating Nina for spending above her household budget. Stormy lowered her hand. Stepping into Nina and Tully's fray would only add to her own melancholy.

She stopped in front of the hall mirror to study her face. Her earlier bout with tears was no longer evident. Satisfied, she slipped out the kitchen door onto the deck.

Tyler was a shadowy silhouette at the end of the walk. She felt all at once lighter, freer, stronger.

The soft spring night was ripe with the expectation of summer. The moon was full, the sky a panoply of stars. Nature couldn't have been more compliant had Stormy gone down on bended knee. It was an evening for lovers.

When she reached him, Tyler said nothing, only took her hand as if it were the most natural thing in the world. Her heart leapt and she doubted she could get through the evening without giving herself away.

Tyler tightened his grip. "Spectacular night, isn't it? We don't get them quite like this inland."

"We didn't get them in prison, either. I missed nights like this. And silverware," she footnoted, so nervously aware of his hand that she had to check a tendency to babble. "Plastic knives and forks and spoons were all we were allowed."

Astonishingly, for so grand a night, they had the beach to themselves. They walked a yard or so along the damp sand before Tyler spoke again. "Prison was hard for you, wasn't it?"

"It's hard on everybody. I can't even watch police shows on television now without shuddering."

"Then let's talk about something more pleasant," Tyler said. He stopped in his tracks, released her hand and slid his arms about her waist, pulling her against his chest. He held her there, certain she could feel his erratic heartbeat.

"This is talking?" Having his hands on her was oddly, wonderfully comforting. And stimulating. And overwhelming.

"It's a language of sorts," he said. Then, as he dipped his head to brush her lips with his, a low moan of pleasure emanated from the back of his throat. "Truce?" he implored, his lips moving to the shell of her ear.

Every nerve ending in Stormy was attuned to his caresses. His lips on her earlobe, his hands slowly moving along her back, the urgency his hips telegraphed against hers—it was a sensual bombardment, and she was undefended. She wore shorts, and even the feel of his slacks against her bare legs took her breath away. Her hands made their way up his chest and around his neck.

"I've been having dreams...." His voice was audible only because his mouth was at her ear.

"Dreams?" Stormy asked, her own words soft, blending with the sound of the waves washing ashore at their feet. His after-shave filled her senses.

"Of waking up mornings...your head on the pillow next to mine, your body fitted into the curve of my arm..."

"Oh."

He lifted his head and gazed at her, trying to discern her expression in the moon glow. "Just, 'Oh'?"

"Tyler," she said, aching to feel his lips on hers, his tongue in her mouth. "If you're going to kiss me, just do it."

He stiffened, then abruptly dropped his arms and stepped back. "A kiss? A kiss! You think that's all this is about?"

Stormy guessed at what he was driving at, but couldn't make herself believe it. It was like having all the luck in the world—wrapped in tissue paper. Tempting but oh, so fragile. She was afraid to succumb to happiness. Terrified, in fact. Besides, what she felt for him was probably just her hormones acting up. "Why are you getting angry?"

He glowered at her. "I'm not angry. Why should I be angry?" He was afraid of his emotions. Should he allow himself to act on his feelings for Stormy, he'd haul her onto a nearby dune and make love to her until the sun came up. He shoved his hands deep into his pockets, as if he didn't dare leave them to their own devices.

Stray wisps of hair had come loose from Stormy's braid. She brushed them back behind her ear. "You're trying to complicate things," she said nervously, uncertain exactly what was going on but feeling a need to rally her defenses. Then her vulnerability, her need of him, panicked her and swept her beyond a boundary she had not meant to cross. "Is this something you do with every woman you meet on a case? Or, since I've been in prison, did you figure that I've been so long without a man that I was ripe for the picking?''

The cap flew off Tyler's frustration at her unjust accusation. ''That's crap, and you know it! You have gall, lady. You really do.'' And he spun on his heels and stalked off down the beach toward his motel.

A half dozen barbs she could fling at his back came to Stormy, but for once, she held her tongue. She looked at his retreating back, and suddenly she imagined that he was walking out of her life forever.

''Tyler! Wait!'' And then she was running to catch up to him.

In his job Tyler had learned to be stubborn and tenacious. He called upon that learning now as he glanced at Stormy out the corner of his eye, taking in her lovely profile. ''What?''

''You did offer a truce.''

He circled around that warily. ''That was a hundred years ago. Flag's tattered to ribbons now.''

''You were going to finish telling me your theory about the robbery.''

''I'll call you when I've got it worked out.''

Stormy felt a dull ache in her heart. ''When will that be?''

''Who knows.''

She slowly turned away and headed for the path that led up to the house.

Tyler watched Stormy's retreat, which was lit by a ribbon of moonlight.

Damn. Falling in love was hell on a man. One would think the powers that be would keep that in mind. It was supposed to be wonderful. Arguments weren't supposed to start until after the honeymoon.

Deep inside, he felt a sensation he barely recognized, but as it became stronger, he knew it for what it was: a mixture of fear, want, need and hope, so deeply embedded, it was engraved on his soul.

The only other time he'd been aware of the sensation was when he'd watched the paramedics working on Priss at the side of the swimming pool. He had needed her to be alive, had stood there begging God to let the paramedic look up and say, "We got a pulse."

But it hadn't happened.

And he'd had to live with the guilt. If only he'd arrived home five minutes earlier. If only his wife had not gone into the house to get a towel. If only...

Stormy had reached the kitchen door. She went in; the deck lights went out.

If only... Tyler thought, then stopped.

He'd be damned if he'd allow Stormy to become another of his if onlys!

He looked up to the sky, taking in the panorama of the heavens and the moon hanging among the stars. Stormy was a woman. She should have known what he was talking about—probably before he did. They *always* knew.

A wave came rushing in and caught him unawares. It soaked him to his calves.

He looked down at his ruined loafers and began to slog up the beach, as mired in confusion as he was in damp sand.

Hell, he couldn't ask her to marry him—not yet. Never mind that this case was like an exploding hand grenade, scattering chaos everywhere he looked.

He needed a real break on this one—in more ways than one.

THERE WAS A HOLIDAY SPIRIT in the air. The flea market was packed with shoppers. Stormy missed having Liane at her side, but the child was thrilled to be spending the day with Janelle. In brief respites between customers, Stormy's thoughts traveled to Tyler.

Life wasn't fair—she knew that with a passion. The man was interested in her, so why did he keep pulling back? He couldn't possibly be as confused as she was. Men never were. They always knew what they wanted and simply took it.

Was he just trying to make her miserable?

"Hi."

Stormy jerked from her reverie. "Sandy! What are you doing here?"

"I'm combining business with pleasure. Meet my children," she said, her eyes alight with pleasure. "Ned and Terry Jean."

The youngsters were towheaded, shy and polite. They shook hands with Stormy.

"I only have them for today, this time," Sandy said. "We're heading from here to Noreen's to dye Easter eggs. But I wanted you to see what I've been buying up with your money." She opened a huge plastic bag and pulled out dozens of stuffed animals and dolls. "These washed up fabulously, don't you agree?"

"They're great!" Stormy said. "You have time to spare? Let's get price tags on them right now and put them on the table."

"You know how you said to keep an eye out for other things?" Sandy said hesitantly while they were pricing.

"You found something?"

"I hope so. I went to a yard sale. The woman was a recent widow, and she was selling her husband's things, including the stuff for his hobby—which was candle making.

For sixteen dollars I got a hundred pounds of wax, all sorts of molds, wicks, dyes, scents, cooking pots—everything we need, including instruction booklets, where to order supplies—''

"Candles..."

Sandy frowned. "Not good?"

Stormy grinned. "Are you kidding? It's super! I can see the display now... candles flickering... cinnamon in the air...."

"We have to make them first," Sandy reminded her.

"We will. You want to hold down the fort a minute? I'm going to the office to get our name on the list for a bigger stall." She pointed out a ceramics merchant who had built display shelves. The man's van was backed right up to his stall on the parking verge for easy access for loading and unloading. "We need something like that."

When she returned twenty minutes later, Stormy was waving a receipt. "I got us one. At the end of this aisle, too. It'll be available in two weeks. That'll give us time to make some candles."

"I've sold forty dollars' worth of toys in the few minutes you were gone," Sandy said, stunned. "I love doing this. Maybe I could help you tomorrow? This is exciting."

"I'm not planning to open tomorrow. I want to spend Easter with Liane. It's our first holiday together since I..." She looked at Ned and Terry Jean. "Well... you know."

"Let me open for you," Sandy pleaded. "I could do it. We don't want to lose momentum, do we? And it'll give me something to do besides feel lonesome and sorry for myself. Unless... you don't trust me."

Stormy looked aghast. "Of course, I trust you. I was just surprised. I can use the help anytime you want to work the stand."

They were interrupted by customers, but once the sales were made, Sandy continued. "You know, on the weekends I don't have the kids, or even some weekends I do, I could work. I think they would enjoy it. It's different."

"Okay," Stormy said, deciding on the spot. "You're on."

"The only thing is, when I work it by myself, I ought to get twenty-five percent of net profits, don't you think?"

"What I think is, you learn darned fast," Stormy said, instantly agreeing to Sandy's proposal.

"I'm an apprentice with a good teacher," the other woman replied, her eyes glowing.

Embarrassed by the praise, Stormy began to rearrange the table. "All this success could just be a stroke of luck, you know. There will be down days...."

Sandy paled. "You're not trying to talk me out of doing this? You regret taking me on?"

"Not a bit!" Stormy reassured her. "It's just that nothing is a sure thing."

"Well, if it falls apart, I'll still be that much further ahead, and I'll have learned something. I hate to leave, but I promised the kids. I don't have to have them back until nine, so I'll see you again at Noreen's?"

Stormy nodded. "I'm picking up Liane at about six."

Sandy beamed. "That will work great. We can unload all 'our' stock from your car to mine, so I can be here bright and early tomorrow."

"*PLEASE*, MOM. Pretty please with sugar on it. Let me spend the night. Janelle wants me to, and Mrs. Byers said it's okay with her if it's okay with you."

"Uh-uh, you little scamp," put in Noreen. "Leave me out of this. What I said was, you're always welcome."

"Including tonight, right?" Liane said.

Noreen shrugged helplessly. "Kids are born despots," she said to Stormy. "They get absolute power over us the minute they're born by looking so cute and innocent and helpless. By the time we catch on to their tyranny, it's too late."

"Tomorrow is Easter," Stormy said. "It's our first holiday together in a long while."

"You can come and get me early in the morning. Just don't let Davie and Tommy get into my Easter basket. And look, here are all the eggs I dyed for them. Please, Mom. While you were in jail, I *never* got to do any fun stuff."

"See what I mean?" Noreen said sotto voce.

Stormy sighed heavily. "Doesn't it matter that I'll miss you?"

"While you're sleeping you won't," Liane said.

"That's the kind of childish logic that has stumped parents since Adam and Eve," said Noreen. "I wonder how *they* handled it."

Stormy turned to her new friend. "You're not helping."

"I confess, I'm not. I'd be delighted to have Liane sleep over. I'll even bring her home in the morning with the hope that you'll invite Janelle and me to sunbathe out on that beach in front of your house. Elise is at Disney World this weekend on a school-sponsored outing. Truth to tell, I could do with a fun day."

"Oh, Noreen, you're welcome *any time.* You don't have to trade visit for visit."

"With Liane spending the night, she and Janelle will entertain each other, and I'll get to curl up with a book I've been dying to read. It's full of sin and sex."

"Liane doesn't have her pajamas or toothbrush or—"

"She can wear a pair of mine," said Janelle. "And we have lots of new toothbrushes."

Stormy plopped down at the kitchen table and dropped her chin into her hands. "Okay, I give in."

"Gracefully done," said Noreen over the whoops of Liane and Janelle. "Now, how about a cup of coffee for the road?"

EIGHT-THIRTY on a Saturday night and here she was bathed and bedded down simply because she was at a loss for what to do with herself. Stormy told herself she was exhausted and closed her eyes. It didn't work. Her adrenaline was racing as if charged by a Niagara Falls power station. It must be Noreen's coffee that was keeping her awake.

Liar! a voice at the back of her mind challenged. *It was the sight of Tyler's car parked at the motel. You wanted to stop. So why didn't you?*

Lack of courage, Stormy answered.

Pooh! Since when have you lacked courage?

Since nice girls can't approach men in motel rooms.

Prison really did a number on you, didn't it? the voice mocked. *You used to snub convention. Remember the day Liane was born? You vowed to take* shouldn't *out of your vocabulary. You went into business for yourself and made a success of it. Now you're doing it again.*

You're forgetting my track record with men. I haven't picked a winner yet.

So? It takes practice. And don't forget, you're dealing with a man who lost a marriage and a daughter. That's big-time rejection. Men don't get over things like that so easily. Could be he's a bit out of practice himself and just waiting for you to take the first step.

Stormy threw off the coverlet and got up.

If she were going to mock herself, she might as well have a good reason.

But what does one wear to a seduction?

Less is better, came the voice, getting in the last word before Stormy shut it out.

A half hour later, holding her breath as if beneath a ton of water, Stormy rapped softly on Tyler's door.

The man who answered was bald, short and shirtless. He gaped at her.

"Lawdy Miss Clawdy!" he said in a surprisingly gentle voice. "I've died and gone to heaven."

"I—I'm sorry," Stormy stammered. "I've got the wrong—"

"Shoot. I thought my luck was changing. You want the guy who runs the place, I'll warrant. Drives that BMW?" He pointed to Tyler's car, parked in front of the door.

Stormy nodded. Running in place sounded like Tyler; a man with excess energy to burn.

"Two doors down," the man said, pointing.

She mumbled an apology and moved off, thankful that the man had closed his door and would not witness her reception by Tyler—whatever it might be.

When he answered his door, Tyler's expression was one of genuine shock, but he seemed to recover quickly.

"This ought to be interesting," he said, stepping back to allow her in.

She looked down at the threshold, sensing that once she moved across it, there was no turning back. "I hope so," she answered lightly as she swept into the room.

Without relaxing the stiff set of her head, she took in his small living space. The bed was most prominent.

The air in the room was redolent with the somehow manly smells of damp towels, soap, after-shave and the sharp tang of graphite from recently sharpened pencils. Aware of holding her breath, Stormy exhaled.

"I'm forgetting my manners," Tyler said, offering her a chair at the minuscule table. He pulled it out and moved some folders and pencils aside. "What can I offer you?" he continued as she sank into the chair. "Diet Coke or a beer?" he asked, reaching into a small refrigerator against the wall.

Yourself, she thought, feeling as if her heart was about to explode in her chest. "Neither, thank you."

"I see." He sat down opposite her, wondering what she was up to. Going through his mind were all the things he had promised himself he was going to explain to her, all the things he had been planning to say, all the words he'd been rehearsing during the long, sleepless nights he'd suffered since setting eyes on her.

"What are all those folders?" she asked, finding it easier to speak of the mundane than of the purpose that had brought her to him.

"Your case, the trial transcript, broken down into bits. The same with Wilson's. And a couple of other cases that need attention."

"You take your work seriously."

"Have to if I want to eat..." he said. His voice trailed off. Her eyes were challenging him beneath her dark brows, yet her neck was so taut, he could see the tendons straining. He sensed an unmistakable sensuous heat, and his mouth was suddenly dry. He bent to pick up a fallen pencil; it got away from him. He looked at his hands; they were shaking.

Ignoring the tautness of her nerves, Stormy expelled a tumultuous breath and scattered a few inane comments. "I had another terrific day at the flea market. Sandy came and helped me out. We're going to add candles to the inventory and..." And suddenly she was out of words.

"Sounds like you've really got the ball rolling." He sat there, across from her, an eyebrow raised in question.

It seemed to Stormy that silence prevailed for an eon. She suddenly felt ridiculous. As if from a distance, she saw herself and Tyler: a pair of stiff-necked mongooses darting hither and thither, arguing over which would slay the cobra that separated them. The picture made her smile.

"What's funny?" he asked, still wondering what her game was.

"This 'n' that," she told him, nervous laughter escaping her throat.

"An impressive reason," he said, miffed. "I could stand on my head and still not get it."

"I know. I'm sorry. The truth is...I came here to make an unladylike, immodest spectacle of myself."

If his mouth had gone dry before, it was now as arid as the Sahara. He reached for a beer, then changed his mind in favor of a Coke. If he were going to navigate an unmapped minefield barefooted, he needed his wits about him. "And?" he said, popping the tab and taking a long, cooling sip.

"I lost my nerve. And then I thought, how funny we look, sitting here—"

Tyler's shoulders tensed. "Find it."

"Find it?" Her voice faltered.

"Your nerve," he insisted. "Look under the table. Under the bed, maybe. I know—in your purse...look in your purse. Women keep *everything* in their purses." He grabbed her small bag from the edge of the table and dumped its contents.

Among other things, a toothbrush tumbled out, more graphic than words.

Tyler circled its significance warily, slowly raising his eyes to Stormy's.

Her face was flushed, the line of her jaw rigid. "I told you it was a stupid idea."

Don't shoot yourself in the foot, Tyler cautioned himself. "What if I told you that I don't think it stupid at all?"

"I wouldn't believe you. You've backed away every time we—" She stopped, appalled.

"I was only being circumspect."

Stormy lifted her eyes to the ceiling. "Very inventive."

"Suppose I told you I was scared?"

Stormy lowered her gaze. "Of what?"

"Well, hell..." He didn't like being pressed to hang out a list of vulnerabilities. It only took one well-aimed poisoned dart to shoot a man down. "Any number of things..." *You. Me. What's happening,* he thought, recalling that the first real crisis in his long-ago marriage had shattered it instead of becoming a binding force.

"Name one."

"Will rejection do? I'd like to get through this with my ego intact, thank you."

"*Your* ego?" Stormy flared. "What about mine?"

"Hold on a second," he said, suddenly twisting around to yank open a dresser drawer behind him. When he turned back, in his hand was a handkerchief. He unfolded it and waved it in front of her face. "I'm willing to negotiate a peace settlement."

"So am I."

"Terrific. I'll just put this toothbrush in the bathroom where it belongs."

This he did so nimbly, Stormy's protest was little more than a strangled utterance from the back of her throat.

Tyler switched off lights, leaving only a small lamp by the bed.

"You call this negotiating?" she said, but she was rooted to the chair in a cocoon of expectancy.

Tyler sat down on the foot of the bed, the space they were in so small, his knees touched hers. He put a hand on her thigh, its imprint burning into her flesh beneath her cotton skirt. She kept her eyes on his hand, watching for any perceptible movement. If it moved, she knew something cataclysmic was going to follow.

"Do we have a cease-fire or not?" Tyler said softly.

Her voice dropped to a whisper. "Are we positive this is something we want to do?" She traced his hand with her fingertips, giving him her own answer. How odd, she thought. On the outside her body felt chilled; internally, she was a furnace.

Now both his hands were on her, his long, strong fingers gently kneading her. "We can stop anywhere along the way...." He reached for the sash of her wraparound skirt and untied it. "Well...maybe not," he murmured throatily at his first glimpse of the beige silk teddy she wore.

From somewhere deep in her soul, Stormy recognized that, regardless of what might come later, this moment was theirs. It was good and right and healing. She lifted her arms toward him....

"I SUPPOSE you thought me timid."

"Never. After all, I knew you had seduction on your mind the instant I opened the door. Uh...could you just...?"

"Oh? You're psychic now?"

"No—wait...not there, not yet."

"But it's waving at me, begging for attention."

"I'm the one who's beg—"

"Would you rather I do this?"

"Ahh. Hold up. I'm—"

"Or do you prefer...here, just put your hands on my hips and let me move..."

"You're not supposed—"

"Don't be so Victorian, Tyler. You did it to me. Fair is fair. It feels good, doesn't it?"

"It feels terrific. Spectacular. Extraordinary... For crying out loud—*wait!*"

"Can't."

"Oh..."

Chapter Twelve

While the last dregs of night were slipping away, Stormy moved quietly so as not to awaken the sleeping household.

She was overflowing with the gamut of emotions that went with making love. Not that she and Tyler had actually spoken the words...

She had her hand on the banister when Nina emerged from the kitchen into the foyer. "I thought I heard you sneaking in," she said, voice and expression exhibiting how strongly she disapproved of Stormy's behavior.

Stormy answered her sister with a smile. No way was she going to allow Nina to undo the happiness she felt at this moment. "You're up early. Did you see the eggs Liane dyed for the boys?"

"Don't talk to me about Easter eggs," Nina snapped. She waved the note Stormy had posted on the refrigerator. "I'll bet I can guess the name of the *friend* you spent the night with."

"I wasn't trying to keep it a secret from you, Nina. Had you been home last night when I left, I would have told you."

"What about your parole officer?" Nina smirked. "Suppose someone told her that you spent the night in a man's motel room?"

Anger flared so quickly in Stormy, it made her tremble. She grabbed Nina's arm, propelled her into the kitchen and shoved her into a chair. Then, knowing she needed to keep some distance, she stepped back and leaned against the sink. Strewed across the counter were dyed eggs, chocolate bunnies, jelly beans and colored grasses. Seen through her irritation, the array of bright colors blurred. "All right, Nina. That was a threat. What do you propose to do?"

"Nothing."

The response was so skimpy, Stormy didn't believe it. Nor did she want to have this conversation with Nina. Especially not now, while she was still under the blissful spell of Tyler. But there Nina sat, waiting, the slight smile on her face mere varnish to hide...what? Stormy wondered. Resigned, she composed her thoughts and put them into words.

"Nina, I've been bullied by the best—women serving life sentences, prison guards filled with so much scorn, they've forgotten they themselves are part of the human race, district attorneys with reelection on their minds—so nothing you say or do can hurt me anymore. I won't let it. You've seen me vulnerable because you're family. I trusted you. But no more."

Nina sneered. "You think tough is talking tough."

"I'm just telling you like it is. And just so you'll know, Noreen Byers and Janelle are coming over this morning—"

Nina arched an eyebrow. "Another jailbird."

"She's my friend. And this afternoon, my *friend* Tyler is coming over. We're looking at some new leads in my case. We'll use Dad's upstairs study, so we'll be out of your way."

"Don't trouble yourself. Tully and I are taking the kids to Washington Oaks State Park, but you knew that."

"No, you didn't mention it." On purpose, Stormy realized, because Nina did not want to include her or Liane in the outing.

"You'd just better make sure your *friends* don't steal anything while we're gone."

Stormy shifted her gaze out the window to the sea. The sun was creeping above the horizon, promising a day of silver sunshine. Then she noticed her own reflection in the panes. There was something—a tilt of the head, the shape of her jaw—that brought her mother to mind.

"Nina, do you remember when we were younger, how we'd sit at the kitchen table to do our homework while Mom cooked dinner? If we had a problem that day, she'd tell us that it was okay to be angry, that it was okay even if we didn't like a schoolmate or a teacher, but that it was never okay to be rude. 'Elliotts,' she said, 'don't compromise their dignity and character.'"

Nina made a derisive moue. "It's obvious you didn't listen, isn't it?"

"I've made mistakes, large and small, but I've learned from them."

"What've you learned? How to steal and sleep around without getting caught?"

Stormy looked at her sister with a sudden and curious sense of detachment. Nina was utterly selfish. She demanded more than a person was able to give. That another might have to make sacrifices to meet her demands caused her no qualms or guilt whatsoever. Stormy gave her sister a sad little smile. "Happy Easter, Nina."

Upstairs a few moments later, Stormy had difficulty dismissing the unhappy conversation with her sister. Foremost in her mind was Nina's blatant threat to undermine her security and freedom. But even Nina wouldn't go that far, Stormy assured herself. After all, what was in it for her? The trust-fund proceeds had already been milked. Revocation of her parole would only mean more scandalous publicity—the last thing Nina wanted.

Stormy began to disrobe, instantly aware that the taste of Tyler was yet on her lips, the texture of his body lingered on her skin. How decadent. How delicious. To hell with Nina, she told herself. Now was a time for reveling in a delighted afterglow.

She had been almost frightened by the passion Tyler had unleashed in her. Neither of them had completely undressed that first time. A mindless urgency had caught at them; they couldn't wait. He took her quickly, pulling her silk teddy aside with his fingers and thrusting into her, engorged, insistent, feverish with desire, murmuring her name over and over.

Even now she could recall the magnificent feel of him as he entered her, how stunned she was at his bulk and readiness, at her own flesh, moist and accepting.

After that first quick coupling, they had not rested, but continued, moving more slowly, exploring each other inch by inch, riding each other into submission after submission, yet each being careful not only to take, but also to give.

Hours later, they had finally slept, naked bodies fitted against each other, arms and legs intertwined. Once, she had awakened to feel him pressed against her back, the hairs on his arm around her rib cage, tickling the undersides of her breasts. A drowsy sense of calm and happiness had engulfed her. Those hours in his arms, feeling so safe and secure, had been the best sleep she'd had in years.

Wonder of wonders, they had parted without a single scathing remark. There had been no barriers rapidly flung to protect exposed vulnerabilities.

Perhaps, Stormy thought now, they had both been too dazed at the heights of emotion and response they had scaled together.

Even in parting, his mentioning her case, her invitation to her home had been spoken in whispers, as if an aura of benediction surrounded them.

"I DON'T KNOW HOW THOSE little twits manage to keep going," said Noreen, shading her eyes to spy out the girls on the beach among a crowd of sunbathers. "They talked and giggled all night long."

Stormy put the lid back on the grill. She was slow cooking a beef roast and potatoes. "They'll putter out soon, I expect." She turned toward the beach to see Tyler splashing into the surf to retrieve a wind-caught shuttlecock. He and the girls were playing badminton, sans net.

"Oh, I wouldn't take bets on it," Noreen said, eyeing Stormy coyly. "If I had a hunk like Tyler paying attention to me, I'd prop my eyes open with broomsticks before I'd admit a craving for sleep."

Stormy grinned at her friend. "Stop fishing."

"Who's fishing? I saw the looks you two exchanged."

Stormy smiled, but refused to satisfy Noreen's curiosity. She still had a sense of reverence about her experience with Tyler. She was afraid that speaking of it might dilute it. Instead she asked, "Does Janelle miss her father?"

A flicker of resignation crossed Noreen's features. "She does, but I didn't realize how much until I saw how outrageously she flirted with Tyler."

"Liane is enjoying his attentions, too. I've always tried to tell myself she wouldn't miss what she hasn't had."

"I think it's biological. But let's not be sad—it's too gorgeous a day." Noreen picked up her beach tote and towel. "You sure you don't need any help with that?" she asked, indicating the grill.

"Positive."

"In that case, I'll go relieve Tyler of the girls. Damn, but I wish I had a pair of legs like his."

"You have nice legs," Stormy told her friend.

"Not wrapped around me, I don't."

"Noreen!"

"I told you—it's biological. Keep me in mind when he introduces you to his friends."

"I haven't the slightest idea what kinds of friends he keeps," Stormy said, knowing it was useless to deny her attraction to Tyler, yet moved to step delicately around whatever the future might hold. She picked up a cooler of soft drinks and a folded lawn chair. "Come on, I'll walk you down to the beach."

Tyler saw them coming. Over squealing protests, he left off cavorting with the girls to wait at the foot of the walk. Under his scrutiny, Stormy was, for a moment, self-conscious. She wore sandals, cutoffs, and a blouse tied at her midriff. Her hair was pulled back and secured with a rubber band. Noreen's swimsuit was modest, but there was an awful lot of Noreen exposed to the sun—and Tyler's gaze. Stormy felt a slight twinge of jealousy, though it faded when Tyler relieved her of the chair and cooler, then bent to briefly nuzzle her neck.

"It's bad manners to display one's wealth to those less fortunate," Noreen teased.

"Can't help myself," he said.

Liane and Janelle got underfoot. "You were kissing my mother," Liane accused.

Tyler snorted. "I was just whispering something in her ear."

"About our secret?"

Stormy intervened. "What secret?"

"Wouldn't be a secret if we told, now, would it?"

"No, but I'll tell you this—I'm *extremely* interested in whatever it is."

"We'll discuss it when the time is right," he said, giving Liane a warning look. He took Stormy's hand and tugged her back toward the house. "C'mon, I'm thirsty." Both of them ignored the cooler.

Stormy stopped to caution Liane to behave and not go into the surf without her water wings. Once out of earshot of the children, she warned Tyler to keep his hands to himself.

"Are you serious?" he asked.

"At least until we're behind closed doors!"

"Lead me to the nearest one."

"We're supposed to go over my case, remember?"

"Afterward?" he said, all hope.

"Afterward, we're eating."

He shot her a sidelong look. "Are we?"

"Vulgarity is not appropriate on Easter Sunday."

"Did you go to church today?"

"No, and neither did you."

"Yes, I did—the minute you were out of my bed. I went to sunrise services at the Castillo de San Marco."

Stormy was flabbergasted. It showed.

"I thought that'd make a good impression on you," Tyler said. "I also go on Christmas, Thanksgiving and my mother's birthday—just in case she still has eyes in the back of her head. And maybe one or two other days that are fixed in my memory.''

The tone of his voice told Stormy that the one or two of those other days fixed in his memory were probably the birth and death of his daughter, Priss. She slipped her hand into his.

''I've never met a man who goes to church without being prodded.''

''Gives me another dimension, doesn't it?''

''*Or* one who can match you in arrogance.'' She gave him a slight push. ''Go get your briefcase. I want to know what information you've been squirreling away.''

The kitchen table was set for dinner, so they sat in the alcove. ''Here's the most interesting tidbit I've turned up,'' he said, passing her a manila folder labeled H. B. Foley.

Stormy's chest constricted. ''Foley is the bank vice president who testified against me. Why are you investigating him?''

Tyler pursed his lips. ''I always take a look at everyone involved. After it became obvious that we seem to have a discrepancy in the money, I took a harder look at our Mr. Foley.'' He pointed out a photocopy in the file.

It made little sense to Stormy.

''That's a credit check. What it says is that before the robbery, Foley was ninety to a hundred and twenty days past due in several accounts. Soon after the robbery, he brought them up to date.''

''You're suggesting that Foley is the one who lied about how much money Hadley actually stole?''

''Let's just say I found Foley interesting enough to track.''

''If it's true, can you prove it?''

Tyler shook his head.

Stormy sighed despairingly. "How is all this going to help me?"

Tyler took a swig of beer. He hated to admit that his ideas had not panned out to his satisfaction. "I don't know yet."

"Lots of people get behind in their bills." She was thinking of Nina and Tully. "That's not exactly a crime."

"True, but it doesn't make good business sense for a banker. On the surface, Foley doesn't appear to live beyond his means, which begs the question of why he gets behind."

"Some people don't know how to handle money."

Tyler's green eyes flashed. "Pretty hard to be banker if you don't, wouldn't you say?"

Stormy rifled the file. "What else is in here?"

Tyler pointed out a copy of the vice president's résumé. Several previous employers had been highlighted with a reference marker. "My client insures any number of banks, savings and loans, credit unions and finance companies—small companies that don't qualify for federal deposit insurance or can't afford the premiums. Outside of a major bank Foley interned at after college, he seems to like working for the smaller companies. Those I've highlighted in his résumé are all insured by my client. I asked them to review their files on those companies during Foley's employment. Guess what we discovered?"

Stormy looked at Tyler. "Other banks were robbed!"

"Sure were. And until you and Wilson came along, the perps weren't caught."

"You mean there might be a conspiracy between Hadley and Foley?"

"That would surprise me. What I think is that our Mr. Foley waits patiently until a robbery does occur and somehow manages to profit by it."

Stormy frowned. "I'd like to believe that, but it's so farfetched."

"On the off chance I'll start a war of the worlds between us—that's what everybody has said about your side of the story."

Stormy closed her eyes. "Touché," she said softly.

Tyler smirked. "I like a woman who can eat crow."

Her eyes settled on him. "Don't press your luck." Then, elbows on the table, she rested her chin in her hands and sighed in resignation. So far all Tyler had was speculation, nothing she could take to her attorney that might get her conviction overturned. "I just don't see how Foley could work it. And I was charged as an accessory to stealing a hundred and two thousand dollars. I couldn't protest the amount, because I had no idea what Hadley was doing. But why didn't Hadley protest?"

"I just found out he did—but only in a deposition to his attorney that said in effect, 'Sure, I robbed the bank, but not of that much money.' Who believes an admitted thief? The bank examiners said how much was missing. That's what the police went with. In your trial, the amount of money stolen wasn't even an issue. And when you were taken to court to testify against Wilson, his attorney didn't raise the issue. Though convicted, you were still protesting your innocence. Once Wilson was convicted, Foley was home free."

"But I sat there and listened to Foley's testimony. He followed bank policy in reporting the robbery, calling in the examiners—"

"Well, yes and no. When he rushed to lock the door after Wilson made his exit, he saw you...."

"I was sitting in the parking lot with the motor running to keep the air-conditioner on because it was hot and Liane was sleeping in the back seat." Stormy shook her head in disgust for her own gullibility.

"A fact you failed to mention at your trial."

"I was scared for Liane. I didn't want to subject her to interrogation." Stormy shuddered.

"Spilled milk now," Tyler said gently. "But, had you, your attorney might have been able to convince the jury that your love and concern for Liane precluded your intentionally putting her in any kind of reckless situation. Many bank robberies, after all, do contain an element of violence."

"I couldn't take the chance." Her eyes appealed to him to understand. "Had I been found guilty anyway, Liane might have become a ward of the state. I could request that Nina and Tully take care of her, but then they, too, would've been subject to an investigation. Nina wouldn't stand still for that."

The ice in her soft drink had melted. She replenished it, offered Tyler another beer. He declined.

"Foley has gotten off scot-free," she mused angrily. "How did he do it?"

Tyler cautioned her. "Don't jump to conclusions. We only have suppositions."

"But you found something that incriminates him. I know you did."

"It's not much. When he called the police, he failed to give them your license number. Had he done so, you and Wilson would've been apprehended within a few blocks of the bank. He delayed giving them that information, using a perfectly respectable excuse. He asked that the police interview him last, as he had to secure the bank, alert the auditors and make a list of customers on the premises at the time of the robbery. He told police that he clearly saw your license plate, but in the confusion, it just wouldn't come to him. However, a few hours later, he recalled it precisely."

"Which gave him time to do what?"

"Well, it was his job to secure the teller stations, which meant removing the tellers at once. Wilson had each teller pass his pack on to the next to fill, so Foley had three teller drawers to play with."

"You mean he just scooped up the money? Where could he hide it? You proved how much space that much money requires. And what about security cameras? They ran the tapes at Hadley's trial—"

"As soon as Foley removed the tellers from their stations, he had the cameras turned off and called for the tapes to be removed for the police. He kept the drive-in windows open and had a bank employee stand outside and refer all arriving customers there. So now we have the customers inside the bank isolated in the reception area, the tellers involved with the robbery off in a tiny room they used for a cafeteria, and the drive-in tellers busy and out of view of the inside teller stations.

"One of the tellers commented that Foley was very solicitous of them, checking to make certain they were unharmed and so forth. That little lunchroom is situated right next to the night depository chute, and Foley had the only key. And, of course, he stayed at the bank long after closing hours to lock up after the auditors had finished."

"And the audit reflected a loss of over a hundred thousand dollars. Isn't that a lot of money for tellers to have in their stations at a small bank?"

"Not on a Friday. People came in to cash their paychecks."

Stormy smoothed out Foley's résumé. "So by the time the police ran my license number, Hadley and I and Liane were at Disney World. And by the time we were arrested three days later, everyone thought that we had hidden the money.''

''That's exactly what my clients thought.''

''Thought? They don't think that now?'' Her eyes were huge, full of hope.

''Let's just say they're mulling things over.''

''Isn't there anything *we* can do?'' she asked forlornly.

Get married, have a few babies, put the past behind us, he thought. ''I'm afraid we're checkmated. Foley hasn't so much as had a traffic ticket—''

''Neither have I!'' Stormy fumed. ''The man is a low-down opportunist! He hid his crime beneath Hadley's, and I'm suffering for it.'' She gazed out at the beach filling with surfers and sunbathers. She searched for Liane and Janelle, finally spying them playing safely in a tidal pool. ''What about a sting?'' she said abruptly. ''Suppose your client *staged* a robbery...''

''That would've been an option, but Foley resigned six months ago and moved on to a facility they don't insure.''

''Don't insurance companies cooperate with one another?''

''They're competitive as hell. If one takes a huge loss, the others gloat—or move in to take them over. The only time insurance companies are in accord is when they want to raise premiums.''

''You know,'' Stormy said, contemplative, ''I met Hadley at a charity event to raise money for a local animal shelter. He was low-key, charming and sincere. He would come over to the sandwich shop and chat with me. Once, I got a quick rush of customers off the beach during a sudden downpour. He came behind the counter and took orders for me. I never actually dated him until that weekend.'' She sighed heavily. ''It was the first weekend I'd taken off in more than a year. I had mentioned that

Liane had not yet been to Disney World. He insisted we take her. He was terrific with her."

She smiled wryly. "I was nervous—I thought it was about leaving the sandwich shop in the hands of a part-time employee. I had this gut feeling I couldn't put a name to." She sighed in despair. "I can sure name it now—stupidity."

"You weren't stupid. You got conned. Wilson was a master. He's under investigation now for a half dozen other unsolved robberies in Alabama, Georgia and South Carolina."

"I'd better check the roast." She got to the screen door and looked back. "Are you absolutely finished with your investigation of me?"

"Unless I get instructions otherwise."

"So you'll be going home? Back to that cabin..."

"Eventually." He was remembering the moist, fiery axis between her legs. He had no intention of going home alone.

Stormy took little heart from his answer. It was too ambiguous. *He's having second thoughts,* she told herself. Or perhaps he hadn't ever had a first thought. She had done the trite thing and thrown herself at him, shedding her determination and celibacy like old clothes ready for the rag bin. "Would you mind leaving Foley's file here with me for a few days?"

"No, but—"

"Want to earn your dinner?" she put in quickly to forestall his mentioning his departure date.

"Sure. Name it." He was worried. The way she had accepted the news that he'd run into a dead end was unlike her. He'd expected her to scream, pound the table, throw something—anything but this uncharacteristic calm she was displaying.

She pointed to the counter where a dozen or so dyed eggs were in a bowl. The girls had played with them until they were cracked and no longer acceptable to decorate baskets. "Would you peel those eggs?"

"I'll do my best."

Irrational as it was, the words finally set her off. "Your best? Damn you, Tyler, you played with me. I was vulnerable, and you played with me. Holding out the hope of vindication, saying all the right things, *doing* all the right things, down to being caring and kind to Liane! I came to trust you but, you're almost as bad as Hadley! You just want what you want when you want it, and you'll do whatever it takes to get it!"

Tyler was on his feet, responding to a Stormy he knew and understood—to a degree. "I can't change the facts. Even if there was a way to corner Foley, even if he walked into a police station and confessed, that doesn't mean you'd be free and clear. Wilson did stage a robbery. You were at the site. You did drive the getaway car."

"I didn't *know* I was doing it, dammit!" she exclaimed in frustration. "I stayed with you last night, Tyler. You know what could've happened to me if my parole officer had decided to check my whereabouts?"

"You invited yourself. And don't tell me now that you were there to sell Girl Scout cookies."

He moved closer but didn't penetrate the frosty shell in which she'd enveloped herself. "I know you're disappointed about the outcome of the investigation, but that's all it was—an investigation. I don't have the authority or the means to put Foley behind bars, or even on the stand. I don't have any method, short of beating the guy to a pulp, to get him to admit he stole that money. I'm an asset-recovery agent. I locate money or stocks or real estate—whatever. Then it's up to the parties involved to press charges, hire attorneys, demand return." He softened his voice. "You've got to have patience, Stormy. Foley will make a mistake and get caught. Believe me, his kind always do. That's the time to press him. When he's already up to his neck in bug squat—"

"Time is just what I don't have! I have to get my life in order."

"You've been managing admirably to do just that," he said gently. "You've got a business off the ground, taken a partner, you're ready to expand...."

Stormy sniffed. "Those are the practical things. Do you realize every time I leave the county, I have to get permission?"

Tyler had the swift intuition that they were getting close to the heart of the matter of why Stormy was suddenly hell-bent for leather. If there ever was a woman who chafed at restraint, it was Stormy Elliott.

"Maybe we can sic your mean old parole officer on Foley."

Stormy gave Tyler a fleeting smile. "No. Mrs. Lowery is nice really—considering."

"Are we still on battle stations?" he asked tenderly.

Stormy's resistance collapsed. It was disheartening to have to admit her life and love could only be lived by the grace and favor of the state of Florida, but, on reflection, taking her anger out on Tyler was as unfair to him as Nina was to her. Besides, what they had shared last night didn't deserve a mantle of shame and guilt and anger.

"I guess not," Stormy said as coolly as possible, clinging to that coolness because she still had no idea if he meant to exit her life at any moment now.

"Good, because I'd hate to be run off before we eat. I haven't had a home-cooked meal in forever." He moved in and put his hands on her waist, holding her that way a moment before he slid his hands around her hips and pinioned her to him.

She tilted her head upward. "Oh, God, Tyler, I had such high hopes...."

"I know you did, sweetheart. Look, I'll suggest to my clients that we do some more checking on Foley."

"Thank you, thank you, thank you," she said, planting damp kisses all over his face and neck. She stopped suddenly. "Who made your last home-cooked meal?"

"My mother."

"Oh. Is she nice? Your mother?"

He brushed Stormy's lips with his. "She has the temperament of a rattlesnake."

"You inherited it, then."

"A minor genetic flaw," he said, taking her mouth as if he'd just invented the kiss and had to keep practicing until he got it right.

Chapter Thirteen

"I have ideas going six ways to a dozen, Stormy. My brain just doesn't want to stop!" Sandy reverently tapped the pocket that held her share of Easter Sunday's earnings. "I have to work three days to earn this much at the plant. Not only that, they know I'm on probation, they know I *have* to work, so I'm the one who's always asked to come in early or stay late. You should've seen the look on my supervisor's face when I told him I was taking the afternoon off."

"The power of money," Stormy proclaimed, passing Sandy another of the copper candle molds to dry.

"Well, it is power of sorts. I mean, if a person has money in the bank or owns a piece of property, they're treated with respect. I'm putting aside some of what I earn flea marketing toward buying a little house." Sandy paused. "But you know what I'm going to buy first, even before new underwear or shoes?"

"I can't guess."

Sandy held out her hands. "See these nubby fingers? Tomorrow I'm going to Perfect Ten to have some silk nails put on. I'm going to stop thinking poor and start thinking elegant. Just because we've been in jail doesn't mean we have to be second-class citizens forever."

"Silk nails are going to change all that?"

"Can't hurt. I'm registering to vote, too. Family court judges in this county are elected. The next time I take Bennie into court, I won't be a scared little mouse. I'm stretching my muscles and expanding my horizons."

Stormy rinsed soap off another mold and passed it to Sandy. "Your strategy sounds good to me."

"More than that, Ned and Terry Jean don't like Bennie's new wife. They're not allowed to sit on the furniture in the living room. They eat dinner alone in the kitchen. Eventually, they'll be allowed to stand up in court and speak for themselves."

Eyeing Stormy, Sandy dried another mold. "I don't mean to pry, but your enthusiasm doesn't seem up to par. Something's on your mind, isn't it?"

Stormy paused, her hands in the sudsy water. "I've got a bad feeling. It's gnawing at me. Scaring me, if you want to know the truth."

"We're not supposed to project. We're supposed to have the confidence that we can cope with whatever lands on our doorstep."

Her worry was more than just on her doorstep, Stormy mused. It was living in the same house with her. But the old adage about hanging out the family's dirty laundry prevented her from discussing her sister. Instead she said, "Well, one of my worries has a name—H. B. Foley." She highlighted the situation, ending with a wave of her hand toward Foley's file on the table in the alcove. "On paper, the man is perfect. Not even a breath of suspicion."

"Maybe you and Tyler are too close to it. Suppose I read Foley's file. I might find something."

Stormy sighed. "You might as well, since I'll probably be obsessed with Foley at our support meetings. Another perspective can't hurt."

Sandy dried another gleaming mold, this one in the shape of an apple. "We're going to do fabulous with candles, Stormy. I just know it." The mold slipped from her hand and clattered to the floor. "Oops. Hope I didn't dent it."

Nina burst into the kitchen, fire in her eyes. "Could you hold it down in here? You know Tully is sick. You're making enough noise to wake the dead."

Sandy froze, darting a look from Stormy to Nina. "Sorry, my fault."

"It's all right," Stormy soothed.

"I'll just take these on out to the garage," Sandy said, avoiding Nina's eyes as she picked up a box of molds and made good her escape.

Stormy whirled on her sister. "That wasn't nice. Or necessary. Tully isn't in the throes of death. He's just got a hangover."

"Why do you have to have Sandy here?" Nina said in a tight voice. "If you wanted a partner, you could've asked me instead of some stranger. You know I could use the extra money."

"If memory serves me right, you suggested flea marketing was only one step away from being a streetwalker."

"How much are you paying Sandy?"

"That's Sandy's business. If you want to work, Nina, what's to stop you from going out and getting a job? Or lending Tully a hand down at the office? Perhaps with the two of you pulling together, you could get his company out of the red. Today is a prime example. With Tully sick—"

"Tully prefers me to be home with our children."

Stormy knew it would be of no use to point out that Nina had just contradicted herself. "Tommy and Davie are in school and day-care. You could put in a few hours."

Instead of spending all your free time shopping or playing cards with your girlfriends, Stormy thought.

"Well, I can't do that, can I? I have to keep an eye on you and the rubbish you invite into my home."

Stormy went rigid. "No one is immune to mistakes, Nina. Don't you have any compassion?"

"I save my compassion for where it's needed—for my sons and my husband. You're going to get your comeuppance, Stormy, you just wait and see. And Tully isn't hung over, he's got the flu. I'm leaving now to pick up a prescription the doctor called in for him." She made an about-face and stalked out, leaving Stormy with an incubus of foreboding.

Trembling, Stormy leaned over the sink, trying to unravel the nervous knot in her stomach. She wanted desperately to believe that Nina's bursts of vitriol were harmless. But even that slim pretense was denied her when she joined Sandy in the garage.

All the candle-making paraphernalia had been sorted and arranged on a makeshift tabletop. Sandy looked up from the instruction booklet. "I overheard everything. Living here must be worse for you than jail."

Quick tears betrayed Stormy's turmoil. "I keep telling myself *nothing* is as bad as prison. All I need is one more weekend and I'll have enough to move Liane and myself out of here."

"My place is hardly more than a cubbyhole, but the sofa makes into a bed...."

"Thanks, but no. It's only for another week or so. Usually I manage to stay out of Nina's way."

They both turned to watch as Nina pulled out of the driveway. She was at the wheel of Stormy's car. Sandy shook her head. "Now that takes more brass than General Schwarzkopf's."

"I think brass was bred into our genes," Stormy said, attempting a smile. She swiped at the tears on her cheeks. "Let's get started. What's the first thing we have to do?"

"Shave wax," Sandy said, handing over a block of paraffin. "And we don't have to worry about making mistakes. We can remelt and start over. The main thing is to make sure the wicks don't have kinks in them."

They pulled up plastic milk crates to serve as stools and got to work. After a few minutes, Sandy said, "Listen, I don't want to butt in about your sister—"

"Then don't," Stormy said more abruptly than she'd meant. "I'm sorry Nina was—"

"Please, Stormy—I've got to say just this one tiny thing."

Stormy inhaled—she felt skinned and nailed to the wall—but finally, she telegraphed a small smile. "Okay. One tiny thing."

"Noreen has lined up a psychologist from the women's center to come and talk to us in a couple of weeks. Why don't you make notes and plan to talk to her. I'm no professional, but from what I overheard, I got the impression Nina is scared of you. She sees you as a threat to her."

Stormy gaped. "That's absurd."

Sandy shrugged. "Maybe. Maybe not. I've always been overshadowed by my older sister. To tell you the truth, it's intimidating."

"But you're doing fine," Stormy countered.

"Well, gee, around you it's easy to be brazen!" She laughed. "I'm not saying your sister is right, or even that she isn't trying to undermine you, but if you understand her motives . . ."

"I can try to defuse the situation?"

"Losing my husband, the house, my children seemed to . . . to sort of highlight the rift between my sister and me.

I mean, she had a longer list of why I lost my family than I did. No matter what she does—and that includes two failed marriages—she seems to land on her feet. I used to resent her for that. You're a lot like her.''

"Then why don't you resent me?''

"You're not my big sister giving me advice every time I turn a corner, or reminding me that I ruined your best blouse when I was in the sixth grade!''

"I just told Nina to go out and get a job,'' Stormy mused aloud.

"I heard. Maybe she panics at the idea of interviews. I did.'' Sandy shuddered.

Sandy's comments were food for thought, Stormy mused, though deep down she knew there was something far more amiss with Nina than mere panic at job hunting. "How do you and your sister get along now?'' she asked.

Sandy giggled. "Darn! I knew you were going to ask that. Let's make candles while I think up some nice things to say about her.''

IT TOOK SEVERAL TRIES and much experimenting, but by the time Liane and her cousins stepped off the school bus and rushed into the garage, Stormy and Sandy had a half dozen apple-and-cinnamon-scented candles standing in a neat row.

"Ooooo, light one, Mom,'' Liane demanded.

The women looked at each other. "We'd better,'' they agreed in unison.

"And time how long it takes to burn itself out,'' added Sandy. "That could be a selling point.''

The wick caught on the first try. They all cheered. Stormy shushed them. "Your dad's sick in bed,'' she told the boys.

"We're really in business," Sandy whispered, watching the tiny flame wobble and grow stronger. "We really are!" She leaned closer to the flame and sniffed. "It really does smell like apples. People are going to follow their noses right to our stand."

"Where's my mother?" Davie asked, reemerging into the garage from the house. "I can't find her. I'm hungry."

Stormy looked toward the drive. Nina had been gone an awfully long time for a wife professing concern about a sick husband. She gave a minute of thought to the possibility of car trouble. No. She had new tires, she'd had the Ford serviced only the week before, and, anyway, the phone hadn't rung. No doubt Nina had run into a girlfriend and was sitting in some coffee shop, complaining how awful it was to have her older sister underfoot.

"She's picking up some medicine for your dad," Stormy finally told the boy. "C'mon, I'll fix you guys a sandwich and get you settled. You can watch television in the upstairs den for an hour before you do homework."

"I want to help make candles," Liane protested.

Stormy eyed the small cauldrons of hot wax. "Not this time, poppet. We're finished for today."

Sandy looked up in surprise. "We are?"

Stormy urged the children into the house with instructions to go quietly to their rooms and change out of their school clothes.

"Can we eat candy out of our Easter baskets?" Davie asked.

"Ten jelly beans apiece until after your sandwich."

"Do I know how many is ten?" Tommy said worriedly.

"Liane will count them for you. Now, scat. On tiptoe."

"Did something go down that I missed?" Sandy asked once the kids disappeared.

"I can't shake that bad feeling. Nina's been gone far too long just to get a prescription filled."

"You think she had a wreck or something?"

"I don't know. I just have a sense of dread. I think I'll look in on Tully."

She rapped on his bedroom door and was rewarded with a muttered reply. She poked her head around the door. Tully had the coverlet up to his neck, his head buried in a pillow. "How're you feeling?" she asked.

He raised his head, revealing an unshaven jaw and bloodshot eyes. "Terrible."

"You want some aspirin?"

"No. Is Nina still in a snit?"

"Did you two have an argument?"

"Nina did. I was too hung over to hold up my end. Where is she?"

"Gone to pick up your medicine."

"Probably arsenic," he said, and dropped back onto the pillow.

"She did call the doctor for you, didn't she? For a prescription?"

"I don't know. I only asked for Rolaids."

Bristling with deepening apprehension, Stormy returned to the kitchen.

Sandy was in the alcove, flipping through Foley's file, the candle they'd lit in a saucer in front of her. The scent was fabulous.

"I unplugged all the wax pots," Sandy told her. "What'd your brother-in-law say?"

"He and Nina had an argument. He's hung over, with an upset stomach. He doesn't know anything about a prescription. Dammit! What is Nina up to?"

"Do you suspect her of being up to something? What are you fixing the kids? I'll help."

"Peanut-butter-and-jelly sandwiches," Stormy concluded, falling back on a mother's tried-and-true standby. Her mind was so aflame with dire possibilities, anything more complicated was beyond her. Still, it wasn't fair to embroil Sandy in any family squabble that might erupt when Nina did return. She said as much.

Sandy nodded. "I know, but I'm staying, anyway. You're worried. I'll worry with you. I'm an expert worrier. I'm a *master* worrier. I can think of things to worry about that haven't even been invented yet."

Stormy laughed. "Earlier, you were telling me we weren't supposed to worry."

"True, but since you insist on doing it, why let good talent go to waste? As soon as Nina is home safe, I'll slip out the garage door." She added bananas to the food tray. "Probably better if you take this up to the kids. The boys don't really know me."

Stormy put the cashbox filled with Sunday's receipts on the edge of the tray. Leaving the money in sight was just another bone of contention for Nina to gnaw on.

She took the tray up, settled the children in front of the television and put Liane in charge.

"Liane's not gonna boss me," sputtered Davie.

"I wouldn't waste my time bossing you. I'm a girl."

"Please," Stormy appealed to them. There was a catch in her voice; the children looked up at her.

"Mommy, is something wrong?"

"No, poppet. I'm just tired. Your Uncle Tully is . . . has the flu. You all have to be quiet. Help the boys with their homework, okay? I'll call you when it's time for supper."

Stormy went through the door that connected the small den—her mother's former sewing room—to the room that had served her father as a study. It had been his quiet space, the place he laughingly said he could go to escape the "caterwauling" of his womenfolk.

And now that she thought about it, much of that caterwauling had to do with Nina pleading with their mother to be allowed something that Stormy was already being allowed—lipstick or use of the family car or a later curfew. Their mother's stock reply had always been, "When you're older and more responsible."

Stormy wondered if that stock reply had fostered the dislike Nina held for her now.

Sunlight poured into the study, catching dust motes in flight. The walls were a soft gray, the leather furniture worn to the suppleness of silk. It *was* a tranquil room, exactly right for a man who spent hours reading, collecting stamps and carrying on a correspondence with philatelists around the globe.

When she left, Stormy thought, this was the room she'd miss most. She moved to the armoire that served as camouflage for the safe her father had used for the rarest of his stamps.

The opened doors of the armoire blocked out the sun, leaving its interior in shadow. For a moment Stormy thought the emptiness of the safe was only a trick of light. She pushed open the doors as far as they would go and bent to peer inside. *Empty!*

But that was impossible.

She ran her hand over the interior. All she felt was cool steel.

She opened the cigar box. Only some loose change tumbled into a corner.

For a few seconds nature provided the anesthetic of disbelief. Then her mind registered the truth, and adrenaline poured into her system.

The money was gone.

Fourteen hundred dollars did not just vanish into thin air.

Nina. There was no doubt in her mind.

Yet there was no logic to this turn of events at all. Nina wanted her out of the house as badly as Stormy wanted out.

Stormy's legs carried her halfway down the stairs, but there she collapsed and buried her face in her hands.

"Stormy!" Sandy whispered urgently, creeping quietly up the staircase. "Mrs. Lowery's here. She's making a home visit. Stupid me, I answered the door. I put her in the living room. I didn't know what else to do."

Stormy got to her feet.

"Wait!" Sandy admonished, still whispering. "That's not all. Tyler Mangus is with her. He said he's been trying to reach you all afternoon, but your phone is out of order. I looked. It was off the hook."

Tyler and her parole officer together in the same room? Her fate was sealed!

She felt sick.

"Nina took the phone off the hook, I'm sure, so Tully wouldn't be disturbed." But in light of the empty safe, it seemed more ominous than that.

"Well, your brother-in-law is disturbed now. He poked his head out and wanted to know what all the commotion was about. What do you want me to do?"

"Do you mind making coffee? No—brew some tea. If my destiny is about to be unraveled, let's do it in a civilized manner."

Sandy backed down the stairs. "What *are* you talking about?"

"And tell Tully to get up and get cleaned up and dressed and join us in the living room." Sandy turned and moved down a step. Stormy grabbed her shoulder. "Call Noreen, too. Tell her if my parole is revoked, I want her to take care of Liane for me."

"*What!*" Sandy squeaked, fear leaping into her eyes.

"Just do it!" Stormy pleaded. Then she approached the living room, terror at her heels.

Both Tyler and Mrs. Lowery were standing. Tyler had his back to her, much the way she had first encountered him in this very room. If only she could turn back the clock!

Mrs. Lowery, though, was on alert for her entrance. "There you are," the parole officer said so firmly that Stormy wondered if she were to be marched off to prison again without so much as a by-your-leave.

She could think of nothing more momentous to say than hello. A stealthy glance at Tyler showed his expression to be carefully devoid of emotion.

"Do I need to make introductions?" she asked, gesturing them both toward the sofa.

"Mr. Mangus and I are acquainted," Mrs. Lowery said.

Tyler remained standing, as if distancing himself.

Stormy had never felt so awkward in her life.

"I'm afraid you'll have to lead me through a home visit," she said, sinking down into an overstuffed chair opposite Mrs. Lowery. "I don't know what to expect."

"This visit is...a bit more involved than usual, I'm afraid. It seems we have some serious matters to discuss."

Stormy sat dead still, bracing herself. "What serious matters?"

Mrs. Lowery reached into her briefcase and pulled out a notepad. "Your sister, Mrs. Dawson—Nina—has called me twice during the past week." She glanced up from the notepad. "Then, today, she came to see me."

Stormy's heart stopped, her vision blurred, her stomach churned and her blood ran cold. Through the haze, she glanced at Tyler, then back to Mrs. Lowery.

All she could think was that it wasn't possible. It just could not be possible. Nina had made good on her threats. Insults Stormy could accept. But this! Not even taking her money compared to this! She did not want to believe Nina capable of such betrayal. It made no sense. Was there any twisted way in which it made sense?

A vision of Liane swept into her mind's eye. Liane looking up over her shoulder, as if to make certain her mother was there, home from prison.

"What did my sister have to say about me?" she heard herself asking.

Chapter Fourteen

"You don't take proper care of your daughter...you stay out until all hours of the night...you associate with un-desirable elements...you sleep around with strange men...you pawned the family's television...you drink to the point of intoxication..."

Stormy's stomach thumped with a sickening heaviness as she listened to the litany of half truths and utter fabri-cations. *Oh, Nina!* she mourned silently. *How am I ever to forgive you for this?*

From beneath tear-dampened lashes, she glanced at Ty-ler. Was he part of it, too? Part of this conspiracy to...to what? Did he still harbor doubts? Why else wasn't he helping her? No matter what, it was awful having him witness her humiliation.

"Stormy?" Mrs. Lowery said. "Did we lose you there for a moment?"

"Yes. I mean—no," she said, indeed lost in inner suf-fering.

"That's about it, then." Mrs. Lowery closed the note-pad with a snap. "However, I like to think I'm fair-minded, so I want to hear your side of this."

Stormy picked over a minefield of possible answers to find one that seemed safe. One that would do no more damage. She replied slowly, "My sister and I haven't been getting along. Beyond that, there's not much to tell."

Mrs. Lowery sat back against the sofa cushions, her eyebrows raised in skepticism. "My dear, I recognize an understatement when I hear one. You're going to have to do better than that."

"Does Tyler have to be here?" Stormy asked.

Mrs. Lowery sighed. "We'll get to Tyler after a bit. For the moment, just tell me about your sister."

Stormy threw up her hands. "I don't know what you want me to say."

"I want you to tell me what is happening in this house. I don't want to ask you questions because that would be leading you. I need to hear what you have to say. No embellishments. The truth. The plain and simple truth."

Stormy closed her eyes against the hot tears surging up. Dear God! She was on the stand in her own defense all over again.

From the hall came the sound of the children clattering down the stairs. Stormy looked their way, but they passed by, hurrying toward the back of the house. Her chin trembled. Liane, motherless again. No! she thought. It was one thing for Nina to hurt *her*, but not Liane. She couldn't allow that to happen. Once was enough. She raised her head and met Mrs. Lowery's watchful gaze.

"Nina has been...vindictive," she began. "She's taken—or at least I think it was her—all the money Sandy and I have earned at the flea market. She—I did pawn the television. It was mine, but I reclaimed it out of my first week's receipts. The kids were just upstairs watching it. I seldom drink—a glass of wine on occasion. As for Liane, when I first got home from prison, I discovered that Nina often slept in and left Liane to get herself and her cousins off to school." Stormy's chin stopped trembling. "Liane did a damned good job of it, too."

"When you were first assigned to me, you said you had the money to get your own place. That didn't happen."

"No. I had given Nina power of attorney over my share of a small family trust that I expected to be available to me—less, of course, whatever Nina had to use for Liane while I was gone. But I learned she had drawn an advance on it—"

"Milked it, in other words," Mrs. Lowery put in, nodding.

Stormy thought she heard empathy in the older woman's voice. It unleashed the courage she needed to ask, "Mrs. Lowery, are you going to revoke my parole?"

"My dear, the recidivism rate for women in my caseload is less than three percent—far below the norm. I do not recommend revocation of parole or probation at the blink of an eye. I work as closely with my probationers as time permits. If there were no such thing as alcohol and narcotics—" She stopped and inhaled. "Well, don't let me get on that bandwagon." Her mouth formed a somber line. "One thing I don't tolerate is anyone trying to undermine a parolee's best efforts."

She sighed. "I won't deny I'm a bit angry with you. Had you not been so reticent and simply called me, I could've put a stop to this the first time your sister contacted me. As it was, I had no choice but to check things out for myself." She waved a thin and elegant hand toward Tyler. "Fortunately, your young man has been keeping me abreast of things, so I was not entirely surprised by your sister's allegations."

Stormy swiveled her head. "Tyler? What things? Since when?"

But Mrs. Lowery went on as if Stormy had not posed any questions. "And, Sandy, too, in a roundabout way. She's determined to regain custody of her children, so she doesn't make a move without alerting me."

"You're Sandy's probation officer?"

"Noreen and Thelma and Janice are also in my caseload. So you see, my dear, when your sister came to me complaining that you were 'consorting with undesirables'—"

"Tea, anyone?" Sandy said quietly, entering the room with a tray.

Mrs. Lowery accepted the interruption and gave Sandy a smile. "I'll have a cup."

They all heard the front door open and slam. Noreen barreled into the room.

"Stormy? Uh-oh!" she said, spying Mrs. Lowery and skidding to a halt.

But Mrs. Lowery was disposed to smile at Noreen, too. "Ah! Reinforcements, I think. Or perhaps you girls are having your support group meeting here tonight?"

Sandy grabbed Noreen's arm and hauled her away. "C'mon, I want to show you the candles Stormy and I made today."

Stormy still felt likely to fragment at any second.

Tyler's cup rattled in his saucer. Mrs. Lowery glanced at him. "Would you like to explain to Stormy your part in all this?"

Stormy turned her eyes to Tyler. "Yes, do," she said.

"I introduced myself to Mrs. Lowery early on—"

"How early on?"

"While you were seeing your father's estate manager, actually. I told her I was hoping to enlist your cooperation in locating the stolen money."

"Is that what you called hounding me? 'Cooperation'?"

"I got more than I bargained for," he admitted with a faintly amused expression.

I'll just bet you did, Stormy thought, recalling the brazen way she'd stormed his motel room. She quickly shunted the memory aside, lest Mrs. Lowery read in her face what was on her mind.

"The long and short of it was that after I ran the credit check on your sister and brother-in-law—"

Stormy was on her feet. "You what?"

"I told you, I look into everyone who's involved."

"Let's not let this escalate into a war," Mrs. Lowery put in mildly, coaxing Stormy back into the chair. "Suffice it to say that since I had met Tyler, had seen his credentials and the authorization from his client, it seemed only appropriate that he keep me informed of his activities, since they involved one of my own—"

"Stormy!" Nina's voice careened into the room before she did. "I want you to get those sluts out of my kit—"

She stopped on the threshold, taking in the tableau of Stormy, Tyler and Mrs. Lowery. Her mouth slowly creased into a smirk. "I see Mrs. Lowery finally caught you at it." Triumphant, she continued into the room, her attention wholly on Mrs. Lowery, as if Tyler and Stormy did not exist. "I suppose Stormy has denied everything."

"Well, no," Mrs. Lowery said affably. "She hasn't."

Nina stopped in her tracks. "You mean she's admitted to it? *All* of it?"

Mrs. Lowery managed to look as if she'd shrugged when she had not so much as moved a muscle. The near smile she passed to Stormy was even less evident.

"Sit down, Nina," Stormy said. "I'd like to ask you why you took my money out of the safe."

"*Me?* Why don't you ask those thieves and worse who are in my kitchen?"

"Because they don't even know the safe exists. They've never even been upstairs."

"Your boyfriend, then." She snapped a frown at Tyler.

He moved behind the chair on which Stormy sat, put his hand on her shoulder and gave it a gentle squeeze. His gesture surprised and pleased Stormy. Though concerned about how it might appear to Mrs. Lowery, she reached up to cover Tyler's hand with her own. "Tyler didn't take my money."

"You can deny it from here to hallelujah, but he's in this with you." She turned to Mrs. Lowery. "See? I told you they were scheming together. They're using the flea market to launder that stolen money."

Stormy gasped.

"I'm afraid not," Tyler said, his voice unbending steel. "But you've had a jolly day with Stormy's money, haven't you? Let's see," he said, staring at the ceiling. "You paid the mortgage due on Tully's office, paid your dues at the country club...had a drink there with your friends, too, as I recall...."

Nina went pale. "You've been following me?"

"Let's just say I have a vested interest in your sister's affairs. Keeping an eye on you seemed like a good idea. It was."

"Where'd you get the money to do all that, Nina?" Tully asked from the threshold. He stood there in slippers, cutoffs and T-shirt, his hair slicked back and wet from a recent shower.

She turned on him. "I had some money put by."

He shook his head. "No, you didn't. You rifled my pockets this morning for the boys' lunch money."

Mrs. Lowery stood up to address Nina. "Mrs. Dawson, I hardly know what to say to you. But there's no doubt in my mind what you were trying to accomplish by your calls and visit. You wanted your sister back in prison. I suspect you thought I'd rush out here and haul her off to jail. But that's not how I work. I also suspect your motivation was greed. And that with your sister out of the way, you wouldn't have to explain your sudden windfall.

"I just stopped by to ask Stormy some questions—and to let her know that she has my full support. You see, Mr. Mangus has almost convinced me that Stormy had nothing to do with the bank robbery she was sent to prison for. However, until such time as she gets something done with her conviction, she is still on parole. I can't change that."

She turned to Stormy. "And one more thing. You do have legal recourse, should you want to file charges against your sister—not only for the money she took from you today, but for abusing the power of attorney you gave her over your trust fund." She then dispensed a look of utter disgust at Nina. "Don't ever again let me hear you calling one of my probationers a slut. If your behavior continues in the same vein as we've witnessed today, *you* might end up as one of my clients." She picked up her briefcase and purse. "I guess that's it."

"I'll walk you to the door," Stormy said, though she wasn't certain her legs would carry her that far.

Before she stepped onto the porch, Mrs. Lowery turned and placed one perfectly manicured fingertip in the center of Stormy's chest. "As for you, my dear, I don't approve of your visiting Tyler in his motel room. I'm not such an ogre that I expect an attractive, healthy young woman to be celibate, but I won't condone blatant indiscretion. Be more discreet—or marry the man."

Stormy's face overflowed with color. "Yes, ma'am."

Stunned, she watched Mrs. Lowery negotiate the drive.

TULLY MET STORMY in the foyer. He held out a wad of bills.

"This is yours," he said. "I don't know how much she took, but this is what was left in her purse." His face suddenly looked rumpled. "I'm sorry. Sorry for the whole mess. I should've put a stop to it." Eyes downcast, he rubbed a knuckle against his mouth. "She convinced me you had that stolen money. I guess I wanted to believe it."

He looked around the hall—at the polished floors, the antique mirror, the cobbler's bench. "Part of the problem is this house, you know. She keeps it as shrine to your dad. I don't measure up. I'm no good at contracting. I'm a good plumber, though. I'm going back to being just a plumber."

"I'll have to talk to her, Tully."

He sighed. "I know. But could it wait? I'm going to pack her and the boys up and take them to my parents' for a few days. The boys love the farm. And Nina needs to be reminded of *my* roots." His breath chuffed out. "And so do I." He paused before shuffling back into the living room. "Would it be too much to ask if you'd keep an eye on the boys until I get Nina calmed down? They're in the kitchen with your friends. Tyler said he'd wait for you there."

The scene in the kitchen was as gay as the one in the living room had been tense. Tyler had Tommy on one knee, Liane on the other. Janelle sat on Sandy's lap. Davie was helping Noreen empty ice trays for soft drinks. In the center of the table, the candle still burned in its saucer, making the kitchen smell good and fine and friendly.

Liane caught sight of her mother. "Hurray! Now we can go eat."

"Are we going out for dinner?" Stormy asked, her eyes sweeping the room, taking everyone in but landing on Tyler. He gave her a smile.

"Tyler has offered to treat us all to pizza," Noreen said. "We were just waiting for you. You don't have to go, of course, but I'm not passing up a meal I don't have to cook."

"What about me and Tommy?" asked Davie, fearful of being left out.

"You boys *have* to come," Tyler told him. "You can't leave me all alone with these women. I'd be massacred."

"You mean all alone with me, don't you?" Stormy said near his ear as they were filing out the door.

"Not at all," he said out the corner of his mouth. "I'm saving you for the last."

He was the Pied Piper of the evening. All four children scrambled into his car.

"Do we really want to do that to him?" Noreen asked.

"Yes," said Stormy, sailing imperiously past Tyler to place herself in the front seat of Noreen's car.

"Now, why do I sense this is going to be an interesting evening?" Noreen cast into the night air.

"After the day we've had," observed Sandy, leaning forward from the back seat, "it can't possibly be more than a footnote. But don't follow too close, in case he tosses one of them out the window."

"Nina stole my money," Stormy said, giving an abbreviated version of what had transpired in the living room. She ended with how like a sphinx Tyler had been.

"You could hardly expect him to cuddle and coo in front of Lowery," Noreen admonished. "Knowing her, she probably laid down ground rules before she agreed to his being there at all."

"You're taking Tyler's side," Stormy accused.

Noreen grinned. "I like him. If you don't, pass him on."
They drove a quarter mile in silence. Noreen chuckled.
"Thought that'd shut you up."

"Speaking of passing," Sandy said, "we just did. Tyler turned into Pizza Hut."

By the time Noreen found a break in traffic to make a U-turn, Tyler had ushered the children into the restaurant and had them seated at a table, where they were pretending to read the menu. He looked wan and shell-shocked.

Stormy pulled Tyler into a nearby booth and slid in beside him. Noreen and Sandy joined the "adult" table.

"Were the kids unruly?" she asked.

"They weren't unruly, no. But the conversation was very...*scientific.*"

"Uh-oh," Noreen groaned.

"We'll explain everything to them," Stormy said. "But a mission like that can't be done on an empty stomach. Let's order."

She felt Tyler's hand on her knee, and a spring of delight bubbled up within her. And while the adrenaline still coursed through her veins, for the moment she could put aside her sorrow over Nina. She smiled at Tyler. "Don't take too much on faith," she warned feistily. "You may have helped, but you haven't exactly been canonized."

"You're upset because I admitted to Lowery you came to my motel room."

"Stormy!" Noreen crowed. "You didn't tell us that."

"It was...just to...talk about my case."

Prudently, Tyler said nothing but, "Cheese and mushrooms for me," to the waitress.

"Could I just say one tiny thing?" Sandy put in after everyone's order was taken.

"Not now," Noreen begged. "Your 'one tiny thing' always ends up a speech."

"I just wanted to tell Stormy I read H. B. Foley's résumé while I was making tea."

"And?" Stormy said, splitting her attention between Sandy and Tyler's hand, which was surreptitiously moving up her leg.

"I'll tell you one thing—if he had kids and was in a custody battle, they'd sure use his work record against him."

Tyler's hand stopped moving on Stormy's thigh. "What do you mean? He has an excellent employment record."

"On the job, maybe," Sandy said. "But as a family man? Uh-uh. He changed jobs twice in one year, both times during school terms. And all his other job changes were during the school year, too. A family-court judge would look closely at that. I mean, you don't just jerk kids out of school year in and year out if you can help it. It's awful for them."

"Sandy's right," Stormy said as the waitress put salads and breadsticks before them. "I've been searching for a place to live, but the only one I liked so far and could afford would've meant Liane had to change schools. It's too late in the school year to do that to her." She turned to Tyler. "Is Foley married? Does he have children?"

"He is, and he does."

Stormy frowned. "But does this open up any new possibilities?"

"I don't know," Tyler admitted, "but I'll look into it first thing in the morning."

"If anything works out in your favor," said Sandy, her voice a parody of innocence, "can we increase my share of the business to thirty percent?"

Stormy thrust her hand across the table. "If I get out of this mess, we'll be full partners!"

Grinning, Sandy shook Stormy's out-thrust hand. "Terrific! But I want it in writing."

At the nearby table, Liane yelped. "Tommy spilled his drink all over me!"

"You look like you peed your pants!" Davie laughed.

Stormy and Noreen rushed to the table and began shushing and wiping and chiding.

Sandy smiled at Tyler. "Don't look so glum. You'll only *have* to be seen in public with them one more time."

"How so?" he said pleasantly, taking a bit of bread-stick.

"You know—ring bearers and flower girls. After that, you're home free."

Tyler choked.

"Hey!" Sandy called. "Does anyone know the Heimlich maneuver?"

"She's a witch," Tyler complained. "All your friends are witches, even the ones only this high," he added, throwing out an arm to measure two feet from the floor.

"Sandy is as sweet as she can be," Stormy countered, kneeling on the floor beside the sofa where Tyler lay. They were in the downstairs family room, where she'd left Tyler to recuperate while she put Liane to bed. Without Nina and Tully and the boys, the house was exceptionally quiet. "How's your throat? Did the tea help?"

"I could've died."

"Of embarrassment, that's all."

At Sandy's shout the waitress had left off mopping up the spilled drink, jerked Tyler out of his seat, performed the Heimlich, and gone back to serving her other customers. The entire episode had taken about thirty-two seconds. Tyler left her a twenty-dollar tip, to which she'd said he could choke in her station any day of the week.

"What were you and Sandy talking about, anyway?"

"Nothing."

Stormy kissed his eyelids. "Feel better now?"

He snaked an arm around her waist. "Maybe. Do that again. Or I might not live till morning."

"I'll do anything I can to help you through the night— I want to know what you find out about Foley."

He opened one eye and gazed at her. "Anything?"

"Within reason."

His hand traveled up beneath her blouse. "Is this within reason?"

She shivered but was not yet ready to abandon her case. "When did you do a background check on Nina and Tully?"

"After you discovered all your boxes in the garage had been rifled." He leaned to begin nuzzling her neck.

"Mmm... Hey, wait a minute!" she yelped, trying unsuccessfully, to evade his wandering hands and lips.

"You thought I had the money and that they had stolen it from me!" she complained weakly as his fingers worked their magic under her blouse.

"I think all sorts of things when I'm working," he murmured idly, fumbling for a moment but finally releasing the clasp on her bra.

"Tyler...oh! Stop...I mean, don't...stop...wait!" she protested feebly, gasping. She straightened away from his probing fingers.

"When...when did you stop thinking I participated in the robbery?"

"After I saw how you parlayed a few dollars into a viable business," he said with a long-suffering sigh. "Smart, stubborn and proud—too proud to steal."

"Did you think that before or after I came to your motel room?"

"Stop splitting hairs, woman, and start worrying about what I'm thinking right now."

"What would that be?" she wondered aloud.

And with a hungry growl, he pulled her up onto the couch and proceeded to show her.

Chapter Fifteen

"Where have you been?" Stormy yelled, hurrying from the garage to accost Tyler the moment he stepped from his car. "You said a couple of hours. It's been half the *day*."

"I've spent a boring two hours hanging around Western Union waiting for a fax. You've had a productive morning, from the looks of it," he said, ushering her back into the garage, where row after row of finished candles marched along one of the makeshift tables.

"I had to do something to keep my mind off—dammit, Tyler, don't keep me in suspense! What'd you find out?"

"We're grasping at straws."

Stormy sank down onto a stool, defeated. "Oh, no! I had so hoped—"

"I didn't say all was lost. I just said we're grasping at straws."

She lifted her head. "Then you did find out something!"

He reached into his pocket and pulled out some folded papers. "This is all I got, and it ain't much."

Stormy snatched the papers from his hand, spread them out on the table and began to read. "These are copies of Foley's credit-card charges."

"Look where they're from. Casinos in Las Vegas. At first glance, it seems meaningless because Foley was there for a banking conference."

"He gambles!" Stormy gasped. "That's motive, isn't it?"

"Those are his wife's charges. *She* gambles."

Stormy glanced again at the printouts. Most of the charges were cash advances ranging from three hundred to five hundred dollars. "Foley steals to cover his wife's gambling losses!" she breathed. "That's it."

"Pretty desperate action when—"

Stormy was shaking her head. "She's his wife, Tyler! Look how Tully went along with Nina."

"Tully didn't do any stealing."

"No, but he *let* it happen. Only after Nina was caught red-handed did he come up with a set of morals. And only after you and Mrs. Lowery got involved. I wasn't going to hang dirty laundry out for the world to see—Lowery forced me to do it. And think. What's the first thing Tully did? He moved Nina out of sight, still protecting her.

"And that's probably what Foley does—why they move so often, why he changes jobs. As soon as his wife—" she looked at the printout "—Cheryl, gets in over her head gambling and puts them deeper in debt, he moves the family. Perhaps he's always hoping for a new beginning.

"Just think of all the potential problems, Tyler. If she gambles away their money, utilities go unpaid, the kids aren't cared for properly, maybe the school counselor alerts social services...it goes on and on. A bank vice president can't tolerate that kind of scrutiny. He's supposed to be a pillar of the community." She tapped the printout with her fingers. "We've got to catch Cheryl Foley gambling."

"And then what?" Tyler asked, shoving his hands into his pockets. "Nothing in those files says she gambles illegally."

"Then we . . . we confront Foley?"

"That's what I meant about grasping at straws. You think if we confront him, he'll confess? This is the real world, Stormy. The man isn't going to destroy his life just to do you a favor. He helped ruin you, remember? He perjured himself in court."

Stormy jumped off the stool and put her arms around Tyler's neck. "Please. Go back to those computer folks and find out where the Foleys live now. We can at least go talk to them."

Tyler sighed. "You think you can get me to do anything you ask by rubbing yourself up against me like that?"

Stormy planted a kiss on the corner of his mouth and pressed herself a little more tightly against him. "It feels that way."

"*That* part of my body doesn't have the sense God gave a billy goat."

"Aren't you the best asset-recovery agent on the eastern seaboard? Don't you have satisfied clients from here to the Mississippi?"

"Stop throwing my bragging back in my face."

She pressed her lips to the vein throbbing in his neck. "Your heart is beating faster."

"All right, all right, I'll make some more inquiries, but—"

"You can use my phone," she murmured between persuasive kisses.

"This isn't going to get you anywhere—except maybe on the sofa."

Stormy began to tingle inside. "That sounds like a reasonable beginning to me."

He was back within twenty minutes. "Okay, I've set some things in motion. Now let's go get . . . *reasonable* on the sofa," he said, his arms snaking around her waist and his hands beginning to climb.

"Could we compromise?" Stormy asked sweetly as she poured a layer of hot pink wax into a mold.

"Compromise?" he asked darkly.

"You can shave wax, and I'll—"

"Unfair, unreasonable and *unlikely,*" he protested.

"Liane will be getting off the school bus within ten minutes."

"You knew that when you were plastering yourself all over me twenty minutes ago," he grumbled.

Stormy tilted her head to one side. "Ah, but it *was* twenty minutes ago. Can I help it if you spent all that precious time on the phone?"

"Dirty, underhanded and low-down," Tyler muttered. "All right, all right, how the hell does one shave wax?"

"Goodness, you don't have to give in so quickly," she said mischievously.

He glared at her. "Forget it. I refuse to start something we can't finish. I'm not in the mood for torture."

"Don't you like the romance of anticipation?"

"Only women think that way."

"You know, you really make it hard to fall in love with you," she said lightly, though part of her was testing the waters.

"If only that was all that got hard," he growled.

"Only *men* think that way." She sighed. Then she plopped a five-pound block of paraffin in front of him. "Just chip it and put it into that pot. How long before they'll call back?"

"Who?" He was thinking about what she'd said about falling in love. He scanned her face. Nah. She'd just casually tossed it out. Better he bank his emotions before he said something stupid.

"The people who're checking out the Foleys!"

"Not for a couple of hours, anyway. Maybe not till morning."

"To pass the time, we can grill some steaks and bake a couple of potatoes for supper."

Tyler scattered wax everywhere, then made a production of picking up every tiny piece and placing it in the melting pot.

"It's a school night," Stormy said. "Liane goes to bed at eight o'clock."

"So?"

"So I thought we ought to stay near the phone."

"Your phone is in the hallway."

"Oh, didn't I tell you? There's a jack behind the sofa."

He looked up. "I'm beginning to see," he said slowly, "how a good man can be lured from the straight and narrow by a devious, underhanded woman."

"Poor Foley," Stormy sighed.

"WHY CAN'T I CALL JANELLE now? If I wait until later, Elise will be on the phone, and she talks all night!"

"Tyler is expecting an important call."

"But he's not even here! He went to the store."

"He'll be back in a minute. After his call, you can phone Janelle. Go sit in the alcove and do your homework while I cook supper."

"What's the use of calling later if I can't get through?" Liane grumbled.

"Since when have you learned to be so sassy?" Stormy countered.

"I'm practicing to be a teenager."

"You have six long years before you get there, kiddo. Keep it up and I may start practicing swatting your fanny."

Liane flounced into the alcove and climbed a stool. "You can't do that," she called from the safety of her perch. "Grown-ups are not supposed to hit little kids. It's against the law."

"Is taking away telephone privileges against the law?"

Muttering, Liane buried her face in her spelling book. Stormy turned back to the sink so the child could not see her smile.

Tyler bustled in and put a six-pack of beer in the fridge. Then he slapped a small paper sack down on the counter next to the salad makings. "This is for Liane—and you," he said quietly.

"Oh, how sweet." Stormy dried her hands to look. "What is it?"

"A book."

"Oh?" She upended the bag. Out slipped a small paperback titled *Where did I Come From? The facts of life without any nonsense with illustrations*. She paged through it rapidly. "Uh-uh. No, she's not ready for this."

Tyler began backpedaling. "I'll check the grill, see if the coals are—"

Stormy grabbed the front of his shirt. "What possessed you to—"

"She's ready," Tyler muttered. "You can't have your daughter going around asking men about sperm. It's not . . . it's not *seemly*, for crying out loud. Hell, it's not safe. Suppose she asked some pervert."

"But this is so graphic." The illustrations were cartoon fashion, but they clearly delineated body parts. The language, too, was quite specific.

"The clerk said it was the bestselling book on sex educa—"

"They don't sell books like this at minimarts."

"I told you I spent a couple of boring hours waiting for a fax this morning. I browsed the bookstore at the mall."

"What are you two whispering about?" called Liane.

"Nothing, poppet. Do your homework."

"If it were Priss, I'd give her this," Tyler said.

"Liane isn't Priss," Stormy shot back.

Tyler picked up the platter of steaks. "I'll just toss these on the grill," he said, and went out to the deck.

Stormy leaned on the sink and muttered an unladylike epithet. She had spent eleven months in prison and survived the experience. Why was she so worried about talking about sex with her daughter?

Because it would mean the end of innocence.

But how innocent were the children of the nineties? Not very. Sex was on television, in the schoolroom, in the movies, on the streets.

Perhaps Tyler was more objective than she. At the least, he had shown a willingness to tread where other men might falter. She picked up the book and pored through it for a few minutes. Then, dry of mouth, she went into the alcove and sat on a stool opposite Liane. She held the book in her lap.

"Poppet?"

Liane looked up.

"You know you can talk to me about anything, don't you?"

"No, I can't. Janelle and I have secrets. I can't tell you or anybody or it wouldn't be a secret anymore."

"I'm talking about...other things. Remember when you and Janelle were talking about sperm?"

"Yes, but we can't find anybody who has any."

"Well, men have sperm."

"What men?"

"All men."

Liane's eyes narrowed to slits. "Tyler said he didn't."

"Well, he does."

"Why did he lie about it, then?"

"He didn't want to lie to you, but he wasn't comfortable discussing it with you."

"Where does he keep it?"

"I have a book here that tells you all about it. I want you to read it, and if you can't figure something out, just ask me and I'll help you."

Liane straightened. "I can read up to fifth-grade level!"

Stormy passed her the book. Liane read the title aloud; her eyebrows shot up. "Oh, boy!"

"We'll talk after you've finished it, okay?"

"Okay," Liane answered absently, already on page two.

Sitting there, watching her daughter silently sound out words, Stormy suddenly felt superfluous. She joined Tyler on the deck. He was stretched out in a lounge chair, eyes closed against the drooping sun.

"I gave it to her," she said.

"Steaks will be ready in about ten minutes," he replied.

"I'm sorry I criticized your choice. You were right. If a child is old enough to ask questions and has the curiosity—"

He raised one eyelid. "I lied. I wouldn't have given the book to Priss. I would've made her mother do it."

"Well."

"But if I ever have a son, I'll—"

"You want more children?"

"A man likes to think he'll leave something noteworthy behind when he's gone."

"So does a woman," Stormy said.

They sat there in silence, both wondering just how far they could carry the conversation. Stormy was also wondering just how far into the book Liane was.

Liane came to the screen door. "Somebody wants Tyler on the phone," she said.

Both adults leapt up.

"Keep an eye on the steaks," Tyler ordered.

He had not returned by the time Stormy judged the meat to be medium-well done. She put the steaks on the platter, took it into the kitchen and began setting the table.

Liane was still in the alcove. She was gazing out the windows, the book closed.

"Do you have any questions, sweetie?" Stormy asked.

Liane emitted a doleful sigh. "I'm probably gonna have to read this to Davie and Tommy," she said.

"Oh, why?"

"They get to keep their pe-nus-es their whole lives."

"Do they think differently?" Stormy asked, pleased that Liane was absorbing everything so matter-of-factly.

"Well, of course, they do, Mom. I told them when they got big like me, it'd fall off."

"Oh."

"But this book says I never had one, 'cause I'm a girl. Is that true?"

"That's true, poppet."

"Janelle only got one thing right," Liane said, annoyed. "Sperm do look like tadpoles."

"Perhaps Noreen will let her borrow the book, then Janelle will know as much as you."

"She won't believe half of this, Mom. She's never even *seen* a pe-nus. It'll gross her out." She sniffed. "I'm starving. Am I gonna get a whole steak all by myself?"

That's all? Stormy thought, baffled. Had one small book of less than thirty pages taken away all the curiosity and mystery of life? No, of course not, she realized, relieved. Liane would have to grow into much of it.

"Yep, you do," she replied, smiling. "Go wash up."

"Is the great debate over?" Tyler said, entering the kitchen as Liane went out.

"For now, anyway," Stormy told him. Perhaps twenty years from now she'd tell him of her conversation with Liane. There was no good reason to let him off the hook any sooner than that. "Any news? What'd your people have to say?"

"Remember when I said I didn't know where this would take us? Now I do."

"Where?" Stormy asked, holding her breath.

"How about a cruise to the Bahamas?"

"Save the jokes, Tyler. My future is at stake here."

"Come Friday, your future—and his wife—are boarding the Star Ship *Atlantic* at Port Canaveral for a three-day cruise to Nassau. One of the delightful adult activities aboard ship happens to be gambling. Among other things, the *Atlantic* is a floating casino."

Stormy sat down with a thud. "How'd you find that out?"

"Told my guy that as soon as he found Foley, to call him and make an appointment for me to meet with him on Friday, ostensibly to apply for a bank loan. Good old Foley declined the appointment—said he was taking his family on holiday. Didn't take much chitchatting to get the particulars out of him."

Stormy's eyes were shining. "Tyler, we've got to be aboard that ship!"

Chapter Sixteen

"Suppose I don't recognize Foley?" Stormy worried aloud, eyeing the line of passengers that formed down the gangway. "There must be over a thousand people going aboard. I only saw him those two times in court."

"The greater worry is that he might recognize you," Tyler said. "That would put him on guard."

The line moved from the shade of the pier sheds into the sun. Sweat began to trickle down between Stormy's breasts. "If we don't get aboard soon, the girls are going to have heatstroke."

"Good," Tyler said. "Then they can spend the trip in sick bay."

"Oh, Tyler, you know I couldn't leave Liane behind. But she and Janelle will occupy each other. Besides, I'm certain that bringing the girls along helped convince Mrs. Lowery of the sincerity of what we hope to accomplish."

Anxiety overrode Stormy's relief at finally doing something concrete about her situation. The past three days had been a whirlwind of activities. She had that feeling one often does when rushed, that she had forgotten something important. She pulled out her to-do list for the umpteenth time and began reading it over.

Sandy was house-sitting so that she could continue to make candles and use the garage to store whatever loot she acquired at yard sales. Noreen and Elise were working the flea market for her on Saturday. Thelma and Janice had volunteered for Sunday. For proof of citizenship she had brought her voter's registration card and the girls' birth certificates. The girls' teacher had been alerted that the children would be absent Friday and Monday. She had paid her parole fee and had some cash in her purse. Stormy twisted in the line to face Tyler. "I wish you'd tell me how much all of this is costing. I want to put in my share."

He grabbed Janelle as she tried to climb the ramp railing to look down between the ship and the pier into the water. "You can pay me back by coming to see me after I have a nervous breakdown," he groused.

Stormy let out an audible sigh and moved the girls in front of her.

The ship's photographer snapped their photo just before the captain welcomed them aboard. Liane and Janelle mugged for the camera. Stormy smiled. Tyler faced the ordeal with all the fluidity of a cinder block.

Theirs were connecting cabins on the Premier Deck. Stormy's was like a minuscule motel room with bath, and a sofabed the girls could share.

On the bed was the ship's bulletin and, for the children, bags of Chocolate Ship's cookies. Stormy picked up the bulletin. "Our luggage will be put in the hall for us to collect later," she said. "Let's go explore the ship. There's no gambling until we're outside U.S. waters. Oh, and there's an orientation in the Club Universe once we set sail. That might be our chance to get our first glimpse of Foley and his wife. We don't have any idea what she looks like."

"You and the girls go explore the ship," Tyler said. "I'll check with the purser, see if I can wrangle the Foleys' cabin number and which dinner seating they have, early or late. There's supposed to be a buffet laid out on the Riviera Terrace. I'll meet you there in, say, an hour."

Stormy followed him into the corridor, pulling the door closed on the girls. "You're not going to be in a bad mood this whole trip, are you? We can have fun and still—"

"We're not going to have a minute's privacy. And I'm not in a bad mood. See?" He gave a toothy grin suited to a corpse.

"Just this once, could you stop thinking with your—"

"I'll try."

She kissed him on the cheek. "That's better."

"No, this is," he said, snaking an arm around her and kissing her fully on the lips. Hearing excited voices closing in, he broke away reluctantly. "If you don't want this happening every two minutes, go wash off that perfume."

Stormy determined she'd wear the same perfume for the rest of her life.

LIANE AND JANELLE'S excitement would not be reined in as Stormy led them on a tour of the ship. There was Pluto's Playhouse on the stern of the Premier Deck and a video arcade and Space Station Teen Center on the same deck as the Lucky Star Casino. They found the ice-cream parlor, the movie theater, the fitness center and three swimming pools.

Children were everywhere: on deck playing table tennis, checkers and cards, and dancing to the band that welcomed them aboard. Stormy learned that there was a full schedule of activities for kids until 10:00 p.m. every night, all supervised by a trained staff.

While on the glassed-in promenade, they felt the ship tremble. The turbines were turning.

"We're moving!" Liane yelped.

"So we are," Stormy agreed. The girls pressed their noses against the windows. Stormy sent up a heartfelt prayer that all would go according to plan.

The Welcome-Aboard Buffet was located in the Starboard Café. Hundreds of people were filling their plates and congregating to dine and tap their feet on the Riviera Terrace, where a calypso band performed. Stormy found a shaded table beneath a ship strut and collapsed into a chair. Tyler would never find them in this mob, she thought.

There was no holding the girls back from the buffet. Unwilling to leave the table lest it be usurped, she let them go through the line on their own. They snubbed their noses at the standing rib roast, baked ham and salads, opting for pastries, cakes and cookies.

"It's all free!" gushed Janelle. "You can go back as many times as you want."

"Just hope you don't get seasick." Tyler warned.

Stormy started. "You found us!"

"I spotted the girls in line and followed them here."

"Smart you."

"Hungry?" he asked.

"Not really. If I eat every meal they serve, I'll go home weighing a ton."

"Drink?" he offered, nodding toward the bar.

"Lovely."

He returned with a pair of tall vodka tonics. Stormy took a sip and sighed. "Delicious. Did you find out about the Foleys?"

"They're in a stateroom on the same deck as we are. P90."

"The purser just told you?"

"I told him I spied Foley and his wife coming aboard ship and that we were old college buddies. I wanted to order a bottle of champagne."

"Did you?"

"Sure. Couldn't make myself out to be a liar."

Stormy scanned faces, worried. "I keep trying to remember what he looks like, but my mind goes blank. Winging it doesn't seem like such a terrific idea now that we're here. I didn't expect such crowds."

"Getting cold feet?"

"No!"

"Look, Mom, there's where you get drinks," Liane said, pointing to a set of self-serve juice dispensers farther up the deck. "May we go get our own?"

Stormy nodded. "Walk! Don't run."

"Crowds are better for us," Tyler reassured her. "We'll watch for opportunity and strike when we can. And if that doesn't work, we'll make our own opportunity."

Stormy took her gaze off the girls and eyed Tyler. "I can tell you're not worried."

"Nope."

"You spotted them already?"

"Nope."

"You've done something sneaky."

He smiled.

"Okay, have your little game. I have some news, too. The ship has supervised activities for kids from ten in the morning until ten at night. We only have to collect them for meals in the dining room."

Tyler's green eyes were suddenly backlit with a gleam of anticipation. "You don't say."

"And after they're in bed, the cabin steward will look in on them as necessary. For a tip, of course. Which means we'll both be free to be in the casino."

"Or to take a nap in my cabin."

Stormy gave him her most alluring smile. "The possibility exists." Too soon for Tyler, a frown replaced her smile. "That reminds me. You didn't forget to pack pajamas, did you?"

"Never fear. I'm going to be modestly covered from neck to ankle as long as I'm anywhere near the girls—the little perverts."

Despite his remark, he was so cheered by possibilities that when Liane and Janelle returned, carefully bearing plastic cups filled to the brim with orange juice, he insisted on challenging them to table tennis on the pool deck until it was time for orientation. Stormy went below to unpack suitcases.

ORIENTATION WAS A SHOW in itself, put on by the ship's staff. One bit of information dismayed Stormy. The emcee announced that once docked in Nassau, the ship's casino closed. Gambling then was done in the hotel casinos on the island. Tyler squeezed her hand. "Not to worry," he said quietly.

Fifteen minutes into his spiel, the emcee called up all the children. Liane and Janelle were out of their seats in a flash. Disney characters and costumed counselors led the children out of the room for a special tour. Parents were told to collect them in Pluto's Playhouse at the end of the orientation.

The emcee then gave out bottles of champagne to newlyweds and couples celebrating wedding anniversaries. Then he called for Henry Foley to come up.

Stormy went rigid. "Tyler!"

"Hush," he said.

There was a commotion in the back, and finally H. B. Foley was making his way forward. "That's him," Stormy breathed when the man came into view.

He was wearing Bermuda shorts, a Hawaiian-print shirt and grinning with embarrassment. He was of medium height with an open, affable face. Seeing him for the first time outside a courtroom, Stormy realized he looked like a friendly neighborhood grocer. No wonder he'd been believed on the stand. He looked so honest!

The emcee teased him. "Now, this is a gift from one of your old pals," he told Foley. "You'll have to guess who. He said you'd know him if you remember a special Friday night in your college frat house."

"There were a lot of special Friday nights," Foley said.

"Whoa!" the emcee joked. "Tell us about one of them."

Foley hedged. "Can't. My wife is here."

The crowd laughed. The emcee gave him the champagne and faced the audience. "Well, old buddy, whoever you are, you'll have to catch Henry when his wife's not looking." Another laugh.

Foley made his way back to his seat. Heart pounding, Stormy tracked him with her eyes. When Foley sat down, she shifted her gaze to the woman at the table with him and imprinted the features in her mind. Small-boned, delicate; chestnut hair piled casually atop her head. She wore earrings that dangled to her shoulders and a bright slash of scarlet lipstick.

"We shouldn't have any trouble picking her out in a crowd," Stormy said. "Not if those earrings and lipstick are her trademarks."

The emcee announced the casino would open in ten minutes, and orientation was over. The audience came to its feet.

As she rose, Stormy slipped her arm through Tyler's. "That bit with the champagne was brilliant," she said admiringly. "Let's go collect the girls."

Her breath caught in her throat. Tyler's eyes were following Foley. He had the stillness about him that reminded her of their first meeting—that hard aura that suggested no quarter. She reminded herself that she was no longer his prey.

H. B. Foley, she thought, didn't stand a chance.

LED TO THEIR DINING TABLE, they were awestruck by the magnificent ice carvings of swans on display. They chatted with the two middle-aged couples, one from Wales, one from Alabama, who shared their table.

Stormy happened to glance up from the menu and spied the Foley family—father, mother and two sons—bearing down on them. She gasped with involuntary panic. Tyler followed her gaze. He put his hand on her thigh and murmured, "Steady."

The maître d' seated the Foleys at the next table. Stormy judged the boys to be about seven and ten. They were no more than seated when the younger boy jumped up and ran over to Liane.

"Hey, Liane, we're goin' to the Splash Down Sunday on Salt Cay—that's where they filmed parts of *Gilligan's Island.* Are you?"

"I don't know. Are we, Mom? This is my new friend, Jason. He lives in Kissimmee and gets to go to Disney World *all the time.*"

Suddenly Foley was on his feet, apologizing and dragging the child away. "So sorry," he murmured.

Janelle snickered. "Liane has a boyfriend."

"I do not!"

"Stuff it, you two," Tyler said in his most authoritative voice, then looked surprised when they quieted down on the spot.

Stormy sipped wine, its chill smoothness an antidote for the hot dryness in her throat. Some of it was from fear, but more, she suspected was from feeling Tyler's thigh next to hers. The sensation was not only incredibly sexy, it was also cozy, comfortable . . . right.

Once, she reflected, she had thought herself in love with Truman Witney. She had had a child by him. Yet, she'd never really, truly trusted him, she supposed. Not the way she trusted Tyler.

The irony of the thought struck her, and she suppressed a delicious chuckle.

He leaned close to her. "You're wearing a Cheshire Cat smile."

"And why not?" she replied lightly. "I'm on a cruise with the most exciting man aboard."

"Hear, hear," said the man from Wales, and everyone clinked glasses.

Stormy chanced a glance at the Foleys. They were silent, unsmiling, and she almost felt sorry for them. No softness now, she commanded herself. This was no time for compassion. H.B. had certainly afforded her none.

LATER, AFTER LIANE and Janelle were snug in bed asleep, Stormy and Tyler went up on the pool deck to watch the moonlight play over the ship's wake. "Foley didn't recognize me," she said with a twinge of anger. "He stole that money, lied under oath and ruined my life. You'd think he'd at least remember me!"

"He focuses on his own problems, sweetheart. Then *and* now."

"I'm scared. Suppose he doesn't break? Suppose..."
Her head was half-turned away from Tyler, exposing the
soft column of her neck.

"Suppose this..." Tyler murmured, oblivious to other
couples wandering the dimly lit deck. His lips placed a kiss
behind her ear, then trailed across her temple to her eyelid. He slid the top of his tongue across the curved line of
her eyelashes. "Delicious," he said.

"Shouldn't we be in the casino?" she whispered breath-
lessly.

"We should," he agreed, feeling her shiver as his strong
hands moved slowly up her back.

"We can't just stand here...necking," Stormy argued.

He sucked gently on her lower lip, loving the feel and
shape and taste of her mouth. "Who would dare stop us?"

"We're going to be miserable, and you know it." But she
moved deeper inside his arms, sliding her hands beneath
his jacket, reveling in the rippling sinews beneath his shirt.

His tongue flicked out, probing her mouth. "I'm made
for misery," he breathed against her lips.

OUTSIDE OF BUYING an occasional lottery ticket, Stormy
knew little about gambling. But the moment she stepped
into the ship's casino, she was swept up in the tumult.

She gripped Tyler's arm. "I can feel the tension vibrating in the air. It's amazing. I can see how people get
hooked."

Gambling had its own sounds. There was the whirring
of slot machines, the rippling tinkle as quarters fell into
metal trays signaling a win. The roulette wheel hummed
like a stick dragged along a wooden fence as its ball went
around and around, seeming to defy gravity. She could
hear the snap of cards at Blackjack tables and the click of
dice being rolled before landing against green felt. Thread-

ed through it all was the reverberation of hushed voices as players placed bets, whispered to dice or cajoled slot machines.

They found Foley playing the slots and his wife, Cheryl, at the Blackjack table. She had several stacks of chips in front of her.

"She's winning," Tyler said. "Maybe on a roll."

"Is that good or bad?"

"Well, if she stops while she's ahead, good for her and bad for us. We'll have to figure another way to put a wedge between her and Foley. On the other hand, if she's got the disease, she'll play until she loses and . . ." He spied the cashier's cage. "Let's get you a couple of rolls of quarters. You play those slots near the cage. Watch how often she hits her charge cards for cash advances."

"What are you going to do?"

"I'm going to play a little Blackjack."

Stormy glanced again at Cheryl Foley. The woman wore a white skirt, a spangly halter top, dangling earrings and false eyelashes out to the end of her nose. "Are you going to flirt with her?"

"I wouldn't dare."

"But you're going to talk to her."

"Only in your interest. Why? You jealous?"

"Don't be silly."

He passed her a twenty-dollar bill. "Get your quarters. You can keep your winnings."

"Generous of you."

Stormy won thirty dollars before it was time to collect the girls for lunch. She caught Tyler's eye across the casino and pointed to her watch. He shook his head.

During lunch, Liane and Janelle chatted away with the couple from Wales like well-seasoned travelers. They wore newly acquired Mickey Mouse hats and pirate swords they had made in a crafts class. They also begged money to play video games in the arcade. "Jason is going," came the predictable plea.

This is how it starts, Stormy thought as she gave them each two dollars of her winnings before returning them to the care of their youth counselors. She freshened up in her cabin and spent a moment debating whether to put on earrings and fix her hair. Maybe put it up? Stupid, she told herself, discarding the idea.

When she returned, Tyler and the Foley woman had moved to the roulette table. Stormy browsed the lounge deck, looking for H.B. She found him hunkered down in the Junkaboo Bar. She ordered a Coke and, braving fate, sat down at the next table. He looked up. She smiled.

"We met last night," she said. "Your little boy, Jason, and my daughter have become great friends."

"Oh, right," he said, and stared past her.

She searched frantically for something more to say. "You were funny in orientation. Did you find your fraternity brother?"

"What? Oh, no. That was just part of their script. I don't know anyone aboard ship."

"You've been on cruises before?"

His brow wrinkled. "A few."

Stormy cocked her head. "You don't sound as though you enjoy them."

"My wife does," he said abruptly.

Stormy exhaled. How much could she get away with? she wondered. If Liane had told Jason that she and Tyler weren't married . . . "So does my friend. He loves to gamble. To excess, I think. He'd rather play Blackjack than eat." She looked down and twiddled her straw. "Tell you the truth, it scares me sometimes. He seems driven. And it takes so much *money.*" She gave a little laugh.

"It does that. Well, if you'll excuse me, I have to check on my boys."

"Oh. Sure. Nice talking to you." Heart clattering, she returned to the casino. Cheryl was in line at the cashier. Stormy moved to the side and watched the transaction. The cashier counted out five crisp hundred-dollar bills. Cheryl crumpled up the credit-card receipt and tossed it toward the nearby trash bin. It missed. Stormy retrieved it and wandered over to the roulette table, nudging Tyler.

"Having any luck?" she asked in her most syrupy voice.

"Fair. You?"

"I won thirty dollars." She bent over and kissed him on the ear. "Our friend just got five hundred," she whispered. "I spoke to H.B., and he's not happy."

"You—" Tyler picked up his chips and put them in his pocket. "Let's go find a cup of coffee," he said, taking her arm, ushering her out of the casino and back into the bar. "You're playing with fire," he said angrily after the waiter took their order.

"And you aren't? Anyway, I feel superfluous just standing around. Everybody has something to do except me."

"Poor baby."

"Don't patronize me." She tossed the credit-card receipt onto the table. "Here, she threw this away."

Tyler smoothed it out. "She'll keep on tossing them. From here on out, we need to stick to her like glue, pick up every one of these we can. They're going ashore to the Crystal Palace tonight. You'd better make arrangements for a baby-sitter."

"You mean leave the girls aboard ship alone?"

He sighed. "Not alone. They have a program for the kids while parents are ashore. They take them to the movies, have entertainment, put them to bed. They'll be fine. It's the done thing.''

"The Crystal Palace, huh? You got that chummy with her."

"She was trying to be helpful—said the gaming tables warm up about ten. Look, I'm taking you on a date. If we were back in St. Augustine and I asked you out, you'd get a baby-sitter, wouldn't you?''

"A date?" Stormy laughed. "After all we've been through? What do you call this cruise, for heaven's sake?''

"Business! Hot damn, but you're stubborn," he fretted, shaking his head. "Just so you don't feel guilty, once we dock, let's take the girls ashore, do the tourist bit, have dinner somewhere local, then bring the kids back and get them settled."

"What about the Foleys? They may head straight for the local casinos."

"I think our long-lashed friend has to maintain the facade that this is a family vacation, if only for H.B. She'll do her gambling at night. Besides, that's when the thrills are the highest. Meanwhile, they'll probably be doing the family scene themselves." He scooped up the credit-card receipt and threw a couple of bills onto the table. "I'd better get back. The broad places bets all over the ladder. She'll be down to her last few chips by now."

"Unless she's winning."

"Sweetheart, she's obsessed. Her kind never win."

She has so far, Stormy thought bitterly.

Chapter Seventeen

She wasn't scientific, quantifiable or expert, but at the roulette table beneath the gleaming chandeliers in the Crystal Palace, Stormy was having beginner's luck.

She felt as if she had crashed through an invisible barrier to the unknown. Whatever gambling fever was, she was touching it, smelling it and hearing it. She didn't know how to handle it.

Tyler was standing behind her stool; she kept glancing back at him for reassurance. All she understood was that Tyler asked her to pick some numbers. Five, nine and thirteen popped into her mind. He placed bets on them. The numbers kept coming up winners. He moved off the stool and told her to play the money she'd won.

There were sidebar bets. She learned she could "ride the lines." She kept expecting to lose, to have the dealer sweep her chips off the board, but he kept coming back to her to pile up more. Tyler kept telling her to play it out.

The Foleys were at a nearby table, but there was no room for another player. Now it was Tyler who dogged Cheryl to the cashier's booth. Only once did he return empty-handed. He asked Stormy to check the women's restroom. Cheryl had not tossed the credit-card receipt but absently held on to it as she went into the ladies' room.

Sure enough, Stormy found the receipt wadded up on the sink amid lipsticked tissues and a paper towel. It was for two hundred dollars.

At midnight Tyler told Stormy to cash in. She put all her chips into a little plastic bucket to take to the cashier. Tyler removed five and passed them to the dealer.

"Why'd you do that?"

"It's a tip, sweetheart."

"Oh. Why are we leaving? The Foleys are still gambling."

"We've got what we need. There's a pattern to how Cheryl uses her cards. She starts out getting five hundred, then reduces the amount. Remember those printouts? How the cash advances gradually lowered? Apparently she's bottomed out on four different credit cards."

"Then why'd you stop me from playing? I was winning."

"You were enjoying it too much."

Stormy paused, stunned. "I was, wasn't I?"

The cashier sorted her chips and counted out her winnings in newly minted hundred-dollar bills. Twenty-eight of them. Stormy's legs suddenly felt like rubber. "How much were those chips worth?" she asked Tyler.

"We were at the five-dollar table."

"You mean each *chip* was worth five dollars?" She thought about her bets, how she'd allowed them to stack up to five while riding on five, nine while riding on nine, *thirteen* while riding on thirteen. She did some quick mental calculations and gasped. "You let me bet three hundred and twenty-five dollars on one spin?" She could barely get the words out. "You *idiot!*"

He grinned. "Does that mean you'll foot the bill for the cab back to the ship?"

She was still trembling with aftershocks as Tyler paid the steward who'd watched the girls.

"Thirteen must be your lucky number," he told her lightly as they stood outside their cabin doors. "We have thirteen credit-card receipts. Don't wake me for breakfast. I'm sleeping in tomorrow."

Finally Stormy let the words tumble out as they came into her head. "I know what she's feeling, Tyler. It's a rush—it's so powerful. It takes over. I was so focused, yet my heart was in my throat the entire time the wheel was spinning.

"Poor Cheryl!" She sniffed to ward off the tears she felt burning her eyes. "I told myself not to feel sorry for them, but I can't help it. In order to put my life right, I may have to destroy theirs." She sniffed again. "And Jason is Liane's new friend. It's awful."

Tyler reached for her and drew her into his arms. "Everyone has a choice," he said softly into her ear. "You, me, Nina, Noreen, Tully, the Foleys—everyone. Some of us, some of the time, don't make the right choices. The Foleys made theirs, and you can't hold yourself responsible for their behavior. You've got to hang tough."

"I thought I *was,* but I don't feel tough now. I feel awful. We won't do anything in front of the children, will we? I couldn't bear it."

"We won't."

"Let's just have fun tomorrow. Let's not go anywhere near a casino."

He pressed his lips to the soft hollow behind her ear. "We'll explore an uninhabited island, swim in secluded lagoons, look for pirate treasure—"

"Can I sleep with you tonight?"

"Choices," he groaned. "And have the girls wake up and find you gone?" He smiled into the dark. "Hardest damned choice I've made in years."

STORMY WAS BEGINNING to believe she had nothing but *bad* luck. Now that she wanted to avoid them, it seemed to her that every time she looked up or turned around, the Foleys were there. On the excursion to Salt Cay, they had chosen a picnic site next to theirs. Jason and his older brother, Hank, had become constant companions to Liane and Janelle, teaming up to pedalboat, ride inner tubes and snorkel.

Stormy was elbow to elbow with H.B. on the tender that returned them to the ship, two steps behind the family as they waited for the dining room to open, and one step ahead as they trudged back to the Promenade Deck to watch as the ship set sail for home.

Though the children chattered among themselves, the adult Foleys remained aloof.

Stormy turned to Tyler. "I feel so awkward. What're we going to do? We can't wait until morning. We'll be back at Port Canaveral."

"The casino will reopen within the hour. We'll—"

"I don't think it's a good idea for me to go back into a casino."

"You might feel better if you lost a few dollars."

"I'll feel better once we get this over with." She called to Liane and Janelle. "I'm going to take the girls down and get them ready for bed."

They howled with protest. "It's too early! All the other kids are getting to stay up till after midnight."

"We have to pack our suitcases," Stormy insisted. "We have to put them in the hall before we go to sleep. You two have been little angels up to now. Don't—"

"There's no such things as angels," said Janelle. "Only ghosts."

"Maybe there're ghosts on the ship!" said Liane.

"One might come into our cabin and get us while we're asleep," Janelle suggested.

Stormy laughed. "Sorry, you two. That won't work. Only the sandman is coming to visit you."

"There's no such thing as a sandman, either," Janelle informed her. "What gets in your eyes in the morning is from tear ducts cleaning your eyeballs."

Stormy groaned.

IT WAS MORE THAN AN HOUR before she could rejoin Tyler on the promenade. When she'd left him, all the tables along the windows had been occupied. Now only a few couples remained, the Foleys among them.

"They've been arguing," Tyler said without ado. "I think we ought to get this done."

Stormy felt her stomach seize up. "Now?"

"Now." He took her arm, strolling her toward the other couple. When they reached the table, Tyler stopped and pulled out a chair. "Mind if we join you?"

Both Foleys were startled, but Cheryl recovered first, recognizing Tyler as her gambling companion and smiling tentatively.

"It's not a good time, pal," H.B. said.

Tyler held out the chair for Stormy. She sat. Tyler took the chair next to her.

H.B.'s face puffed up. "Listen, buddy, I don't think you understand. We're having a private conversation."

Tyler reached into his pocket and pulled out the charge slips. He spread them out on the table one by one. "Your argument wouldn't be about these, would it?"

Foley glanced at the credit-card receipts, then up at Tyler, then back at the receipts. He picked up one, then another, and another. His mouth went white around the edges.

"They represent forty-eight hundred dollars in cash advances," Tyler said softly.

Cheryl grabbed them. "What the hell? These are none of your business!"

Tyler leaned back. "That's where you're wrong, Mrs. Foley. You see, I'm wondering how the vice president of a small bank branch can afford such extravagance."

Foley's breath came in rapid puffs. "Who the hell are you?"

"Gee, I thought you'd never ask. Stormy, sweetheart, introduce yourself to these nice people."

"My name is Stormy Elliott."

H.B. thrust his head forward. "So?"

Stormy licked her lips. "Mr. Foley, you testified against me in court. You said I stole, or rather, that I helped steal one hundred and two thousand dollars from the Beach Coast Savings and Loan."

"What—?"

"And I'm Tyler Mangus," Tyler said. "I'm an asset-recovery agent working for the company that insured Beach Coast. A funny thing happened when I started tracking that money, H.B. I discovered that most of it never left the bank. At least, not with Hadley Wilson and Ms. Elliott here."

Cheryl's hands flew to her mouth. "Oh, my God!"

H.B. turned on her. "Shut up."

"That's not a nice way to talk to your wife," Tyler cautioned, his voice like tempered steel. He gazed at Cheryl. "You know how he works the scam, don't you? Gambling is a terrible disease. It eats at you. You gotta do it."

Cheryl started to cry.

Stormy sat rigid, unable to breathe.

Tyler leaned forward, the cords of his neck taut. "Ms. Elliott spent eleven months in prison on your testimony, Foley. She was separated from her little girl all those long months. You've met Liane. She's been playing with your son Jason. Ms. Elliott told the truth when she said she knew nothing of the robbery. She never saw that money. But, of course, no jury believed her. After all, how can you hide over a hundred thousand dollars?"

"Oh, God, Henry!" Cheryl cried. "You told me nobody would get hurt."

"She was there!" Foley growled. "I saw her drive away with Wilson. She's a criminal."

"Ms. Elliott thought Hadley Wilson went into the bank to get a cash advance on his credit card—just like Mrs. Foley has done so often over these past few days."

"It's my fault... my fault," Cheryl sobbed.

Foley raised his hand as if to strike her. Tyler grabbed his arm. "Tut-tut, none of that."

Foley yanked his arm from Tyler's grasp. "You can't prove a damned thing," he said, flinging the words recklessly at Tyler.

Tyler leaned back, crossed his legs and tented his fingers. "You know, I think I can. After you stowed all that cash in that night-deposit chute, you failed to collect it all. I guess you were in a hurry. You left several twenties Beach Coast could never account for. All the night deposits added up, and no one claimed the overage."

Foley looked at his wife, sobbing softly at his side, then beyond her out the windows. The moon was slanting across a calm sea. Before Stormy's very eyes, the man appeared to shrink as if something had died inside him. "I'm glad it's over," he said. Then he stood up and looked sadly at his wife. Then he shook his head as if all his pleas had been used up.

They watched him until he turned the corner to the stairwell. Stormy felt not the remotest sense of satisfaction.

Cheryl's head drooped dejectedly.

Tyler took Stormy's hand and squeezed it. "You okay?"

She shook her head. "I'm staggered. You never told me about those twenties."

"Didn't I?" he said, and smiled. "Do you mind sitting here with Mrs. Foley while I see the purser?"

"Are we to be arrested?" Cheryl asked. "What about my children?"

"When you and your husband disembark tomorrow, you'll be met. But I'd like to take a statement from you."

"Would it help Henry? It's my fault, what he did."

"It might," Tyler said.

Stormy knew vindication was finally to be hers. Still, she lay awake most of the night, feeling ineffable sadness for the entire Foley family.

THREE WEEKS LATER, Stormy sat in the courtroom where she'd been convicted, before the judge who had sentenced her, and listened to him set her conviction aside and order a new trial. The district attorney announced that, in light of the new evidence obtained via depositions from Henry B. Foley and wife, Cheryl Foley, his office would not retry Ms. Elliott.

The judge looked down from the bench and smiled at Stormy. "Ms. Elliott, Mr. Mangus, I'll see you in my chambers in ten minutes."

They both nodded. "I'm free," Stormy said softly, a little fearful that if she became overly jubilant, she'd awaken and find it was all a dream.

"Only for the next ten minutes," Tyler reminded her as she accepted congratulations from her attorney and Mrs. Lowery.

The wedding party awaited them in the hall. Noreen handed Stormy her bouquet and pinned a boutonniere to Tyler's lapel.

"You two are the most efficient people I've ever met," she teased.

"Only because I never want to set foot in a courthouse again as long as I live," Stormy told her.

"Am I adopted yet?" Liane asked, hanging on to Tyler's hand.

"That comes after your mom and I are married," Tyler told her, swinging her up into his arms.

"Are you and Stormy going to have intercourse now?" Janelle asked.

Tyler sputtered.

Noreen shot a hand over her daughter's mouth. "You started this," she told Tyler. "You bought the book."

"Burn it," he said, releasing Liane and backpedaling to stand near his parents, who were chatting with Mrs. Lowery.

Sandy touched Stormy's arm. "Your sister just got off the elevator."

Stormy went to meet her. "I'm glad you could make it, Nina."

"Me, too." She took a breath. "I'm sorry for everything, Stormy. I . . . You know I have a job now, and Tully and I are seeing a marriage counselor?"

"I heard. I hope things work out for you both."

"We're putting Mom's things in storage and renting the house out."

Stormy nodded. "Ben told me. He said you'd instructed him to use your portion of the proceeds from the rent to repay the advance you took against my income from the trust." Stormy had wanted to forgive the fifty-four hundred dollars, but Ben had wisely talked her out of that. It wasn't fair to Nina, he said, to put obstacles in the way of making amends.

Nina suddenly burst into tears. "I hate it that you'll be living so far away."

"A three-hour drive, that's all." Stormy put her arms around her sister. "And I'll be in St. Augustine often. Don't forget, Sandy and I have a business to run. Now stop crying or you'll have me doing it, and I don't want to mess up my makeup. I'm the bride."

Nina smiled through her tears. "Finally."

A few moments later, Stormy found herself standing hand in hand with Tyler before the judge, getting married.

When the judge got to the words "love, cherish and obey," Stormy balked. "Not 'obey'," she said.

"Right on!" chorused Noreen, Sandy, Thelma and Janice.

The judge frowned and spoke to Tyler. "Son?"

"Love and cherish will do. She's not going to listen to me, anyway."

Next it was Liane's turn in family court. Tyler signed her adoption papers, making her Liane Elliott Mangus. She was offended because she wasn't asked to sign anything. "I've been practicing writing *Mangus* all week!"

Tyler let her sign his copy beneath his name.

The reception was held at Noreen's.

Elise caught the bridal bouquet, only to have it snatched away by her mother. "Don't even think it!" Noreen said.

Stormy had a tearful moment when Liane climbed happily into the car with her newly acquired grandparents, who were taking her home with them so that she could meet her new uncle and his family.

"That's it, folks!" Tyler said, hooking Stormy with his arm and ushering her into his BMW before anyone could stop them.

The next thing Stormy knew, they were in their hotel's honeymoon suite and Tyler was undressing her. His tongue flicked into the hollow of her neck. "No kids, no folks, no candles, no Lowery, no interruptions," he murmured. "I'm in heaven."

"Do you think Liane will be okay with your parents?"

"They raised *me*, didn't they?"

She slid her hands down his hips. "That's a recommendation?"

"Do we have to talk?" He gently pushed her onto the bed.

"Not if you don't want to. Can we turn off the light?"

"Not a chance. I want to see every inch of you." He watched her face as he ran his hands over her skin, trying to satisfy his visceral, bone-deep craving. "I love you," he said. "I think I was a goner from the first moment I saw you."

"Really?" she murmured, shifting her hips so that he could slide her panty hose off. "I thought you were dangerous."

Tyler began to bask in one delicious sensation after another. "Dangerous? Me? I'm a pussycat."

Naked, solemn and clear-eyed, she looked up at him. "Put your arms around me, Tyler."

Moments later, as he buried himself deep within her, he knew he was never going to turn her loose.

IT WAS HOURS LATER that Stormy remembered. She shook Tyler awake. "What'd the fax say, the one you had to pick up this morning at Western Union?"

"Sleep," he mumbled.

Stormy turned on the light and elbowed his chest. "I know it was about the Foleys. Tell me."

He opened his eyes a sliver. "I might be *persuaded* to tell you."

Stormy straddled him. "Tell me . . ."

"Foley was bonded while working for Beach Coast. The bonding company is reimbursing my client for the ninety-eight thousand he admitted stealing. The other four thousand or so was chalked up to Wilson."

"So what's going to happen to him?"

"Beach Coast brought charges against H.B. for theft. He's copping a plea, so he'll probably get probation, plus he'll have to make restitution. Nothing's going down with Cheryl, as far as any charges. They're selling their house and extra car to show good faith on restitution. No more cruises or holidays in Vegas." He put his hands on her hips. "Satisfied?"

"Well, now that we're married, don't take any more jobs like this one. We'll go broke."

"Broke?" He laughed. "I collected, sweetheart. My clients are happy as hell. Why, they're so happy, you might even find a nuisance settlement in our mailbox when we get home."

"A nuisance settlement? From whom? What for?"

"Why, Beach Coast, of course. After all, Foley was their employee. He stole most of the money and lied about it to your detriment."

"Will Hadley get a nuisance settlement, too?"

"I don't believe so," Tyler said dryly. "He did, after all, rob the bank, even if he didn't get as much as H.B. did.

Now, are you going to find a better place to park that pretty behind of yours or—"

Wearing nothing but a smile, Stormy slowly began sliding down his body. "You mean here?"

He closed his eyes and arched his hips, forgetting all else as her hot, moist flesh enveloped him. "Exactly," he managed.

"How much?" Stormy asked.

"What—?"

"That nuisance settlement."

"A pittance," he groaned.

She stopped moving, leaned forward, buried her elbows in his chest and propped her chin in her hands. "How much?"

"Do you promise to love, cherish and *obey?*"

"Unfair!"

"Shove off. I need my beauty sleep."

"All right." She sat up, put her hands behind her back and crossed her fingers. "Love, cherish and obey."

Tyler lifted his head and looked beyond her into the dresser mirror. "You're cheating." He switched off the lamp. "Five thousand," he said anyway.

"Dollars?"

"This is our wedding night. Can't you think of anything more interesting than money?"

"Do you think your parents liked me?"

Tyler sighed. "All right, that's it. I'm taking charge."

Stormy smiled into the dark. "Please do," she said. And she gave herself up to his loving.

Following the success of WITH THIS RING,
Harlequin cordially invites you to enjoy the
romance of the wedding season with

BARBARA BRETTON
RITA CLAY ESTRADA
SANDRA JAMES
DEBBIE MACOMBER

A collection of romantic stories that celebrate the joy,
excitement, and mishaps of planning that special day
by these four award-winning Harlequin authors.

**Available in April at your favorite Harlequin
retail outlets.**

"GET AWAY FROM IT ALL" SWEEPSTAKES

HERE'S HOW THE SWEEPSTAKES WORKS

NO PURCHASE NECESSARY

To enter each drawing, complete the appropriate Official Entry Form or a 3" by 5" index card by hand-printing your name, address and phone number and the trip destination that the entry is being submitted for (i.e., Caneel Bay, Canyon Ranch or London and the English Countryside) and mailing it to: Get Away From It All Sweepstakes, P.O. Box 1397, Buffalo, New York 14269-1397.

No responsibility is assumed for lost, late or misdirected mail. Entries must be sent separately with first class postage affixed, and be received by: 4/15/92 for the Caneel Bay Vacation Drawing, 5/15/92 for the Canyon Ranch Vacation Drawing and 6/15/92 for the London and the English Countryside Vacation Drawing. Sweepstakes is open to residents of the U.S. (except Puerto Rico) and Canada, 21 years of age or older as of 5/31/92.

For complete rules send a self-addressed, stamped (WA residents need not affix return postage) envelope to: Get Away From It All Sweepstakes, P.O. Box 4892, Blair, NE 68009.

© 1992 HARLEQUIN ENTERPRISES LTD.   SWP-RLS

"GET AWAY FROM IT ALL" SWEEPSTAKES

HERE'S HOW THE SWEEPSTAKES WORKS

NO PURCHASE NECESSARY

To enter each drawing, complete the appropriate Official Entry Form or a 3" by 5" index card by hand-printing your name, address and phone number and the trip destination that the entry is being submitted for (i.e., Caneel Bay, Canyon Ranch or London and the English Countryside) and mailing it to: Get Away From It All Sweepstakes, P.O. Box 1397, Buffalo, New York 14269-1397.

No responsibility is assumed for lost, late or misdirected mail. Entries must be sent separately with first class postage affixed, and be received by: 4/15/92 for the Caneel Bay Vacation Drawing, 5/15/92 for the Canyon Ranch Vacation Drawing and 6/15/92 for the London and the English Countryside Vacation Drawing. Sweepstakes is open to residents of the U.S. (except Puerto Rico) and Canada, 21 years of age or older as of 5/31/92.

For complete rules send a self-addressed, stamped (WA residents need not affix return postage) envelope to: Get Away From It All Sweepstakes, P.O. Box 4892, Blair, NE 68009.

© 1992 HARLEQUIN ENTERPRISES LTD.   SWP-RLS

"GET AWAY FROM IT ALL"

Brand-new Subscribers-Only Sweepstakes

OFFICIAL ENTRY FORM

This entry must be received by: April 15, 1992
This month's winner will be notified by: April 30, 1992
Trip must be taken between: May 31, 1992—May 31, 1993

YES, I want to win the Caneel Bay Plantation vacation for two. I understand the prize includes round-trip airfare and the two additional prizes revealed in the BONUS PRIZES insert.

Name _____

Address _____

City _____

State/Prov. _____ Zip/Postal Code _____

Daytime phone number _____
                              (Area Code)

Return entries with invoice in envelope provided. Each book in this shipment has two entry coupons — and the more coupons you enter, the better your chances of winning!
© 1992 HARLEQUIN ENTERPRISES LTD.   1M-CPN